"Think of the An
he will only pour out

The late Travis Duncan,
an unusual 37-year old woman,
bequeathes an estate worth over $23,000,000
to her ex-lovers. Her will stipulates that these men
must meet for one night and answer one question.
The man who answers the question correctly, wins.
The question is:
WHAT DO YOU ALL HAVE IN COMMON?

Seven men arrive in
Portland, Oregon to hear the terms of the will.
Five men stay to share their lives
in an effort to determine their commonality.
Each man is both despicable
and likable, depending on *your perspective.*

DID SHE LEAVE ME ANY MONEY?
is a rollicking ride that reinforces the
precious spirit of nonconformity.

by
ALYCE CORNYN-SELBY

"A female Tom Robbins."
--*St. Martin's Press*

"Plot is unique, writing style is enticing."
--*Atlantic Monthly*

"The ending just right...make a fine film!"
--*Downtowner*

BEYNCH · PRESS

Published by BEYNCH PRESS PUBLISHING COMPANY
1928 S. E. Ladd Avenue
Portland, Oregon 97214

503-232-0433

DID SHE LEAVE ME ANY MONEY?

Second printing 1994

Copyright © 1991 Alyce Cornyn-Selby

Also by author Alyce Cornyn-Selby:
Procrastinator's Success Kit
Teamwork & Team Sabotage
Take Your Hands Off My Attitude!
Alyce's FAT CHANCE
Why Winners Win
I Don't Have To & You Can't Make Me!

ISBN 0-941383-11-3

See you at the movies!

Alyce

Dedication

You know who you are.
See you at the Pittock.

Alyce

"If I have to cry,

I think of my love life.

And if I have to laugh,

well,

I think of my love life. "

--Glenda Jackson

Chapter 1

*Everything is funny as long as it happens
to somebody else.*

— Will Rogers

"They're going to take a ginzu to my gizzard tomorrow and I don't care," sighs Timothy, throwing his head back on the white hospital pillow. "At least I'm not in the office and I'm not anywhere near Travis Duncan."

A pleasant Puerto Rican nurse smiles as she pours a dose of Maalox into a paper cup. "Dreenk up!" she sings. Timothy smiles a broad smile under his salt and pepper moustache and holds the cup champagne-style. "And here's looking at you, kid!" he says with great relish, downing the lemon-flavored goo with a great "Ah!"

The nurse fluffs his pillows and regards his happy face. "I haf never seen someone so hoppy to be ein the 'ospital," she remarks. "Esspecially for ul-sirs."

"*It* can't get me when I'm in here," he smiles, closing his eyes, drifting into the pillows.

"*What* can't get you in here?" the nurse asks, puzzled.

"Travis Duncan's money."

Chapter 2

*Women live longer than men because they
haven't really been living. Better blue-in-
the-face dead of a heart attack at fifty
than a healthy seventy-year old widow who
hasn't had a piece of life's action since
girlhood.*
                              — *Tom Robbins*

Three floors down and half a wing away, a blaring ambulance bucks into the emergency room stall and the rear doors spring open. Two attendants pull on the gurney and it flies out with a slam, its passenger groaning.

"Is this the one from the airport?" a hospital person asks.

Watching from the waiting room picture window, a tiny Japanese gentleman wearing a white linen suit, his Panama in his hands, watches the rushing nurses. His almond eyes widen and his teeth tug on his lower lip.

The gurney makes it over the indoor-outdoor carpeting and through the automatic doors. Someone stands with a clip board and gives traffic signals to the ambulance boys. The cart and its passenger go into ER-3 and a white-coated medical student rushes in after it.

The Japanese walks slowly to the door of ER-3 and the medical student barks in a breathy whisper to the nurse, "Get Dr. Peterson! Stat!" The nurse vanishes without a sound. The student turns to the door and sees the Japanese man. "You can't come in here," he says quietly while pushing his hornrims up onto his face.

"I'm her brother, I have to see her," the Japanese says with the innocent face of an infant.

The student hesitates and starts to recite a regulation but thinks better of it when he sees the fistful of $100 bills unfolding in the visitor's hand. The Japanese has not taken his eyes off of the student. "It's worth half your student loans," he says very evenly, thumbing the bills.

"I didn't see you," says the student as he flies out the door, catching the money in the large pockets of his intern's coat.

The Japanese man steps into ER-3, closes the door and moves swiftly to the bedside. One look at the red and yellow skin and he knows that he has only moments with her. She is obviously Caucasian, despite the discoloration, and her voice sounds like a dry wind through winter wheat. Her grey eyes open. "Two things," she begins.

George Sam wants to touch her hair but checks himself. Tears begin to fill his black eyes. "Travis," he says, then stops.

"First, take this damned St. Christopher's medal and pitch it," she says.

The little Japanese nods quickly and more of his lower lip disappears between his teeth. His eyebrows squeeze deep furrows in his forehead.

"And about the will," she whispers in a harsh tone... "I meant it *then* and I mean it *now*. Do it for me. Play this last game."

Several seconds pass as she blinks her eyes one time. Auburn ringlets crowd her head and appear golden in the overhead hospital light. The color of her cheeks begin to match the grey of her eyes.

"Play it for me, Sam." She looks at him while she speaks, then her gaze goes through him and stops. A tear from his face drops onto her cheek.

She does not blink.

Chapter 3

*Too much of a good thing can be
wonderful.*

— Mae West

It had taken George Sam six months to locate, contact and noti-fy the beneficiaries listed in Travis' 37-page will. As her attorney and executor, it was the little Japanese who held the purse strings to Travis' twenty-three million dollars. He and Timothy (and Timothy's ulcers) had presided over the money for Travis when she had lost her patience with having it.

"I'm not meeting in any more office buildings," she had said to George Sam while they were looking at street rods at the Portland Roadster Show. The little Japanese attorney was on his back under the suspension system of a '29 track roadster when she made her pronouncement.

"How is this money supposed to do me any good if I have to spend all my time in office buildings?" fumed Travis.

What she got from George Sam was his characteristic almond-eyed stare. He brushed the floor crumbs from his white linen suit...he always wore white and carried his light straw hat..."makes you look like a pint-sized Charlie Chan," Travis observed. Together they strolled by a '50 Merc with purple flames and Frenched headlights. "Like the lead sled," she said.

"Just one thing," George Sam said with a little brown finger raised. "A will. You must have a will. Write one. Go to the beach and write a will."

Travis' grey eyes flashed at the sound of yet another assignment. She had no sons or daughters or nieces or nephews to pour the money down like so many yapping holes. She had an aversion to traditional institutions who could have used the money. Truth: She had an aversion to traditional anything. That's how she attracted money to her in the first place.

Travis had indeed become one of the richest single women on the

West Coast but she was ill-prepared to have it. Except for her passion for old cars and travel, Travis had no outlet for the kind of cash she now commanded. The stock market and the language of investments gave her a temporal headache. Income tax evasion, the seemingly Grand Prize of Financial Planning, did not delight or intrigue her. She had no desire for a second or third residence, instead preferring to stay roosted in her old 3-story Portland home. She could get seasick in a backyard swimming pool and so had no need for a yacht. And a Mercedes was out. "That's a standard design solution for wealth," sighed Travis. "It's too obvious." She settled for a red deuce roadster with a stroked and bored 283 small block for the sunny days and a maroon '37 Packard sedan for the rainy days.

She was eccentric even before the money.

"Eccentricity" is a word used to describe odd or whimsical behavior among the very rich or the very old. Being neither and intending to become both, Travis thought it wise to practice being eccentric until either riches or old age set in. Travis was not one to wait.

George Sam had met Travis because of Timothy's ulcers. There was no proper profession for Timothy; no matter what career path he chose, he would have brought his stress with him. Had he been a musician, a gravedigger, an air traffic controller or the Maytag repairman, Timothy would have turned it against his own stomach. He had the misfortune to be Travis' financial advisor and banker. And *this* job would have turned even Mr. Rogers into Rambo. Mixing Travis with Timothy was like mixing razor blades into toothpaste, nothing good was bound to come of it. Before Timothy's intestines could blow up in his face, he called on the mild-mannered and competent little Japanese-American estate attorney to run interference for him. George Sam was everything that Timothy was not...and he was a car nut who could keep Travis entertained with street rod jargon.

Why Travis couldn't just settle down into a Mercedes was beyond Timothy. To Timothy, chopped was something done to liver, not to cars. And pinstripes were on Timothy's business suit where they belonged, not painted on the side of an old automobile. Running board to Timothy was jogging when you didn't want to and small block was a short neighborhood street, not an engine. When Travis said, "Look at that bowtie shine," Timothy looked around for someone in a gold lamé tie, not knowing that "bowtie" was the slang term for the Chevrolet logo.

"Deuce is *not* a card in a deck," explained George Sam. "It's her *car*."

George Sam was a card-carrying member of the National Street Rod Association and his own ride was a '34 Ford three-window with a 327 V8. For what he billed to the bank in the first month of helping to organize Travis' money brought him a '46 black Caddy convertible with wide whites and red leather interior.

When George Sam and Travis talked with each other, frequently Timothy didn't know (or care) if they were talking about the inside of a car or the outside.

A seemingly innocent call from Florida on that seemingly innocent November morning would change Timothy's banking career and would eventually necessitate the services of the gastro-intestinal physician at Providence Medical Center and that would lead to George Sam for help. Travis had made the call to Timothy from Florida.

"Timothy, I need you," she had said.

Timothy's crotch had begun to swell. His spine gave out a little shiver in his three-piece pin-stripe and he reached for another cigar from the top of his banker's desk. It had been four years since he had received a call from Travis Duncan and her voice activated him.

"Lady, I'll go anywhere with you, you know that," Timothy purred from his office in Portland, Oregon.

Two days later Timothy stepped into the Florida sunshine and pulled at his tie. His briefcase was heavy with estate books and he was already weary with Travis' mystery. When the magnitude of Travis' situation was explained to him, he could not rely on his years of corporate calm to sustain him. And Travis' years of practicing her eccentricity were fine-tuned enough now to cause him real stress. Huge amounts of money had been lying idle in banks in Canada, Switzerland and Florida...and it was about to move. Timothy sat in the cold air-conditioned Miami office building and sweated through his pin-stripe.

Even though Timothy was the kind of person who would let a piece of egg shell in his scrambled eggs ruin an entire day, Travis had made a wise choice in choosing Timothy. He couldn't handle life, but he could handle money. "Although you're a chauvanistic cretin," she said, "I can count on you with the money."

"How the hell did all this *happen*?" blurted Timothy the minute the elevator doors pressed together and they were alone. He had grabbed her arm in a very un-banker-like gesture.

Travis no longer wheezed in the Florida humidity. She was adjusting...to everything. Accustomed to thinner and cleaner air however, she was anxious to conclude the business and head back to Portland. "It takes a little getting used to, doesn't it?"

Timothy chewed at his moustache; he regarded Travis as if she were a financial grenade with the pin slowly working itself out. He jabbed three times at the "L" button and looked at her to re-ask his question.

Without taking her eyes from the elevator doors she said simply, "I made love to a Cuban."

Chapter 4

Timothy worked his pocket calculator at 30,000 feet and wrote numbers down on a paper pad sliding over the airline's lap tray.

"According to my calculations, Travis," he said, finally, "that's about a million and a half dollars per...ah...encounter."

"Don't be vulgar," said Travis.

Chapter 5

I've made this letter a little longer because
I lack the time to make it shorter.
                              — Blaise Pascal

When Travis handed over her 37-page will to George Sam, she apologized, "Brevity has never been my long suit."
George Sam weighed the document and weighed her demeanor.

"I'm pleased you restricted yourself to a two week assignment," he said.

"My dear friend-in-Zen," she said, "I walked on the beach, ate only natural foods and microwave popcorn, woke every morning at four, meditated thrice daily, refrained from alcohol, drugs and the hardest part — I stayed away from the second hand stores. This is what I want. Put it in legalese and make it happen for me, George Sam. I know it's a tad odd, but can it be done?"

The little Japanese shrugged delicately.

"Can you put a 427 big block in a 1948 Anglia?" he asked.

Travis pretended to light an imaginary welding torch and grinned at the standard streetrodder answer. "Mister," she said, "it's only a matter of time and money."

George Sam smiled a very good natured smile. Travis was a good student.

"Master," she asked, "why is there evil in the world?"

"To thicken the plot," said George Sam.

Chapter 6

After all, what is reality anyway? Nothin'
but a collective hunch.
                                    — *Jane Wagner*

An Oregon autumn sun winks through the west hills and tips the cornices on the Pittock Mansion. The Pittock's front yard overlooks the city of Portland, the ship repair yard and Mt. Hood. H.L. Pittock had been a very large and important brick in the foundation of Portland at the turn of the century. Newspaper magnate, politico and general wealthy person, he built his mansion in Portland in 1911. Now the city owns and cares for the parquet floors, the stained glass, the marble stairs and all the fine, untouchable furnishings. It's a paradox that the city gets your property if you're either very poor or very, very rich.

The thing that Travis had liked most about the mansion was Pittock's seriously engineered approach to bathing. The upstairs bathroom in the Pittock Mansion has no modern-day equal. There are oddly shaped porcelain receptacles for doing things like washing feet. But it is the shower, a small room actually, that holds the tourist's attention. Pittock himself designed it. Chrome tubes surround the white-tiled shower stall and by opening valves at various heights, warm water sprays appropriate parts of the body. One handle is marked, "kidneys." Looking like a Star Trek "transporter," one expects to hear, "Scotty, beam us up." Pittock obviously took his showering very seriously and such engineering and attention to detail had fascinated Travis.

She had also admired the intricate woodwork, the game tables, the wallpaper preserved to perfection, the decorative trim on beds, pots, carpet, hair brushes...it was as if the Pittock family had just stepped out for a Sunday buggy ride. The mansion is 16,000 square feet of old world elegance and craftsmanship, as much as was available in Portland around 1900. The mansion is also well-known and easy to find. Green and white directional signs point the way up Burnside Street and onto the winding West Hills road.

The other thing that made the Pittock Mansion attractive for Travis' purpose was that it was *rentable*. Travis knew the mansion was available because she had attended a feminist Christmas party there. The contrast that evening was heady. All the women were dressed in navy blue or gray business suits with maroon bows tied to their necks. Their fast-tracking, mentoring, upwardly mobile conversations were exchanged in the men's smoking parlor. How many of them, Travis thought, would know how to get tea stains from a silk, beaded dress, or what an antimacassar was for, or how to cut the tip from hubby's cigar?

Travis had not taken the time during the months that she had the money, to buy a mansion of her own. "You can sign all the paperwork you want," said Travis, "but all things in Life are leased, rented, borrowed or swiped, including each adventure, each treasure, each moment, and each other." Travis needed a mansion, or the use of one, for the reading of her will, and she had specified the Pittock Mansion.

The October date was set. A rusted-out Volkswagen rattles its way up the twisting Pittock road and squeals to a jerking halt next to a blue-gray Mercedes with diplomat plates. A thin man with a hook nose steps barefoot from the VW and gathers his caftan around him. He leaves his keys in the ignition as a demonstration of his detachment to the material world, but also because there are no pockets in his caftan. The computer locking system on the Mercedes lights up a warning when The Wizard leans on the door to get a better look.

"And you must be The Wizard," says George Sam as he holds the large oak door open for what looks like a string bean in a bedsheet.

"If you insist," comes a high-pitched bird-like reply.

George Sam slowly closes his black eyes. A tuxedo'ed waiter approaches The Wizard with a trayful of chopped vegetables and tiny handwrapped sushi. Standing next to a marble column in the foyer is the handsome white-haired diplomat, the consul to El Salvador. Something about his stance is both tense and rested, like a marathon runner in a hammock. The Wizard's quirky bird-like glances take in the opulent surroundings. He eyes the older man with unrestrained curiosity. The diplomat gazes back — he's seen plenty of people wearing bed-sheets before. George Sam still stands by the door, quietly observing the action. "Travis is setting the stage," he says to himself.

A piped-in classical violin filters down from above as if a demented violinist is locked in a chamber somewhere. The faint clicking and thudding of silverware on white linen can be heard as the caterers prepare for dinner. The waiter approaches the diplomat who raises his right hand gently, obviously a man who has consumed and turned down a lifetime of canapes.

Tiny broccoli pods bounce away from The Wizard's face as he munches. His bare feet leave steamy footprints on the marble floor.

"Must be cold," remarks the diplomat finally, with warm good humor.

"If you insist," comes the reply.

"I'm Edwin Burroughs," presses the older man extending his hand. A great smile stretches across The Wizard's thin face as he reaches for the hand, graciously ending the masculine dance of suspicion. "If you insist!" The Wizard's voice is now a warm, laughing song. Edwin Burroughs laughs, too.

"I didn't know that this was to be a costume event," remarks Edwin across the foyer to George Sam.

"It's OK," says The Wizard. "You're in costume."

The diplomat adjusts his Phi Beta Kappa key on the chain across the vest of his $700 blue suit. A faint blush crosses the top of his head barely visible through his thick, white hair.

Again the oak door opens and George Sam welcomes a guest in uniform. The black leather shoes reflect the light from the Pittock Mansion's chandeliers. More light flashes from the brass on the Army green suit jacket and from the military buttons. Reflections glance off the bill of his hat as if it were a black mirror. The tie is pulled snug around his neck causing the reddish skin to overflow his collar.

"Colonel Williams, welcome," beams George Sam, extending his hand.

"Mr. Sam," returns the Colonel, holding a letter out to the attorney before taking the handshake. "Then I'm in the right place."

George Sam looks curiously up at the hand-carved ceiling of the mansion's foyer and wonders to himself how many other Portland houses could possibly be mistaken for the Pittock Mansion. He recognizes his legal firm's stationery in the Colonel's hand.

"Oh, yes, yes, you're in the right place," George Sam insists, as he winces from the strength of the grip around his right hand. He sighs a little when the pumping vice releases its hold. He takes the letter pointing at him.

"The order of the day," says Colonel Williams to the paper. His bulldog chest presses against his uniform jacket straining the brass buttons in their holes.

"You've got to admit," whispers the colonel to the little attorney, "this evening is hardly...regulation."

"Although it will be legally correct in every way, Colonel," says the polite George Sam, "there may be some interesting surprises..."

The colonel removes his hat, tosses it gently in his hands as if it were a Frisbee, keeps his head lowered and his eyes move to George Sam.

"We don't have a Pearl Harbor brewing here, do we?" asks the Army officer with a faint grin that says this is anything but an old joke.

Muscles in George Sam's neck tense and then release. With a look of inspiration, George Sam quotes: "The invincible warrior invites surprise and turns it to his advantage."

The eyes under the military crewcut narrow slightly and the colonel asks, "Confucious?"

The sweet bow lips of the tiny attorney says, "No. George Patton."

Chapter 7

If there's a will, I want to be in it.
— Anonymous

A black and yellow taxi enters the circular driveway of the Pittock and slowly stops on the damp pavement. The October sun now just tips the landmark pines. The young cab driver helps pull an old pot-bellied man from the back seat passenger door. Then he waits as much for the tip as to see if the old brown man can negotiate the car's door. He stands, stooped to two-thirds his height, eyeing the cabbie for a moment and says, "Want a tip?"

The embarrassed cab driver shifts and holds out his hand.

"Wash your white walls with Spic and Span," says Hershell as he dotters away towards the mansion's door, the cuffs of his baggy brown pants brushing the wet pavement.

"Have a good time," says the cabbie, sarcastically, pulling at his cap and circling the yellow car.

"Of course I haven't much *time,*" snaps the slightly deaf Hershell, "I'm *old*!"

The old man's wide-angle tennis shoes thwock-thwock up the steps to the Pittock Mansion's oak door and he stands like a plump goose, webbed feet at a 90 degree angle, head tossed slightly back searching for the doorbell. He locates the ivory and brass button but just before he starts to press his vanilla bean finger to it, the large oak door opens.

"Ah, Mr. Hershell Kaye, welcome, sir," the polite George Sam says, "No need to ring the bell."

"Now that I *found* it, I'm bloody well going to ring the god-damned thing," says Hershell, sending chimes echoing through the foyer. The melody in tinkling brass continues for a lengthy half minute as all eyes are now on the doorway. Hershell looks around the foyer at the surprised faces. He pulls back and examines the double oak doors. He pats the wood gently with his withered hands and says, "Just makin' sure they aren't the pearly gates in disguise. I thought the music sounded familiar."

Hershell slaps one of his snowshoe-sized feet into the foyer and takes George Sam's arm to pull himself over the threshold. Colonel Williams offers his braided arm to help ship-assist docking the old man.

"ARE WE TO BE UNDER GUARD?" demands Hershell, eyeing the uniform but unable to identify it. Hershell's ancient, drooping eyelids look like melting vanilla frosting on a hot cake. His bushy eyebrows go north when he understands something and his filmy eyes somehow sparkle through their normally cloudy blue haze.

"No, no," soothes George Sam, "these are invited participants, as you are, sir."

Hershell winces at the decoration on Col. Williams' chest and like a gun turret, he turns on the Japanese. "You the attorney?" he asks, his voice being pressed through sandpaper.

"Yes, sir, I'm George Sam and this is..."

"Don't like attorneys," Hershell snaps. "I used to be one."

"And this," continues the patient George Sam, "is Col. Bobby Williams, United States Army..."

"Don't like the military either," Hershell spits gruffly. He takes a step closer to the Japanese-American and studies him for a moment. "And you shouldn't either," he advises. Hershell totters past the two men and into the foyer where he spies the tray of hors d'oeuvres. The palm tree print in Hershell's Hawaiian shirt billows around his stout body giving the illusion of a hurricane in progress.

"I *like* food," he says as he chomps a cucumber and ham dip cracker.

There is a slight jingle of a Phi Betta Kappa key as the white-haired diplomat extends his hand in warm greeting to Hershell.

"Edwin Burroughs, good evening, sir," says Edwin.

"One thing about getting *old,* Edwin," quips Hershell as he focuses on Edwin's white hair, "everybody calls you 'sir', sir,"

Edwin's diplomatic training allows him to appear to ignore the remark.

"Let me introduce you to The Wizard," says Edwin, a slightly sadistic tone in his voice.

The Wizard bounces playfully in his caftan and shakes Hershell's brown hand.

"You a *real* wizard?" Hershell askes.

"If you insist," says The Wizard.

"Act more like a kangaroo."

"Travis called me 'The Wizard.' "

The foyer is silenced. The name had not been spoken before. Even the clattering of silverware ceases. George Sam reviews the four faces. Hershell pulls himself erect and looks hard at The Wizard.

"Then for tonight, sir, you most certainly are a wizard."

Hershell pulls a dripping champagne glass from a serving tray and lifts it in the direction of The Wizard in salute. Edwin repeats the gesture.

"You're very tan, Mr. Kaye," the diplomat observes to Hershell. "You must not be from Oregon. What do you do?"

"I run a nudist camp outside of Phoenix," responds Hershell without the slightest hesitation.

Colonel Williams turns abruptly to George Sam.

"Who *is* this guy?" he whispers loudly into George's ear.

"He's Hershell Kaye," said George Sam, "and he owns a nudist camp just outside of Phoenix."

Chapter 8

If you don't know where you're going, any
road will take you there.
                                   — *Lewis Carroll*

It's a narrow, twisting road that brings the tourist up the West Hills of Portland to the Pittock Mansion. An easy jaunt for the horse and buggy it originally served, the Pittock Road, although paved, is still worthy of slow going. Several turns resemble the vertebrae of a dying snake, doubling back and to the left up the steep hill. Once past the gatekeeper's house, there is only one more severe left turn.

A white Jaguar turns right off of Burnside onto the West Hills road and confidently makes its way up the entrance road. The evening sun is now nearly gone and the Jaguar logo is nearly invisible on the engine hood of the car. A blaring, trapped Vivaldi is muffled behind the black glass. The car begins to take the turns a bit too fast and slips, spraying gravel into the tall pines.

Back on Burnside, a red Kenworth semi truck catches the last of the sun on its goldleaf lettering: Lindsay Trucking, We Go All The Way! A cab with no trailer or cargo, the truck downshifts as it approaches the first right turn but it doesn't come to a stop. The large decorative chrome lugnuts spin fancifully as the truck lunges up the incline. The squirrels in the pines overhead jerk and twitch to the unfamiliar sound of a grinding Caterpillar engine, the howl of a Hank Williams, Sr. song and the spatter of the CB radio.

Although the sports car started the climb up Pittock Drive first, the Kenworth soon overtakes it. The steep grade, usually no challenge for a Jag, seems not to have sapped any of the strength of the Kenworth either. The delicate hum-hum of the English pistons are easily drownd by the diesel orchestra of the Cat V-8.

The Jaguar slows on a curve and the Kenworth logo fills the rear windshield of the sports car. The car leaps forward like a scalded puppy and nearly loses control on the next turn. The truck maintains its grinding pace and soon reappears in the side mirrors of the sports car above the type that reads: OBJECTS MAY APPEAR CLOSER.

The high, wide tires of the Kenworth nearly fill the path of the narrow one and a half lane road. Soon the tires are spitting tiny flecks of gravel onto the chrome and black bumper of the Jaguar as it tries to escape up the hillside.

The gatekeeper's house in sight, the white car grabs for branches on the left side of the road and flings itself into the last curve, now heading into the parking lot straight toward the Mercedes with the diplomat plates. There is a brief squeal from outside the car and inside the car. The Jag does a 180 and stops abruptly parked backwards next to its European brother.

Chapter 9

*Those who flee temptation generally leave
a forwarding address.*
— *Lane Olinghouse*

George Sam, who had been standing at his post, is thrown into the wall as the oak door flies open and a bear-like man takes one giant step into the foyer.

"I WAS NEARLY RUN DOWN BY A TRUCK GETTING HERE!"

Holbrook Biasi stands, wobbly, in all his rumpled splendor, his announcement and entry gaining everyone's attention. He moves like a pirate who has suddenly been dropped into the twentieth century and dressed by an amused Edith Head. His head and face are framed in a mass of salt-and-pepper curls. In the darkness, his navy blue sweater almost passes for a priest's collar, disappearing under his beard. The wrinkled and well-worn cashmere jacket seems to be in a sitting position while he is standing. . .reeling actually. He seems to have experienced a close call in his drive up to the Pittock, but then most things in Holbrook Biasi's life are close calls.

George Sam regains his balance and adjusts the gold rims to his nose.

"How could you be run down," asks George Sam, "by a truck *while going up* Pittock Drive?"

The large man whirls as if he were a Brahma bull taking the last bit of guff from a pesky cowboy. He stares wild-eyed at the attorney and lowers his head for a fatal horned attack.

"Pardon me, Mr. Biasi. . .it is Biasi, isn't it?" George begins. "But the truck in question, sir, it was a Kenworth?"

Holbrook looks at the little Japanese as if he is reciting nursery rhymes in surgery.

"WHAT ARE YOU TALKING ABOUT? The nose cone of that 18-wheeler was so close to my bumper that I couldn't make out the brand *name,* for Chrissake!"

"Then if I don't miss my guess, Mr. Biasi, right behind you should be Lash Lindsay. George points towards the door. Holbrook Biasi's eyes move like popcorn popping in slow motion. In another bull-like gesture, he turns angrily towards the door, his arms slightly outward from his sides.

"LASH?!" roars Biasi.

The door gently opens and a petite figure of a boy-man enters wearing pale blue jeans, boots, plaid shirt, sunglasses and a cowboy hat. He is barely five feet three, a miniature person.

"Someone call me?" says Lash.

Biasi expects to see someone behind the boy and looks out into the parking lot. He glares at the back of the little trucker who is now shaking hands with George Sam. George Sam begins cleaning the smudge from his glasses, put there while he had been part of the foyer's wall.

"A Kenworth," confirms George Sam.

The silvergrey cowboy hat nods one nod, the little smile grows broader inside the little brown beard and his miniature thumbs hook in his belt loops.

"I am George Sam," the lawyer begins. "I am kind of...your host...this evening and I would like to introduce you both...to the other guests. Mr. Lash Lindsay, please meet Mr. Holbrook Biasi."

Biasi comes to from his rage for a moment and he studies the boy-man.

"Are *you* the one who brought that goddamned semi up Pittock Drive?"

"Yeah," says Lash Lindsay modestly, then adds, "but it weren't no trouble with no trailer on 'er."

"Don't you have a *normal car*?" hisses Biasi.

The front of the cowboy hat dips ever so slightly. "Mister, that's my car, my home, my business and my lady. What can you say about *your* car?"

Biasi's upper torso expands.

"Only that it's the finest engineering..."

"Oh, was that you in that tin can car?"

The six-foot-four frame and thickening middle-aged body dwarfs the driver.

"That Jaguar is hardly a 'TIN CAN CAR'!" sputters Biasi.

"Understand they have a pretty good sound system," comments Lash, stepping past Biasi into the foyer with the discussion over.

The heels of his cowboy boots make ka-lunking sounds on the white marble floor. Lash crosses the foyer and waves to his audience of four stunned faces, champagne glasses in each of their hands. He spies the champagne bottles and touches the sleeve of the waiter. "Got any beer back there?" he asks, pointing towards the dining room.

"I'll see what we can find, sir," says the waiter arching his neck and blinking his eyes at the same time.

The little trucker adjusts the Kenworth belt buckle at his waist.

"You appear to be a diplomat," says Edwin, the diplomat, and he extends his hand. "I'm Edwin Burroughs. Good evening. And this is Col. Williams. Hershell Kaye. The Wizard."

Lash shakes the colonel's hand and nods his head. He shakes Hershell's old, brown hand and the tip of his cowboy hat again dips slightly. He sees The Wizard and both of his hands stay at his waist. "Howdy," he says.

"How is it that you came to be known as 'Lash'?" asks Edwin.

The cowboy hat dips low this time and perhaps there is even a slight blush. "I don't know, sir, it's just a nickname I picked up." The little trucker removes his sunglasses and reveals his namesake when he again looks into their eyes.

What Sissy Hankshaw was to thumbs, Lash Lindsay is to eyelashes. Their length and weight wave like fronds of a palm tree. Every few seconds his warm brown eyes are basked by the feathered fans that line his eyelids. Lash Lindsay has the longest eyelashes in North America.

The other four men stare unabashedly and even Hershell's eyebrows go up in amazement.

"I go out to drinkin' with my buddies and they say that the first thing they got to do to get anywheres with the ladies is to blacken both my eyes."

Chapter 10

Experience is a hard teacher — because she gives the test first and the lesson afterwards.

— Anonymous

"**M**r. Biasi!"

Holbrook Biasi wheels and gives a pirate squint to the voice just coming through the oak door. The last guest has just arrived.

"I've met you before, Mr. Biasi," says the newcomer, a shorter and younger man, extending his hand to Holbrook. "We were at a reception featuring your drawings of the memorial. I'm Chadwick Ollander."

Biasi relaxes slightly. He adores being recognized.

"I'm sorry," he says, sincerely, "I don't remember. . ."

"Oh, there's no reason why you should," says Chadwick, "but it was at the Design Gallery in Toronto. I really enjoyed your work. Great design. Superb craftsmanship."

Biasi seems reluctant to release the handshake now that there is someone there who is familiar with his work and appreciates it. His bear-like shoulders drop a little and his eyes crinkle good-naturedly at Chadwick.

"I really don't remember much after those openings," apologizes Biasi. He self-consciously touches his red nose and rubs the side of it. "And what do you do?"

"A little land development," Chadwick answers, waving his hand to dismiss any importance. A cuff link flashes as Chadwick folds his arms casually. Even in this posture, Chadwick's suit fits perfectly. Biasi, feeling hulk-like next to the diminutive Chadwick, begins studying the younger man's suit, whose measurements are on a computer disk at Nordstrom's. His 36 Short appears to have been tailored by a surgeon. If Chadwick were a building designed by a competitor, Biasi, an architect, could not have studied the detail more closely. The petite developer has no imperfections; his body proportions — length of arms to height, his head size to his shoulder width — are classical, like the Parthenon. Not a single whisker has escaped the blade; it is as if there are no hairs on his face ever. There is not a freckle, a bump or a dot on his skin showing anywhere. His crystal blue eyes look like a sky showing through the back of his head.

"Oh, this is the attorney, here," Biasi finally comes to from his fascination.

George Sam extends his hand and bows slightly to Chadwick. "I am happy to meet you, Mr. Ollander; I am George Sam. We talked earlier this week."

"Yes, yes, Mr. Sam," Chadwick says, giving the attorney the same blue-eyed focus he had given Biasi.

"I understand that you do well with Japanese businessmen," says George Sam, "perhaps it is because you see eye to eye with them."

Chadwick's half smile is precisely a half smile. It isn't a three quarters length grin or a slight Mona Lisa rendition either. It is not 49% or 51%...it is a half smile.

There is only a faint guess of thinning brown hair at the back of Chadwick's perfectly sculpted skull. Just as there is only the faintest unidentifiable scent coming from him. Chadwick's pale blue eyes, located precisely and evenly at the top of the triangle above his cheekbones take in, edit and process information about George Sam and Holbrook Biasi.

There is a trace, and just a trace, of a New York accent. It is more like a hint of sage in a good garlic sausage...just the merest indication of a street fighter in impeccable tailoring.

Biasi straightens himself and pulls the tire he wears around his waist in slightly. He feels bulkier than his sweater...so far, everyone he has met in the mansion has been five feet seven or shorter. He catches the glimpse of a twinkle of light reflecting on a champagne top and his mouth begins to water.

"Well, join the party, Chad, how 'bout a glass of champagne? I know *I'm* ready."

The perfect half-smile on Chadwick's face goes down to 42%. "Chadwick," he says, barely audibly, but the architect has already directed his course to the bottles and glasses.

"Mr. Ollander," purrs George Sam, "may I introduce you to the other guests...?"

The smile drops to 33%. "Yes," says Chadwick, "You were sufficiently vague in your letter about this evening, Mr. Sam. I don't go into many situations not having a full accounting of the proceedings."

"I know and I appreciate that," George Sam apologizes with a slight bow. "The timing of your arrival and your recognition of Mr. Biasi was perfect, Mr. Ollander, and I'm grateful...you saved a situation from escalating..."

Chadwick looks at the Japanese as if nothing less than perfection is possible and why be surprised. The attorney accepts the surprise and he waves his left hand to welcome Chadwick Ollander into the foyer.

"Is this everyone?" asks Chadwick, his glance taking in micro-information about the other six men.

"Yes, you are the last participant to arrive..." says George Sam. "But a banker will be making a short guest appearance pretty soon...I hope." George Sam pulls his white linen sleeve back and checks his gold watch.

Chadwick sees the time piece and lifts his wrist to check his Rolex, pausing purposely to make sure that George Sam notes that it is not an imitation.

Chapter 11

*A mind, like a parachute, has to be open
to function properly.*

— *Anonymous*

Sheets washed and dried in the summer fresh air feel and smell
differently than those tumbled dry in a Maytag. It is as if dry-
ing by a manmade method is somehow fake to the bedsheet. Such is the
"warmth" in the foyer of the Pittock Mansion on this Wednesday
evening in October. The conversations among the guests
("participants" as George Sam calls them) is like the air from the Maytag — warm, but a piped-in, trumped-up warmth.

They hold their champagne glasses gently but firmly and those that
have pockets, play with their change. Most stand equally on both feet
so as to avoid being thrown off balance. The hors d'oeuve tray comes
around again and again until its entry into a conversation becomes a
welcomed interruption. Questions punctuate the low rumble that is a
roomful of men talking.

They ask, "And where are you from?"

"And what do you do?"

"And what do you think the Lakers will do this year?"

No one asks the question, "What the hell are you doing here?"

As if by some unspoken direction, they group in three's and question and answer some time away. They compare and categorize each
other by success and stature as they gather information, their egos di-
viding each other into "threat" or "no threat." The sugar plum waltz
of communication continues smoothly until an occasional discord can
be heard. The misplayed chord is ignored until it becomes more and
more obvious that the song is changing from a major key to a minor
key. The disharmony is barely audible for a while, taking place only
within their impressions of each other. Then it begins to squeak out in
the reed section and slip through in the strings.

Edwin Burroughs and Col. Bobby Williams get into it over global
politics...

"If you goddamn political types would only let us do our jobs, the military could solve problems in about a week. Instead, we drag out death tolls while you discuss the size and the shape of the table!''

"It is the military mindset that brings us to the table and requires its creation in the first place.''

"We cannot experience peace without first creating it within,'' interjects The Wizard.

Hershell Kaye and Chadwick Ollander discuss corporate life...

"I used to be a corporate, high mucky muck,'' says Hershell, reading Chadwick's exterior. "I was on the board of directors for the Southern Pacific railroad.''

"Why did you decide to...ah...change and start a nudist... resort?''

"'Cause I looked around the boardroom one day,'' says Hershell, his slug eyes blinking, "and I noticed that the best dressed ones died first.''

Chadwick's creases twitch just slightly. He touches his maroon silk tie.

Just when Chadwick is about to risk the indulgence of a second glass of champagne, Hershell explains how he put his UGN contribution on his corporate expense account.

"They ordered me to give money. It wasn't *my* idea,'' says Hershell, "so I put it on my expense account.''

"You *what*?''

Chadwick Ollander is irritated at Hershell because Chadwick hadn't thought of doing the same thing *first*. It was clearly the act of a creative man.

Biasi camps next to the champagne service. George Sam has strategically positioned himself between the architect and Lash Lindsay, who sucks easily on a beer can and wipes his moustache with his tongue.

The threesomes break apart and reassemble like square dancers on the mansion's floor. With each regrouping there is greater opportunity for values to find conflict. No one is intent on polite expression of brotherhood except The Wizard, who seems to irritate everybody.

"Haven't met an architect *yet* who could design a building with a decent ventilation system,'' Hershell Kaye grouses to Holbrook Biasi.

"You a land developer...?'' muses Lash. "How do you guys manage to manhandle the environmentalists when the loggers can't get to first base?''

"Man must have space to commune with Nature,'' The Wizard interjects.

"Why don't you ask Hershell here about that...he *really* communes...'' says Edwin Burroughs.

"Know the definition of a diplomat?'' Hershell says, peering up at the tall, white-haired gentleman. "That's a person who can tell you to go to hell in such a way that you enjoy making the trip. Diplomats! Responsible for more wars than religion!''

"And I suppose taking your clothes off and simply wandering off into the buckbrush...no pun intended...is a solution?'' returns the consul.

"Get to see a lot, huh?'' Lash asks, licking beer foam from his beard and nudging old Hershell.

"Joe Sixpack!'' Hershell retorts, "it's not like you imagine at all!''

"Pervert,'' Biasi says but no one knows if he means Lash or Hershell.

"Pervert? Being nude is a natural and beautiful experience. Perversion is left to us by the neurotic military and their fascination with violence and paranoia!'' barks Hershell.

"You *want* to speak Russian?'' protests Col. Williams, his bulldog neck flashing red.

"Something the matter with Russian?'' asks The Wizard, rocking playfully on the heels of his bare feet.

"There's a bit more at stake here than language...'' adds Edwin.

"Speaking of steak...when's supper?'' asks Lash. "Most of this stuff here,'' he says pointing to the sushi, "wouldn't make good bait!''

"Oh, for Christ's sake,'' Hershell groans.

"A little politeness, *please*,'' twitters The Wizard.

"Interesting thing for you to say, standing there in your bare feet while there is food being served. Aren't there laws about that...?'' says Chadwick, flaring his symetrical nostrils.

"Government regulations are killing private enterprise.''

"The whole system is based on who can regulate who...''

"And you know who pays...''

"Only the lawyers get rich.''

"If they'd do something about foreign imports.''

"Just cut military spending...''

"Just tax the churches...''

"Refuse to pay...''

"Bunch of moochers on welfare.''

"We must take care of the...''

"Nobody took care of *me!*''

"We must...''

"They should...''

"We ought to...''

"You can't...''

"We simply have to...''

George Sam checks his watch, listens for its ticking and checks it again. He checks with the supervisor of catering and he checks the darkening driveway for headlights. He checks behind a low table for his thick brief case and he checks the copies of his legal papers. He checks on the seven men in the foyer and he is suddenly, terribly, reminded of his '29 roadster just before it blew a $600 rod. He watches from his spot by the door, in horror, as both Col. Williams and Edwin Burroughs step back from each other with fists clenched...aiming for The Wizard.

Chapter 12

Women have served all these centuries as looking-glasses processing the magic and delicious power of reflecting the figure of a man at twice its natural size.
— Virginia Woolf

"**E**vening, gentlemen!" Timothy barks as he steps into the foyer, across it and into the dining room. His simple announcement carries with it the demand for all to follow him. They do.

Lash Lindsay, who has a history of knowing a punch before it happens, is the one who snapped the colonel's fist in mid-air as deftly as a frog plucks a mosquito from pond water. Biasi does not understand how Lash could have seen the punch coming.

Edwin Burroughs had amazed and frightened himself. He studies his fist incredulously. In thirty years of protocol, negotiations, offers and counteroffers, egomaniacs and dictators, coups and embassy dinners, terrorist attacks, espionage, sabotage and incompetence, he had not raised an eyebrow, much less a fist. But then, after thirty years, the arguments, the strategies and the approaches to solutions came in neatly wrapped packages. The opinions expressed by the military colonel weren't new to Edwin; it was boring in its familiarity and Edwin had his script memorized to respond to it. The Wizard, however, had spoken and asked questions from a basis unknown to the diplomatic corp — the spiritual dimension. Edwin had broken a perfect record of control.

"I apologize. I am so sorry," Edwin says with the dismay of it still on his face.

Col. Bobby Williams adjusts his jacket and growls slightly. "Yeah," he says to The Wizard. Hershell Kaye is disappointed that someone hasn't rearranged The Wizard. The Wizard is the only one *not* surprised and has not moved. His belief system allows for the smashing in of his enormous nose and the absolute acceptance of that. In return, however, he would also allow for the kicking of the colonel's balls into his military belt buckle and could feel the same sense of perfect acceptance.

Like a platoon of Boy Scouts, they follow Timothy into the dining room.

Chadwick Ollander has a new respect for Lash Lindsay, who had snatched the colonel's fist. "How did you know that was going to happen?" he asks the trucker, who is nine inches shorter than the military man.

The little trucker shrugs. The Wizard hears the question and his quirky expression grows to a serious wisdom as he says, "Intuition is never complicated."

George Sam takes his small brown hands down from in front of his glasses. He looks from side to side and wonders how Timothy had managed to change the scene so quickly. Timothy, of course, hyper and head down, is oblivious to any friction. He always carries his own.

When George Sam enters the creme-colored dining room, Timothy is unpacking his brief case at the head of the table and the seven "participants" are looking to George for direction.

"Oh, sit anywhere, gentlemen," he says, still a little mystified.

A wide oval table with pounds of gleaming silver half fills the high-ceilinged ballroom, converted for this evening into a dining hall. Tall, ornate candelabras support a dozen lit white candles that cast thousands of tiny lights on the china. The warm candlelight softens the whites into cream. Three waiters in tuxedos pull chairs ceremoniously, candlelight reflecting in their shirt studs. There are display cabinets in the room depicting historical Portland, but no windows. Two French doors, located at either end of the room, open into the smoking and card rooms.

The Wizard spreads his caftan as if it were an evening dress and lowers his tush into a needlepoint padded dining chair. Edwin Burroughs adjusts the key over his vest when it clanks into the edge of his dinner plate. Col. Williams settles his ample chest inside his uniform and keeps his coat buttoned. Chadwick takes his place next to the colonel and realigns his tie when he is seated. Biasi, still feeling some comfort from Chadwick's earlier comments, chooses to sit next to the land developer. Hershell, having difficulty with his large tennis shoes on the thick wool carpet, kicks both Biasi and Lash Lindsay as he docks himself into his dining chair. Lash looks irritably at Hershell, winces, but doesn't complain. George Sam stands behind his chair to Lash's left.

"You have all been most patient," George Sam begins.

"No, we haven't," corrects Lash, a toothpick magically appearing from his lips. Edwin Burroughs drops his head slightly, still embarrassed. Col. Williams frowns at Lash.

"Am I going to live long enough to see the end of this stupid mystery?" asks Hershell.

Biasi looks across the oval end of the table at the old man. "That depends," he teases, "how's your blood pressure?"

Hershell harumphs impatiently.

"You do *old* real good, you know that?" Lash says to the octogenarian on his right. "You got it *down,* know what I mean?"

The Wizard bounces in his chair rhythmically and giggles, "You're right! He does!"

Lash zaps a look across the other end of the table and says, "I don't need no agreement from some dude in a dress."

Timothy is still standing with his brief case next to George Sam, The Wizard to his left. He clears his throat abruptly and looks to George Sam. "I see they've all met each other," he comments. "Gentlemen, this is a business meeting. I am Timothy Anzil with the U.S. Bank. My office is here in Portland, Oregon. I am here to assist George Sam in the disposition of property...and to serve as a possible resource for your...ah, challenge...this evening."

"What the hell do we need a banker for?" asks Biasi. Bankers had foiled many an architectural plan in Biasi's past.

Chadwick Ollander's left forefinger touches the sleeve of Biasi's right hand, a champagne glass in it, half empty. "Holbrook..."

"Biasi!" says Holbrook Biasi. "I'm just called *Biasi.*"

"Biasi," repeats Chadwick, patiently, "we're all here for reasons that I assume we are only vaguely aware. It is a pleasant evening in a pleasant, historical place. Now unless the food is substandard, I suggest that we have nothing to lose this evening by going along with what these two have to tell us. We can only extend the drama by interrupting."

"I have to pee," says Hershell, pulling his chair away from the table.

"Jeez." "Oh, for cryin' out loud." "Sheez." The six others raze Hershell.

"Well, just get started without me," says Hershell. "I'll catch up."

"I am afraid, Mr. Kaye," George Sam explains to Hershsell, "that we can't do that. Everyone must be here for all words stated. It is part of the agreement and it is what Timothy and I *must* do."

"Well, then, serve the salad."

Chapter 13

Monotony is the awful reward of the careful.

— Anonymous

Gold plates with lettuce leaves appear at each elegant dinner setting. Champagne glasses are refreshed. The fat white chrysanthemums in the center of the formal table drop a few more petals on the linen tablecloth. In the distance, the violin renews its melodies. Small clear ice cubes tinkle like wind chimes in the crystal drinking glasses. "No more for him," says Lash Lindsay, pointing to Hershell's drinking glass, "or we'll never get out of here."

Timothy waves his salad away and opens the plastic wrapper on a Maalox tablet. He chews it and sips a little champagne. He looks at The Wizard who is happily munching to his left, croutons falling in his lap. Timothy's moustache twitches like a restless caterpillar. "For a holy man, you're kind of a slob, aren't you?" he asks.

A piece of Romaine disappears between The Wizard's thin lips. The fact that he has no chin is exaggerated by his large Arabian-type nose. "Uh-hum," The Wizard bounces in agreement. Timothy watches the gas bubbles in his champagne glass and then turns to George Sam.

"Can we get on with this?"

George Sam has still not taken his seat, preferring to stand. "Yes," he says, then there is a large sigh as he picks up his legal sized pages.

"In my practice," he begins, "I have been asked to do a variety of unusual things. People are very creative with their legal requests when it comes to estate law. This, however, is perhaps the most unusual, the most intricate and the most challenging since even I won't know what is to be awarded until tomorrow morning."

The seven guests look at each other and then to the attorney. "What?" "Then why are we here now?" "Thanks for the grub, call me in the morning." "What the hell...?"

"AND..." George Sam again gains control, "the men in this room will determine the amount and the proper recipients of the award."

Chadwick's jaw muscle is working and his plate is empty. "Let's cut to the chase," he says. "How much 'award' are we talking about?"

"TWENTY-THREE MILLION DOLLARS," snaps Timothy. Seven forks hit seven plates. George Sam flashes a look of disapproval at Timothy. "This will be difficult enough to explain if we don't do it chronologically..."

"I just thought you'd like their undivided attention," Timothy replies with a shrug and a low burp.

George Sam's right hand pulls at the lapel of his white linen suit. "It's like this then...you're all here because you all know or have known...Travis Duncan." Seven pairs of eyes study their dinner plates. "When Travis died six months ago she left this sizable estate and no living relatives. She came up with this rather creative will that leaves the monetary part of her estate...as stated, twenty-three million dollars...to you seven..."

Seven pairs of eyes dilate.

"But there are *conditions*!" he rapidly warns.

Seven heads cock slightly.

"You've met the first part of the conditions. You arrived here this evening for this dinner at the Pittock Mansion and your expenses for getting here have been paid by the estate."

George Sam shifts to his left foot.

"Why don't you sit down," says Timothy, "we're going to be here awhile anyway."

George Sam pulls at the back of his chair.

"Good Lord, man, what do we have to do for the money?" asks Biasi at the opposite end of the table.

George Sam nests in his chair and sips at his water glass. "Well," he says, a little more relaxed now, "you have to compete for it."

Seven pairs of elbows hit the linen table top. "What?"

"I'll fill you in on the details," says the little attorney, "but basically, it's this: you all have three things in common...you all knew Travis Duncan, you're all men and the last thing...you have to figure out for yourselves. The question before you is: what do you all have in common? The correct answer wins."

Chapter 14

*And think not you can guide the course of
Love, for Love, if it finds you worthy,
shall guide your course."*
                                    — Kahlil Gibran

The witnesses for Travis' will had been Dr. Robert Frye, head
of the psychiatric division of the Oregon Medical School and
Justice Harold Prine, Oregon Supreme Court judge. There would be no
contesting Travis' intricate legal request.

" 'I, Travis Afb Duncan, presently of Multnomah County, Oregon, do hereby make and declare this to be my LAST WILL AND TES-
TAMENT. I direct that my just debts and funeral expenses be promptly
paid.' "

George Sam stops reading aloud and explains that Travis had no
formal funeral, as was her request, and that her final "arrangements"
and debts were insignificant and had been honored immediately upon
her death. The estate was free and clear of obligation. Her large old
home had been a gift to the Women's Phoenix Program, an organization providing shelter for abused women and children on the run from
"unfortunate circumstances." The house was now part of the nationwide underground railroad of women creating new identities for themselves and their children. When Travis had owned the house, she had
cocooned in it; now it was filled with noise and toys and counselling.

"If there is anything that you do not understand, or anything that
requires additional explanation, please ask. It is imperative that you all
understand the elements of this...ah, well..."

"Predicament," finishes Timothy. He looks around the table at
the seven faces and his moustache twitches. "This money has been *my*
predicament for the last year, now it's your turn," he says, sarcastically.

"You should have called," says Lash, "I would have taken it off
your hands."

"Can you just shut up until we get the whole picture here?" snaps
Biasi, gripping the arms of his dinner chair.

George Sam's black almond eyes return to his papers. "You have only this night to complete your assignment, gentlemen."

"What assignment?" asks Col. Williams.

"I am serious when I tell you that this is a contest, of sorts," explains George Sam. "And the time frame is from this moment until sunrise. Timothy and I are here to explain the perimeters and to give you information and then we will leave. You will stay and confer with each other...decide among yourselves how you are going to handle this...ah...challenge. Timothy and I will return at dawn for your answers..."

George Sam looks at the duffle bags under Timothy's eyes and sees that the banker's dinner this evening will once again be Maalox and alcohol. "How you all choose to go about your research is your own affair. But the question is this: what do you all have in common? The man who answers that correctly will leave this room a millionaire."

"What if nobody gets the answer?" asks Chadwick, drumming his knife on the table.

"There is a provision for that possibility. If a correct answer is not given by any of you, then the award goes to a scholarship fund to support college-enrolled women, with children, who find themselves in financial need while filing divorce proceedings."

"I beg your pardon," says Edwin, "you did say to interrupt when we didn't understand something..."

George Sam looks over the tops of his gold-rimmed glasses patiently at the consul to El Salvador. "Yes?" he purrs.

"A scholarship fund to...what was that again?"

Timothy interrupts, "A difficult thing to monitor, I know, I've been all through this...but it gives money to women who, employed or unemployed, have children and attend college. If, part way through their education, they find themselves in need of a divorce, this fund pays their legal fees and for expenses of child care and tuition. Don't try to make any sense of it..."

"But that would actually *encourage divorce!*" says Edwin.

"How well did you know Travis?" asks Hershell from the other side of the table.

"Oh." Edwin moves stiffly in his chair.

"Yep, that's Travis. I'd recognize her anywhere," says Hershell, smiling to himself and shaking his head.

"What time is sunrise?" asks Chadwick. Timothy and George Sam look at the blue eyes of the developer, now turning from sky blue to steel blue.

"On with the hunt, eh?" says Timothy.

"You have approximately eight and a half hours to come to some sort of conclusion and each of you must *write* your guess.

"Confer with each other or don't. There are no rules. You have the use of the Pittock Mansion for the night. Enjoy your dinner, gentlemen.''

"This is really ridiculous," says the Colonel. "We don't have *anything* in common!"

"Travis selected the menu for tonight's dinner in her will," says Timothy, side-tracking. "I hope you like it...Pacific Northwest baked salmon with a dill sauce, green beans almondine, new potatoes and a really special dessert..." He smiles maliciously.

"At least she didn't cook it herself," shudders Chadwick.

"Right on!" they all agree.

"She could take normal potatoes," Lash says, "and turn 'em into hash blacks."

"Actually I got kinda used to having 'em that way," muses Biasi sadly.

"Until you leave, we can ask questions...I've got several," says Chadwick to the attorney and the banker.

"I'll just bet you have..." says Timothy.

"You said that each of us has known Travis Duncan. Do you mean that...in a, ah, biblical sense?"

"Precisely," growls Timothy, remembering Travis in her grey crepe dress in Florida.

Six heads turn slowly towards Hershell and six pairs of eyes widen. Hershell leans back slightly and he pulls at his Hawaiian shirt. "There may be snow on the roof," he says indignantly, "but there's still a fire in the furnace!"

There is an uncomfortable silence punctuated by a blush here, a paleness there, hands stop moving and other hands are wiped dry on cloth napkins. Biasi's beard rests in his hands and he looks very tired. The Wizard has stopped his rhythm bouncing and his thin face looks drawn. Edwin is pale, matching his hair. Lash Lindsay tips his cowboy hat back and runs his hand across his forehead to loosen the hair stuck there. Col. Williams' cheeks puff out like a children's illustration of wind and he finally unbuttons his jacket. Chadwick hasn't moved a muscle.

The three waiters serve the salmon in the silence with dill sauce and they look from face to face, mystified. They vanish quietly like frightened little animals, return to deliver the dessert cart, set up the coffee service, nod to George Sam and disappear. The engine of their departing panel truck can barely be heard from within the thick walls of the Pittock Mansion.

Chapter 15

Never grow a wishbone, daughter, where
your backbone ought to be.
                                    — C. Paddleford

"How did Travis get that much money and how did she die?" asks Col. Williams, loosening his tie and resting his fork.

George Sam turns to Timothy for the explanation. "I knew Travis for quite awhile," Timothy begins, "but, not, of course, as *you* knew her." At this, he fondles his champagne glass and his moustache hides a smirk of deep disappointment. "She was financially OK before the money came anyway. She took care of business, paid her bills, stayed out of debt, had no great compulsions..."

George Sam's head goes up slightly.

"...except for old cars," Timothy adds.

"She had a '40 Ford when I knew her," pipes up Lash Lindsay.

"She had a burned up Volkswagen when I knew her," says Col. Williams.

"She had a bicycle when I knew her," puts in Edwin Burroughs.

"She didn't have a pot to piss in when I knew her," says Hershell Kaye.

"Hold your personal stories until I'm out of here, PLEASE!" gnashes Timothy. "There *is* a limit..." Timothy's mind is once more in Florida, in a Miami bar, sitting across from Travis. The bottom button on her skirt is unfastened and she is unaware that the second button is slipping from its hole. Timothy's memory is fogged by the three Scotches already consumed. Travis is leaning forward towards him across the tiny round cocktail table. "How about you and me between the sheets?" he hears himself saying. The button loses its grip on the buttonhole and Timothy loses his grip as more of her thigh is exposed. "I've always thought of you that way," Travis purrs, raising his hopes and the bulge in his pants. Her vertebrae twitches and she sits up a little higher, her breasts expanding like a time-lapsed film of baking dinner rolls. "Oh, you did mean *balance sheets,* didn't you?"

"She inherited the money, OK?" he snaps.

George Sam begins more formally. "About a year ago, Travis received word that she was the beneficiary of several insurance policies as well as a cash estate. Timothy here travelled with her to Florida to claim the estate which involved international deposits. The benefactor, a man, had a French name, but he was Cuban. Travis inherited nineteen million dollars and despite taxes, Timothy's care of the money has seen it grow. Travis was not a numbers cruncher. She not only lost interest in the manipulation of the money, she began to despise it. . .the manipulation, not the money."

"She even started giving it away!" protests Timothy. "She had this ridiculous scheme one day that if everybody in Oregon would think positive thoughts about the economy, then the recession would end. She printed up little cards called 'Santa Cash' and paper clipped them to greenbacks and started leaving them on park benches, on buses, in restaurants, in public restrooms, on elevators. . .all over the city! The little card asked people to change their attitudes about 'abundance in Oregon'. Well, it wasn't long. . ."

"It wasn't long until the economy turned around," says The Wizard.

"Say *what*?" says Lash Lindsay, leaning forward on his elbows.

"That's a coincidence," says Timothy, dismissing The Wizard.

"That's my Travis," says The Wizard, smiling to himself.

"Anyway," continues Timothy, "the *Oregonian,* that's our local metropolitan newspaper, ran a story about who on earth could this Santa Cash person be and that's when Travis split for South America."

"Why South America?" asks Lash.

"Her original destination was Macchu Picchu in Peru. . .mystical energy field. . .or some such fruit loop nonsense. Anyway, she took a detour to Rio for a festival and she was in a marketplace when she was bitten by a coati mundi."

"The bite didn't kill her. . ." George Sam interrupts.

"No. . ." says Timothy with a real sadness breaking his voice.

"Excuse me. . ." Biasi raises a finger as if in school. "But *what* is a coati mundi, a Portugese desk clerk or what?"

Edwin Burroughs turns in his chair and responds to the architect. "A coati mundi is a ring-tailed relative of the raccoon and anteater family. They can be quite tame but usually exist in the wilds of Brazil and Argentina." Eyebrows are slightly raised at Edwin. "I know, I've lived there," he explains.

"What was she doing with a coati. . .whatever?" asks Lash.

"She was buying it," says Timothy. "This will explain. I received this post card from Travis *after* she had already returned to the United States and in fact, died here in Portland."

Timothy pulls a folded post card from his suitcoat pocket. A Brazilian native woman in festival dress smiles at everyone around the oval table while Timothy reads the message: "Dear T.A., Bought a coati mundi yesterday at the festival market. I am going to turn it loose in the jungle today. So I didn't really *buy* a coati mundi, I bought its freedom. Only it may just walk right back into another human trap. So I haven't bought its freedom...I have bought its *choice*. I bought a coati mundi its personal choice in the festival market yesterday. You wouldn't like it here at all...there is loud music, beautiful women and free booze. Stay home. Travis."

Timothy stops to get a check on his sadness.

"Why that old freedom fighter..." says Col. Williams, quietly gazing into a candle flame. "I gave her that idea in a conversation that we had about the military draft. Freedom. And choice. I remember the conversation."

A minute passes in silence. Even the violin is gone. The coffee service gurgles to itself. The Wizard looks around at the other faces and then to the crumbs in his lap.

"So how'd she die?" he asks.

"After the animal bit her, she cut short her South American trip and flew to Miami. She got medical treatment there in between airline flights. Some Miami medical moron gave her penicillin tablets which she took on the plane. She's allergic to it. By the time the flight crew recognized she was in trouble, they radio'd for an ambulance to meet them at Portland International, but it was too late."

George Sam sits up like a school boy. "I met the ambulance at the hospital," he says, "but our last meeting was quite brief. All she said was that she wanted the will carried out as written." He picks up a pen and marks a line off of a lined pad.

"So...I got you all together and I've explained part of the mystery to you. You all understand the challenge now. I also have additional information for you that may help you in your quest."

"Doesn't anybody want to know more about the Cuban guy?" asks Hershell.

"NO!" they all say in unison.

"Wouldn't do you any good to ask anyway," says Timothy. "His money, her part of it anyway, was in Canada, Switzerland and Florida. He was a soldier, an old boyfriend, and she wouldn't tell me much about him. I got the impression that he didn't know what he had or he wasn't willing to admit what he had. I don't think he was *supposed* to have it. Travis did say that she hadn't seen him in more than 15 years. So the ill-gotten gains of God only knows what kinds of dealings ends up in Oregon and now its destiny will be determined by seven ex-lovers who have something in common, but heaven knows what...and if they *don't* figure it out, the money will get carved up into little pieces and wind up in divorce courts and college campuses all over the country! Makes sense to me!"

"We *said* we didn't want to know!"

Timothy's old facial tick is back and his grief has moved from Travis' memory to Travis' money. George Sam pats Timothy's hand. "Well, I've taken such good care of it..." Timothy wails.

"I know you have," George Sam whispers, then he looks up and says, "Please understand. Timothy and the money have been very close this past year. It has been one of the most wonderful accounts at U.S. Bank, a true customer-service organization. The money has done well in his custody."

Timothy wipes his face with his napkin and The Wizard is touched by his pain. "Well," says The Wizard, "if I get the money, Timothy, you can take care of it for me!"

The tears in Timothy's eyes roll back into their ducts and he grabs The Wizard's hand, pumping it until his boney elbows knock against the table. The Wizard smiles as big a grin as his thin lips will allow and his head bobs up and down like a mechanical doll. "Right after I get back from taking my crystals to Peru," The Wizard beams.

Timothy stops mid-shake and his caterpillar moustache jerks rapidly to the left and then to the right.

"Excuse me...before you go counting your account numbers too quickly..." says Chadwick, "there is a small matter of the other six of us."

"You said that you had more information," pipes in Edwin. "What is it?"

"You seven arrived here this evening," begins George Sam, "but you were not the only ones invited."

"Jesus Christ! You mean there are more?" says Lash.

"How well did you know Travis?" asks Hershell again, playing now with one of his big tennis shoes. "Is there any coffee?"

"Do you have some sort of inside knowledge about all of this?" asks Biasi to Hershell. "You act for all the world like you already know what the answer is. Don't you care that we get started on this?"

"We obviously do not have *patience* in common, Mr. Biasi," says The Wizard. "Or the love of cherry cheesecake," says Hershell approaching the dessert cart. "Ah, my favorite, and it's New York style too. Years ago, Travis used to make this for me."

"That's why it's there," says George Sam, "she was hoping you'd make it."

"Make it? I wouldn't know how to make it. I said *Travis* used to make it! You deaf?"

"Cheesecake break!" sings The Wizard, jumping to his bare feet and swishing towards the cart.

Timothy gives a weary look to George Sam. "Suppose we could wrap this up sometime soon?"

"Take notes, if you want to," advises the attorney. "I can only say this once."

"Thank God," sighs Holbrook Biasi at the other end of the table.

Chapter 16

One man's ceiling is another man's floor.
— Paul Simon

"There was a pilot who lived in Alaska...a bush pilot," says George Sam. "He isn't here."

"Why not?" asks Lash.

"Because he's dead," says Timothy flatly.

"But because of him," George Sam raises the point, "you can eliminate race as a common factor. He was black. You see, all of you are white. That might have been someone's guess. But had the pilot made it...he died about a year ago...he would have been of a different race attending this dinner. You see?"

"Got it," says Chadwick jotting sketchy letters on a note pad.

The Wizard stabs and slurps at his cheesecake and he notices Edwin, to his left, staring at the dessert plate in his hand. "You OK, Edwin?" The Wizard asks.

"Oh, uh, yes," says Edwin, sitting up and taking a drink from his water glass. "It's just something Hershell said about the cheesecake..."

"Wha— was that?" The Wizard mumbles through a mouthful of melting cream.

"Well, baked salmon in dill sauce was *my* favorite," says Edwin, sweetly, "and Travis knew that..."

Biasi throws down his fork. "Well, I *hate salmon* and *Travis knew that*...so freaking what?!" he says.

Hershell, sitting at Biasi's left, pats the architect. "Now if everyone would speak up like that, it'd be wonderful," he says. "If nobody else wants their cheesecake, I'm going to have another piece..."

"Have mine! Take his! Have all the cheesecake you want! We'll send out for more! Let's just get on with this! Why can't you just sit still and get the information! We only have until dawn!"

Biasi's curly hair flops around his furious face and he pulls his cashmere jacket off and not finding a coat rack, tosses it to the floor. He pulls the sleeves of his navy blue sweater up on his forearms. "What is *with* this old man?" he says to Chadwick on his right.

"He might not live long enough to spend twenty three million dollars," shrugs Chadwick. "I don't know. Maybe he's already *got* millions..."

Biasi glares at the dottering Hawaiian shirt leaning over the desserts. Hershell is humming.

"Too much of that stuff isn't good for you," teases Col. Williams to the old man.

"There's plenty of the gooey stuff over here!" sings Hershell. "How would you like to wear some of it on that fancy uniform!"

Timothy: "George!"

George Sam aligns his pages and continues.

"I really can't tell you much about Alex Smith, the bush pilot. He had been a highly successful attorney in Chicago before he just bagged it all, apparently, and left for the high country. He evidently loved to fly and didn't want to be in civilization anymore. He flew in the most dangerous areas of Alaska...mountains that eat planes."

"Is that how he died?" asks The Wizard.

"No, he stepped in front of a bus in downtown Anchorage. The bus won," says Timothy.

"Question..." says Chadwick, raising a finger. "Did he make his move to Alaska before or after having known Travis?"

"Couldn't say," responds George Sam.

"Um," notes Chadwick, scrunching his lips, rubbing his chin and making more notes. Biasi watches Chadwick intensely, wondering what conclusions Chadwick may be coming to. He can't help but notice Chadwick's perfect shirt collar, not the slightest fray, not a hint of lint. Despite the candlelight, the shirt collar is stark white, a perfect snow white, a center-of-the-sun white.

"Something else," continues George Sam. "Alex Smith was the youngest black man to argue before the United States Supreme Court. That's like playing Carnegie Hall for an attorney. He was the youngest and only black to be named a partner in Chicago's most prestigious law firm."

"So has anybody else here ever argued before the Supreme Court?" asks Biasi, sarcastically.

"Don't even know the address," says Lash.

"Never married, no kids," finishes George Sam. He shuffles his papers, turns a page over in his file and picks up another sheet. "Then there's Norman O'Seek..."

The seven listeners register alarm. "Excuse me!" says Chadwick looking at the stack of paper in George Sam's file. "But how many more *are* there?"

"How well did you know Travis?" chuckles Hershell again. Both Biasi and Chadwick shoot maddening glances at Hershell.

"This is it," continues the little attorney, adjusting the heavy glasses on his improbably small nose.

"That's a total of nine, right?" scratches Lash.

"You missed the Cuban," says Hershell.

"Norman O'Seek," begins George Sam again. "He's a hermit. Refused to come. Lives in the mining hills behind Wallace, Idaho with no telephone, no running water, no indoor bathroom facilities..."

"And no sense," adds Timothy.

"Guy just wants to be left alone..." says Lash, "I can dig it."

"He's a miner?" asks Chadwick, still taking notes.

"He's an author," George Sam says, his arched eyebrows making hairy half moons over his glasses that say, "Go figure."

"He powers his word processor with a solar battery system on top of his cabin. His watch dog is a coyote and he drives an orange Jeep. I had the displeasure of having to visit Mr. Norman O'Seek because he would not respond to my communiques and I knew he was alive. A four-wheel drive vehicle was necessary to just get near his shack. He can't even get his Jeep close to it. I had to hike the last half mile."

"And this accomplished by a man whose idea of camping out is when room service is late..." says Timothy, pointing and grinning. George Sam tugs a little at his white linen lapel.

"Did you wear that suit?" asks Lash.

"As a point of fact, I ruined a suit finding Mr. O'Seek, yes, but there were provisions for such expenses in the will...Travis thought of everything. Anyway, he refused to leave his...ah, domicile and forfeited any legal claim to the estate. He's an author...I mentioned that... I read a couple of his books. Quite good, I thought...a little on the outdoorsy side. Three of his manuscripts have been sold for movie rights but I doubt he'll ever see them if they are produced for the silver screen. That might require going into town, or something, God forbid and who would take care of the coyote in his absence...?"

"So what else do you know about him?" asks Chadwick, attempting to make sense of George Sam's account.

"Married; separated, never divorced; seven children, all grown..."

"So he's not a spring chicken..." notes Hershell, smirking.

"He's 57 now," recites George Sam. "He's tall...looks like a mountain man, sounds like a Buick in need of a new exhaust system, stubborn as an ingrown toenail and...I don't know, I kind of liked the guy, despite the inconvenience of having to travel to Wallace, Idaho."

"Wallace, Idaho..." muses Lash.

"I-90 runs from the Pacific to the Atlantic and there is only one stoplight on the entire route. The stoplight is in Wallace, Idaho."

"Thank you for that brilliant piece of trivia," says Biasi. "I'm sure it will come in useful later in the evening...or in my life, whichever comes first. For crying out loud, is there anything else about the man that we need to know?"

"To summarize," begins George Sam, "You can eliminate race, height, weight, marital status, color of eyes and creed from your list. You have none of those things in common. You can eliminate love of flying (Mr. O'Seek will not fly and Mr. Smith loved to fly), writing, fatherhood, profession, astrological signs, educational background and birthplace. None of your parents are related and you don't drive similar vehicles. Your economic and social status are different and in fact, you're not all U.S. citizens."

"Huh?" says Chadwick. "Hold it, I can't get that all down so fast. Who isn't a U.S. citizen?"

"I'm Canadian," waves The Wizard, smiling. "Eh?"

"Anything else?" grumbles Biasi.

"I would venture to say that you have varying I.Q.'s," guesses George Sam, looking straight at Biasi. "Your talents and temperments appear to be different on the surface. Your passions and prejudices are dissimilar. Perhaps your ethics are the same..."

There is a short silence, like the breath Lena Horne takes just before the last stanza of the national anthem.

"I have an announcement to make," says Edwin Burroughs. "I'm leaving."

Chapter 17

Diplomacy is the art of saying 'nice doggie' until you can find a rock.
— *Wynn Catlin*

"Was it something we said?" whimpers Timothy sincerely.

Edwin Burroughs stands and pulls at his nose. "No, no," he says. He looks around the table, at each individual, then tugs at his ear.

"So you don't want your cheesecake?" asks Hershell.

"Would you knock it off with the cheesecake!" says Biasi.

"I bequeath my portion of the cherry cheesecake to the estate and stomach of Mr. Hershell Kaye," says Edwin, fumbling with his Phi Beta Kappa key. His left hand, tan and muscular, fingers the linen tablecloth. He is slightly stooped and looks like a politician resigning before he can be impeached.

"I don't know any of you," he begins, "and I don't need to and I'm not required to explain anything to you all but I seem to want to, for some reason."

"Spit it out, Edwin," encourages The Wizard. "What's up?"

"Of course, you're free to go...you are all free to go," says George Sam. "You'll sign a sort of 'quit claim' deed to the estate, however. Only those who stay the night and make a guess in the morning are eligible for the award."

Edwin holds his right hand up to George Sam. "It's all right; I understand all that." Edwin selects his champagne glass and pours from a bottle. He swirls the bubbles and begins, "I'll make this short."

He begins to walk around the table as if walking will somehow release some words stuck in his neck. Perhaps the champagne bubbles will scrub syllables from his voice box. As he paces, his shoulders grow and he seems more energized.

"Two things," Edwin pauses. He stops behind Biasi's chair.

"I've been sitting here wondering what I would do with twenty-three million dollars. I asked myself that question and I got an answer. I don't care for the answer."

"So what would you do?" asks Lash Lindsay, leaning back in his chair until it creaks.

"I've been in the diplomatic corp since the Johnson administration," says Edwin. "I've spent most of my life negotiating, coaxing, massaging and humoring Latin American dictators."

"Ass-kissing," interjects Col. Williams.

"And with excellent results!" defends Edwin. "My mediations have saved thousands of lives. If you think it's a mess now, you have not the tiniest notion of what it could have been!"

"Excuse me," says Biasi, "you will spare us a governmental lecture on the political and economic state of Central America, won't you?"

"Yes, yes, yes," says Edwin, studying the yellow bubbles in his glass. "It doesn't matter now anyway." He picks up his pace and walks behind Hershell's chair.

"I was thinking about the money. And I was thinking about the next time I'm in the middle of some frustrating negotiation with some emotional, thick-tongued national wearing ammunition across his chest and possessing the I.Q. of a tortilla...and I imagined just simply buying his country from him. 'Excuse me, Miguel, Your Most Exalted Poobah, but how much do you want for your country? Would a few mil take it off your hands? Can I write you a check? Can we just end this word game with a little Yankee cash, Miguel?' "

A tiny "Whew!" comes from the lips of Col. Williams and his eyebrows shoot up in surprise.

"Exactly!" shouts Edwin. He spins and his shoulders square with the colonel. "I can't say that I'm very proud of that idea, gentlemen...it goes against all my training, not to mention all my efforts over the years. But they've been long years. And I'm tired."

Edwin walks again, passes Lash Lindsay's chair and approaches George Sam.

"To control that amount of money would be delicious. But, in all honesty, I wouldn't have the control for long. See that chandelier? It's made of Austrian lead crystal, I'll wager, and probably weighs over 500 pounds. If it were made of diamonds instead of glass, would you be any happier? Would it make you feel any better? There's an interesting nonprogression with money. Money is extremely important until your basic needs are taken care of...$50 is a joyful thing. Then there reaches a point where $50 is not such a big thing. And a bed is a bed...it wouldn't give you any better night's sleep if it cost $10,000 more."

"So you're saying that you don't need the money?" asks Timothy.

"If a man can't use some extra money," chuckles Edwin, "then he isn't very creative."

"I was going to say, Edwin, that if you're turning down a chance at all this loot, then we really *don't* have anything in common," says Col. Williams.

"You said that you wouldn't have the control for long..." notes George Sam. "What does that mean?"

Edwin blushes slightly and a red sunset zips across his head showing through his white wisps of cloud hair.

"I'd like to have you all think that this is a noble gesture...my leaving," begins Edwin again, now moving to Timothy's chair. "It's been an important part of my life...seeing to it that people thought well of me. Uh, it took a little courage to admit that nastiness about buying off a dictator, you know? Anyway, I'm not noble or generous or any of that. I have a medical problem...and the prognosis is not good. I won't live long enough to spend 23 million dollars. I've got two, maybe three months. So where do I sign off this ship, George Sam? You said I needed to sign a form, I believe?"

George Sam starts in his chair and finally turns to his fat brief case full of file folders. He flips through the folders and pulls a two-page form but holds it to his chest and looks, very wide-eyed at Edwin. Feeling awkward sitting down, he scoots his chair and stands, still not extending the pages.

"Mr. Burroughs, I am terribly sorry to hear this news," says George Sam quietly, graciously breaking the silence for the rest of them.

Edwin reaches for the papers, knowing the discomfort of the little attorney, having seen it often enough in others who learned of his situation.

"Look, I've been through all this. I'm resigned. I think I'm grateful that I know. It gives me an opportunity. That bus in Anchorage robbed Smith of his opportunity. Then there's the coati mundi, the medical moron and the penicillin." Edwin shakes his head as he draws a pen from an inside pocket of his blue suit.

"The United States is the only country in the world that places such an inordinate amount of respect on death. *That,* gentlemen, is what we all have in common...we will all die. It's been a full life, for this man, a fine life. And who do I have to give this amount of money to? I have a wife who disappeared into tole painting years ago and two grown youngsters who were raised as spoiled yuppies who somehow turned out to be self-sufficient achievement mongers with no time for parents...while all the other kids on the block were shooting or snorting or inhaling or injecting something..."

Edwin leans over the table and begins to sign the pages on top of the soft linen tablecloth. The pen pokes through the paper and Edwin takes the pages to the wall. He finds a smooth place on the doorway trim and scratches a flamboyant signature on the second page.

"Gentlemen, if I came back from Portland with 23 million dollars in my pocket, my wife would want to know where I got it. And if she knew, she'd kill me. I have handled a bunch of grief lately and I am not prepared to handle much more of it. Now...*I'm* going to wander off into the night and get a good night's sleep while you all ponder this delightful little problem..."

Edwin's words had been slowly squeezed from his throat, at first then they began to run on their own and by the time he had finished, the words were merrily flushing themselves. He had taken the group from surprise to discomfort to acceptance.

Biasi sat motionless once Edwin had spilled his news. The architect still held his curly beard tightly in his hands, elbows propped on the table. "So what's your guess? What do you think we all have in common?" he asks.

Edwin shrugged a sigh and looked at the curved white ceiling and its sparkling crystal light fixture.

"Travis was a trickster, all right. She had the mind of Orson Welles, the heart of Will Rogers, the morals of Miss Piggy in the body of a young Julie Christy. Occasionally, she would lapse into global philosophical observations...armed with only tiny scraps of information ...and she'd make a comment about all of man and womankind. Maybe what we have in common is that we have nothing in common."

Edwin looked at the six faces.

"I have been wondering for the past couple of days, anticipating this unusual dinner, wondering about what Travis meant in my life. You do things like that...in my situation. But that information wouldn't help you much, even if I could be very clear about it, which I can't. The more important question is, what did *I* mean to *her?* Evidently more than I realized...because I'm flattered as hell that she even remembered me. It was so long ago...

"Well, ENOUGH!" he finishes. "Are you two leaving soon?" he asks the attorney and the banker. "I could follow you down this hillside."

"Of course," says George Sam still standing. Timothy stands and unrumples his suit. "Is that it?" he asks his shorter partner. "Have we covered it all?"

George Sam leans over his notes and scratches more lines off his yellow page. "That's it," he says to Timothy. George Sam stops and seems reluctant.

"Gentlemen, it is up to you six now. I have executed every request so far. Travis was special to me and for some reason, I have transferred some of that feeling to you all. I sincerely wish you a pleasant night and we will reconvene at dawn."

George Sam and Timothy pack pages of paper into their cases. Edwin waits in his relaxed and athletic way next to the door of the old smoking room. The colonel walks to the diplomat and extends his hand. "I don't know you, Edwin; I suspect that I would have liked to," he says.

"Probably not," smiles Edwin.

The Wizard stands and he too shakes the tall man's tanned hand.

"May your transition be smooth and easy," he says. "White light of love to you, Edwin."

"Thanks," says Edwin. "Believe it or not, I understand your message. The New Age religion in the U.S. is the ancient religion elsewhere in the world."

Chadwick, Biasi and Lash Lindsay line up to shake Edwin's hand and wish him well.

Hershell's tennis shoes make streaks in the thick Oriental carpet as he shuffles over to Edwin. The film over his old eyes clears just slightly as he stares into Edwin's face for several seconds.

"I suspect that you're wrong about that noble part," Hershell concludes. "What's wrong with you anyway?"

The others hold their breaths in a collective stop action.

"Cancer," Edwin says.

"Ah, then," acknowledges Hershell, nodding his craggy old head.

George Sam walks to the entryway of the ballroom and turns to the group.

" 'You have three things in common,' " he reads from his notes, carrying his attache case in his left hand. " 'You all knew Travis Duncan...' "

He glances briefly over his glasses as if for disagreement. There is none.

" 'You're all men.' "

Every eye turns to The Wizard in the bedsheet, then turns back to George Sam as if to say, "OK, if you *say* so."

" 'And the third thing, you must figure out for yourselves.' " George Sam snaps to attention in his now only slightly wrinkled white suit and he reaches for his Panama on the entry table. He adjusts the hat over his stiff black hair, touches his glasses one last time.

"See you in the morning!" he chimes merrily, a happy camp director leaving his Boy Scouts in their encampment.

Edwin gives a raised hand wave to the six. "And don't forget what I said about the chandelier," he says.

Chapter 18

In the parking lot of the Pittock Mansion, Edwin unlocks his silver-blue Mercedes in the pale light.

George Sam and Timothy stroll slowly, letting Edwin get outside ear shot.

Timothy hands George Sam his bulging brief case so that he can unwrap another Maalox. He puts the wrapper in his pocket and there is a plastic crinkling sound of many wrappers making room for another.

"Quite an evening," he says to George Sam. "*Quite* an evening."

George Sam lifts his head and snifts the cooling October air.

"They're a lot alike in their differences," he says.

Chapter 19

Never jump out of a perfectly good airplane.

— *Bill Sellers*

1948
When test pilot Willy "Lump-Lump" Duncan looked out of the maternity ward window at the base entry sign, the nurse was pestering him with the paperwork, something he detested intensely. Even flight plans annoyed him. He frequently wrote "Katmandu" or "Oz" or, his favorite "To Hell If I Don't Change My Ways." His temper would blur the lines on military forms...in triplicate. He grabbed the fountain pen away from the pesky nurse and stabbed at the paper until the space was sufficiently filled. "There," he said, as he swaggered out, zipping his flight suit up to his neck and heading for the flightline. The nurse in the starched white uniform rubbed her forehead and then the bridge of her nose.

"Something the matter?" another nurse asked.

"He just named his daughter Travis Afb," she answered.

"Lucky I wasn't born at the Air Force Base in Tachikawa, Japan," Travis said years later.

She was in grade school before someone told her that "Travis was a boy's name, not a girl's name." Travis could not understand sexes owning things like names.

To say that Travis was well-travelled was like saying Richard Nixon was just a little dishonest.

When they studied *Uncle Tom's Cabin* in school, Travis told the class, "I've been there." And when they studied Paul Revere's ride and the Old North Church, Travis said, "I've been there." And when they got to the cliff dwelling Indians of New Mexico, Travis said, "I've been there."

Travis knew how to collect maple sugar and what real cotton plants looked like. She had sat on a jellyfish on a Virginia beach. And she knew what the Corn Palace was in Mitchell, South Dakota. She could name all 50 states and all the capitals because she had been there. It seemed that she had sat for much of her young life in the back seat of a 1951 Hudson Hornet seeing the USA on the way to Willy's next tour of duty.

"If the people in Maine don't know what grits are...and the people in Texas don't know what an egg cream is...then they can't know much else about each other either," Travis observed. One thing she knew from being on the road, everybody had a different idea of what was right and what was wrong. And if everybody knew, but what they "knew" was different, then nobody knew.

Chapter 20

*She can't take you any way, if you don't
already know how to go.*
                                           — *The Eagles*

1984
      Travis was practicing archery in the backyard when the detective arrived. She wasn't really sure that she liked archery yet, but felt compelled to try it since she was a Sagittarius, the sign of the Archer. And she thought that it might improve her bust.

Travis practiced her Zen meditation while pulling back on the bow string. With eyes gently closed she released the arrow from her fingertips. Well, it had worked in *Star Wars* for Luke Skywalker...

The red-tipped arrow hit the fence with a vibrating thwang an instant after the door bell rang. Travis grimaced. The haybale with the paper target on it was the safest place in the yard.

"I'm out back!" she called to the unknown ringer of the bell. She wasn't concerned that no one was expected. "Who would bother an eccentric holding a bow and arrow?" she thought.

Mr. Peepers unlatched the gate and entered the backyard with his wallet unfolded and held at arm's length. Travis focused on him and slid the end of another arrow into the bow string. Detectives were supposed to look like Bogart, but this one looked more like Mr. Peepers. Holding his I.D. like he did, though, unnerved Travis and her sore biceps tensed.

"Are you Travis Afb Duncan?" was his first question.

Travis's imagination raced through the computer cards in her brain — her last year's income tax forms, her parking tickets and then through the married lovers that she had known who might have been wealthy enough to have wives financially equipped to hire a detective. Everything seemed neat and clean to her. And yet she felt like she was in a red sports car and a police car had just appeared in her rear view mirror.

"Who wants to know?"

The man set his wallet on the top of the dog house and stood with both hands up in a gesture of disarmament. His ashen little face gave an expression that seemed to indicate that he wished he had taken up a different line of work. He looked exasperated to Travis and she lowered the bow slightly. His little eyes blinked slowly behind his glasses and he sighed, losing an inch from his already short, thin stature.

Travis never did warm to the man. Even while he explained how he had been hired by the estate to find her. And when he reached inside his coat pocket to get the lawyer's business card, Travis' planted feet didn't move. When Travis didn't understand something, she said so; it was her policy. She could tolerate a great deal of redundancy until there was finally understanding. After the fourth explanation, the detective said that he really didn't have any idea how much the inheritance was worth, but that he had been paid well for his five months' work to find her. He insisted that she call the lawyer in Florida so that he would know that the detective's job had been completed.

When he said, "Lady, you're going to be one of the wealthiest women on the West Coast," *that's* when the arrow went through Travis' foot.

When Travis became a millionaire, and she had successfully recovered from a little foot problem, she immediately quit work. There wasn't much to quit. Travis had earned her living as a consultant to consultants. She had filled an unusual and almost secretive position for American management consultants — Travis created the seminar exercises or "games" for high level management retreats.

A facillitated game at a management retreat is intended to give the executives "hands on" learning with the information they've been given about the art and science of management. This time is an interactive time...it breaks up the monotony of lecture and gets the group to communicate and "skill build."

A "game" is supposed to be a game, but it never is. And the executives believe that the games are spontaneous, innocent assignments to afford them the opportunity to express their abilities and their new knowledge.

In reality, the games are deadly serious and engineered like a Dolly Parton bra...for strength and seduction. A national management advisor might call Travis with this scenario: "We have a structure of six vice-presidents and two co-owners. The vice-president of one of the production divisions has gotten his area in the black but at the sacrifice of key management people. Morale is deteriorating and beginning to spread to other divisions. The vice-president is aggressive, abusive *and* he's effective. We want to create a situation where everything will come to a head, his managers will all quit en masse and the co-owners will have justification to accept his resulting resignation. What can you do for us?"

Frequently an American executive is too expensive to keep...and too powerful to just get a pink slip.

Travis would ask dozens of questions...what kind of car does he drive? How old is he? How many marriages? Any children? What does he spend his time doing when he isn't working? What are his politics? What does he wear? How tall is he? What was his birth order in his family? What reading material is on his night stand? What does the top of his desk look like? Any behavioral quirks? What photographs, artwork or symbols are in his office?

With the questions answered, Travis would take two weeks to devise a plan for the desired outcome, severing someone's Achilles tendon. The date would be set and the nationally known management consultant would lead the executives through a training session at a local hotel seminar room. A month or two would pass while "additional analysis was done on the company." Then the executives would attend another session — this time at a retreat center, a coastal or mountain retreat hall, sometimes a lodge, sometimes a small convention spot, always with trees and cottages where the senior management would share rooms in two's. The scene would be bucolic and restful, the air always wet and fresh, the pines soothing and stately. A golf course might be nearby and the landscaped burms would obscure any automobiles.

The management consultant, complete with impeccable credentials and possibly one best seller on the *New York Times* business book list, would lull the now casually dressed executives into his management aria. The flip charts of analysis would be flipped and the coffee and rolls would be served. The vice-presidents and the senior managers would almost be able to forget that the silver-haired grandpa in the Izod golf shirt was their chief executive officer. Here, he just seemed one of them, enjoying the same rich coffee from the hotel urn and breathing the same mesmerizing air. All their Reeboks crunched the same pinecones and all their heads slept on the same expensive down pillows.

"Like lambs to slaughter," Travis observed with eyebrows that said, "What can you do? Executive and execution — they're related."

Before the fresh fruit plates were served for lunch, the management consultant would propose the "game" and divide the group into "teams." (They would become anything *but* teams.) The ground rules were always different, intricate and interesting. That was Travis' gift. She could create a challenging game that played with their psyches like a good fly plays with a trout.

Part of the challenge of creating the "game" was to establish the innocence of the management consultant. As the "game" would progress, cross purposes, personality conflicts, value and power battles would develop as they always will in groups. Like an oily salve brings pus to the surface of a skin boil, the "game" would bring the corporation's poison to the surface. All blemishes, pockmarks, scars and weakened veins would be exposed by the "game." An efficient, aggressive executive might be shown as a vulnerable, hot-temperred baby with the right "game." Even to the conclusion of the "game," however, the consultant must look like the surprised, benevolent catalyst to the scene.

Management consultants paid Travis well for these complex and superbly orchestrated executive games. The outcomes affected manufacturing companies, financial institutions, the military, high tech firms, import/export agencies and health care organizations. American management retreats are being held daily and of those that chose correctly, the sting of Travis's special cunning gift would guide their course.

Part of Travis's appeal was that she chose to stay out of the limelight. She didn't share her gift with Prentice-Hall or the American Management Association. She headquartered herself in Portland, Oregon — not New York or Los Angeles. Travis's phone number was only known by the few management consultants who had become household names. It wouldn't do to advertise her talent, in fact, it was imperative that it not be known. Travis was only too happy to oblige. Her expertise was in making things look like they "just happened."

Travis was a corporate assassin who was never around when the deed was done.

"You don't take courses to learn how to do this," Travis said.

Travis had synthesized her degree in communications, her advanced degree in behavioral psychology, her certificate in neuro-linguistic programming and her independent research on American corporate cultures. "The first thing you do is forget all that," she said. "That's been the hardest part."

"American corporations are male-oriented," she wrote in her private journal, "not male-dominated. And to get to know the American male, you need to think of him as a teapot. He will only pour out the truth when he is tipped over. He is such a mess of complex defenses that his only connection with reality comes when he is spent. It appears that it's only after he has achieved orgasm that he can have an intelligent conversation containing any honesty. It isn't prudent to believe everything he says prior to that. Perhaps that's true of the American female too. I wouldn't know. I have only made a study of the males."

So when Travis inherited the money, she quit work. "I guess you're just going to have to learn to screw *yourselves*," Travis said to the video-king of the management consultants, known for his brash style and demeaning tone. "Travis, you're worse than I am," he said. "Thank you," Travis replied, genuinely flattered by the compliment.

Chapter 21

*The greatest difficulty with the world is
not its inability to produce, but its
unwillingness to share.*
— *Roy L. Smith*

In the Pittock Mansion dining room, the silence hangs like sticky raspberry syrup hangs from a stack of six fresh, hot dollar pancakes. Their yellow butter dilemma melts through their minds and moods and drips over the whole mess, a cholesterol nightmare served to a heart patient. Occasionally a sweetwhiff of steam rises from the ooze, a hope, an idea, a sigh. Just when the plate is swollen with the goo of silence and the fried griddle cakes saturated with hardening raspberry thoughts, Chadwick stabs a fork into it.

"Gentlemen, we need some ground rules," he says.

"What we need are some ideas," says Lash, pulling another toothpick from his plaid pocket and jamming it in his teeth.

Hershell pats Lash's forearm. "The ideas will come from the ground rules," encourages Hershell.

Biasi rubs his face and beard, squeezes his eyes and yawns. His hands return to their former position under his chin and he says, "OK, so what you got in mind?"

"Well, foist off," Chadwick begins, the first time his Eastern accent has shown itself, "nobody speaks unless we are all in attendance. It wouldn't be fair to everybody. Even the tiniest detail could be a clue . . . may lead to an idea. We need to stick together . . . everybody sees the same things, everybody hears the same things . . ."

"Hears what?" asks Col. Williams, drumming his silver salad fork on the table.

"Our stories, of course," says Hershell, extending his hands in exasperation.

"I don't wanna tell you guys anything," the colonel retorts, dropping the fork and leaning back in his chair until it touches the wallpaper behind him.

"But that's the whole point," says The Wizard, pressing his boney elbows on the table and thrusting his nose into the center of the group. "We've got to know about each other before we can guess what it is that we might have in common. It might be obvious! It might be something minor...something we never think about...something that we might even take for granted. But we've got to share information...or we might just as well donate the money to that whacko college fund."

The colonel's chair hits the floor and he leans forward, his hands on his knees. "Did I hear *you* call something *'whacko'*?"

"Gentlemen," begins The Wizard, "*Brothers*. If someone in this room doesn't come up with the answer, then approximately 4,600 women will be cut loose from their marital bonds *free of charge* while we are left holding our collective bags and having invested and lost a night's sleep. The twenty three million will be carved up like so much filleted tuna, packaged and canned and distributed nationwide...and of course, end up in bank accounts of approximately 4,600 lawyers."

"He's right," says Biasi. His hands flop to the table. "How'd you figure that out?"

"He used to be a math teacher," says Hershell, sarcastically.

The Wizard's arms fold up to his sides and he gasps at the old man. "How did you know? Do you know me?"

"Huh?' blinks Hershell. "What are you talking about?"

"I taught Statistical Analysis for Marylhurst College!" says The Wizard. "You didn't know that?"

"'Course I didn't *know* that!" barks Hershell. "How the hell should I know that? I've never seen you before in my life!"

"YOU USED TO TEACH STAT?" exclaims Chadwick. "You are the fartherest thing from a stat instructor I could possibly imagine!"

"If you insist..." chirps The Wizard, back into his wizardry.

"Oh, so what!" says Biasi, "The point is, he's right. If we don't buckle down and ask ourselves some questions, we're all gonna lose. And Chadwick's right too. We've all got to see and hear the same things or it isn't fair."

The syrup of silence, now heated, begins to ooze again. It makes runny red-purple waterfalls over the six hot cakes and the fork sticks in the pan-fried muck. Chadwick takes another stab.

"Rule Two," begins Chadwick again. "We have to tell the truth."

The word "truth" halts the raspberry sorghum in mid-drip. Twelve eyes refuse to touch each other. Lash Lindsay chews his toothpick and examines it in detail. Col. Williams rocks back in his chair and it creaks a protest. Biasi scratches his beard vigorously and inspects his fingernails. The Wizard goes back to staring into the candleflames, watching a white wax drip travel to the tablecloth and leave a puddle there. Chadwick pulls at his college class ring, picking imaginary crumbs from its deep gold embossing. Hershell taps his thumbs together while his pudgy fingers interlace with each other.

Chadwick stabs again:

"Men do not share things well, least of all — information and women."

The whole platter of hot-buttered pancakes and its mantle and pools of raspberry syrup flips in the air and lands upside down on a white wool carpet.

Chapter 22

*If you know you're going to win, then it
isn't a game.*

— Homer Groening

A nasty element in the Pittock Mansion's puzzle is the lack of
necessary *inequality* that makes groups function so well.
With all due respect to Abraham Lincoln, equality is a ludicrous concept in a group dynamic. To have equality is to have chaos and anarchy.
The military could not function if everyone were of equal rank. So it is
in business. So it is in any small group function, whether it is the PTA, a
sewing bee or the U.S. Senate.

But at the Pittock, no one can pull rank on anyone else because
there is no rank to pull. Rank and inequality do not exist in this dilemma — none of them will take orders. "Shit flows downhill," is a common U.S. military phrase. That is an apt description of how action occurs. With no "downhill" the shit has nowhere to flow. So it sits. Structure, rank — inequality — creates the "downhill" and then action can
take place.

"Human beings appear to require structure, like they require food,
air and water," wrote Travis in her private journal. "They create it incessantly; they create it where it isn't even necessary; they create it at a
moment's notice. It is as if we, as human beings, cannot *see* without it."

A cherrywood grandfather clock begins its midnight song in the
foyer of the Pittock Mansion. Its sound is like a cattle prod to those
who hear it. The internal white rabbit of their psyches sings menacingly,
"I'm late, I'm late..."

The constant cliff wind that circles the sandstone mansion dies
down to an unusual calm. The city below sleeps this night to wake and
put on its underwear and then its work boots or business suits and go
make a living while six men at the Pittock put their stubborn minds and
creativity to the task of earning in one night what could sustain them a
lifetime.

"OK, then, Colonel, what do you suggest that we do?" asks

Chadwick. "It appears that we have two choices. . .one, make wild-ass guesses based on no information, or, two, share information and make, or try to make educated guesses. I, for one, do not make business decisions on intuition. I'd say that we would increase our chances if we shared something, *anything*, with each other. These are extenuating circumstances. I'm not one to talk about myself much either in a room full of strangers, but, Good God, man! It's twenty three million dollars! You could buy your own battalion for that kind of money."

The colonel rocks defiantly in his dinner chair.

"So what if I don't get it. . .you going to give me part of the money if *you* win? If I help you win the money by talking, what do I get out of it?"

"Colonel, you fool!" says Biasi. "You get what Travis gave that coati mundi in Brazil. . .you get a *chance*!"

The next silence lasts about as long as a burp.

"Reminds me of a story about a wooden Indian outside a cigar store. . ." says Hershell, ambling into the conversation. "Pretty lady passes by in front of him and he speaks! He says, 'Chance.' The lady stops and stares at the wooden Indian and says, 'Aren't you supposed to say, "How?' And the Indian replies, 'I already know *how*. . .what I need is a *chance*.'"

The group laughs but the colonel blinks lazily like a python snoozing on a hot rock.

Biasi grabs the end of the table, pulls the remaining silverware, the chrysanthemums, the candlesticks and The Wizard's elbows with him. He stands bolt upright, taking advantage of his height and he fills his navy blue sweater with his chest. "I'VE HAD ENOUGH!" he roars.

"I've had enough jokes! I've had enough *salmon*! I've had enough stupidity and stubborness! The thing I hate about this situation the most is that even if I killed every one of you, which sounds wonderful to me right now, I still won't be the last possible beneficiary of this loot. And I want it! I WANT THE MONEY! And, by God, Colonel, you're either going to help me get it or you're going to get *out*! If you don't tell your tale, then you have no reason to stay here and hear *ours*. You can bloody well come back at dawn and make a wild-ass guess on your own!"

Biasi throws his palms on the table and glowers at the center of the oval where the Army colonel sits wide-eyed. "Are you in or are you *out*?" demands Biasi.

Colonel Bobby Williams is on his feet in an instant. He shoves his face at Holbrook Biasi and lunges at the table. "I'm *out* and I'll tell you why!" shouts the blond colonel, face inflamed.

"Damn you, Biasi, you push my buttons and I hate that!" The Colonel makes a fist about seven inches from his own nose. He is shaking and his fist turns from crimson to yellow-white as he attempts to get a grip on his temper.

The colonel pulls his military jacket from the back of his chair and he drapes it over his left arm. He begins to take breaths again, as do the others in the room. The Wizard is holding two water glasses that he lifted when Biasi moved the table. Lash Lindsay continues with his toothpick, obviously resigned not to break up this fight.

"I can handle war, gentlemen," Williams begins. "I can handle losing twenty-five pounds in a week, sweating in the jungle. I can handle the nauseating amount of military paperwork and bullshit. I can handle not knowing where I'll be a year from now...or even one week from now. I can handle jumping backwards out of a C-plane at 15,000 feet into a forest full of machine guns."

The colonel's chest presses against the seams in his tailored shirt and sweat rings grow under his arms as he speaks.

"What I can't handle is intimate conversations about anything. When I met Travis, I wanted to know *her* well — not you guys. I didn't sign on to get to know you guys. I've got my own memories of Travis and I don't want that little golden package with her name on it...the one on the inside of me...touched by any of you. It's mine. I own it. I couldn't open it in front of you anymore than I could wear that bedsheet out in public..." He points to The Wizard, who sets the drinking glasses down and pulls his caftan across his knees. The colonel picks up his hat from the entry table and looks carefully at the black mirror brim. He puts the hat on but tips the bill way back, looking jaunty now. One hip goes out to the left and his right hand rests at his waist. His well exercised body looks like its ready for a drink at the Officers Club bar. He looks at the carpet between his shiny shoes and he shakes his head.

"Travis...God, she used to irritate me!"

"Well, we have *that* in common," says Biasi, who has stopped leaning on the table and stands with his arms folded, listening to the colonel.

"She'd be down at the goddamned peace rallies all afternoon and then spend the evening listening to me tell fishing stories. Such a contradiction! We'd talk about freedom and rights and patriotism and duty and honor...and...she was just this beautiful little space of time in my life. I guess I wondered in those days and for all the years since then if I had only dreamed up a character known as Travis. If nothing else happens this evening, I guess I have been rewarded by just knowing that I wasn't crackers...that she really did exist."

The colonel steps to the table and picks up one champagne glass that hasn't tipped over and he drains it.

"Gentlemen, I *don't want* to hear your stories. And I don't think that I have anything to tell you that would help with your guesses. Biasi, you're right, if I don't give, then I shouldn't get."

He clears the champagne bubbles from his throat.

"Men, I'm good at what I do. And what I *don't* do is discuss Travis Duncan with anybody."

"You think it's going to be easy for the rest of us?" asks Lash Lindsay, repositioning his cowboy hat and folding his arms across his chest.

"Can't say," says the Colonel with a smile. "But I'll be back at dawn. "I'll have a guess thought out by then. I mean, what the hell, what have I got to lose by writin' something on a piece of paper?"

Lash sits up in his chair a little and asks, "Colonel, you got more doodads on that uniform than a Christmas tree. What do all those ribbons mean?"

The Colonel sets his hat square on his head and pulls his jacket on over his rolled up shirt sleeves.

"Means it takes him a long time to get dressed in the morning," says Hershell.

Colonel Williams, looking tired but younger, flashes a great smile to the old man. "That's right," he says, "that's exactly what it means."

Chapter 23

*If you don't want 'em to get your goat,
don't tell 'em where it's tied.*
— *Linda Pfeiffer*

"Now we are five," says Biasi, before the sound of Col. Williams' car door could be heard ker-slamming in the Pittock's parking lot.

"I guess we need to back up and decide if we want this to be a group project or not," says the architect, scratching at his beard again.

"We haven't got a prayer otherwise," says The Wizard sadly. "I still say that we up our chances for one of us getting the money if we share information."

"I never thought I'd hear myself say anything like this," puts in Lash Lindsay, "but I think The Wizard's right."

"Hershell?" asks Biasi, looking at the old man at his left.

"I'm in. It only makes sense. Col. Williams exemplifies the pre-60's macho male persona. I bagged that stuff long ago, along with my stationwagon, my metal TV trays and my plastic turquoise patio plates. He's actually an antique, our friend the Colonel; he should be put under glass somewhere."

"Look who's calling who an antique..." teases Lash.

"Age *is* a matter of mind," reminds Hershell to the boy-man at his left, "providing one *has* a mind."

"How old are you, anyway?" asks Biasi.

"Older 'n dirt," blarneys Hershell. "I knew Mother Nature when she was a virgin."

"OK," continues Biasi, still standing from his confrontation with Col. Williams. "That leaves you, Chadwick. What's it going to be? You going to leave?"

"No way," emphasizes Chadwick. "Remember me? I was the one who tried to talk General Westmoreland into staying..."

Hershell has been resting his interlaced fingers on his pot belly among the palm trees of his Hawaiian typhoon shirt. He begins to play with the koa wood buttons and studies the wave pattern off Kuaui.

"Chadwick...you want to go over those ground rules again, now that we seem to finally have a quorum?"

"Let's see...oh, yes. Ground Rule Number One: Nobody speaks unless we are all in attendance. Ground Rule Number Two: Tell the truth. I haven't gotten to Rule Number Three yet."

Chadwick raises his gold Mont Blanc pen from his note pad and says, "I'd like to comment on Rule Number Two. It's been my experience that men don't tell the truth even when they know it. And we don't *know* the truth; we can't possibly know Travis' truth about each of us. In other words...just a little disqualifier..even if we all speak the 'truth' as we know it, it may not lead us to where we want to go."

" 'There's no such thing as truth, only perspective,' " quotes The Wizard, his eyes stuck mesmerized by a candle.

"Oscar Wilde?" asks Hershell.

"*Travis Duncan!*" exclaims The Wizard. "*That* was one of her favorite sayings!"

"You know," says Hershell, "I don't think that what we have in common has anything to do with Travis. I understand what you're saying Chadwick. And you're right, no one can know the 'truth' about a relationship, however enduring or brief or significant. I have a sneaking suspicion that if we concentrate on Travis, which would be like trying to nail jello to a stucco wall, then we'll be wandering down a blind alley."

"But—" warns Biasi, "we need to agree to tell the truth as we know it...about ourselves. No saying you were born in Kansas, when you were really born in Hoboken...OK? Can we agree to that much?"

The four nod their heads in agreement. "We all agree not to give false statements, right? Raise your hands on it," Biasi asks and they all respond with raised right hands.

"I just thought of Rule Number Three," says Chadwick. "Everything said in this room should *stay* in this room. After tonight, nobody remembers anything."

Biasi looks around the table. "Agreed?" he asks. "Agreed," they answer.

"Rule Number Four," interjects Hershell. "No hitting below the belt. What I mean by that is...we can insult each other all we want... but tread lightly...in fact, don't tread at all...on areas involving Travis. We're men, we have egos, this is a raw subject; let's just show a bit of respect for some old memories, eh?"

"No insults, huh?" asks Lash.

"Insult all you want...just stay out of that territory of insults that includes relating to Travis. I'm not in the mood for it...and it's the reason the Colonel left. Just nothin' below the belt, understand?"

"I understand," admits Lash.

"OK, that's Rule Number Four," prods Biasi. "Agreed?"

"Agreed."

"Rule Number Five," continues Chadwick. "We go around the

table and tell our stories. While each man talks, there's no interruptions. When he's finished, we can ask questions. But everybody gets a free forum to say what they want. Somebody ought to keep track of the time. We've wasted enough of it already. Everybody gets an hour... that's all we can afford. Then on to the next story. That's how we ought to do it, gentlemen.''

Chadwick checks his Rolex. ''I'll keep the time,'' he offers.

''OK, then, are we agreed?''

''Agreed!'' they chime.

''Any more rules?''

Silence.

''Well, Chadwick, you've put us on our way. It's almost as if you go to the reading of your old girl friends' wills every day...''

Chadwick doodles a square with the tip of his Mont Blanc. ''In a way, I do...'' he smiles to himself.

Chapter 24

Time flies when you're unconscious.
— Matt Simek

"Ladies first," says Lash, tipping his hat at The Wizard. The three others look to The Wizard first to see how he'll take the barb and secondly to see if he'll begin for them.

The Wizard presses his two hands flat on the oval table and pushes himself to standing. He waves his Arabesque beak in the air like one would wag a stick at a playful dog.

"All *right*," he says. "I'll begin...since nobody else wants to..."

He pulls the sleeves of his caftan up to his boney elbows. A thin stringy ponytail wiggles its way over the collar of the frock as if it were a silkworm, escaping from the black and white Japanese fabric. The Wizard's thinness is detectable by the looks of his thin, long face, the sheet so envelopes his body with textile design. His size 13AAA feet have not seen shoes for several years. The toes are scarred and bent, a thick layer of callous padding the soles of his feet. If walking barefoot connects The Wizard more directly with the planet, then the ironic result is callousness.

"I am The Wizard," he says.

"What's your real name?" asks Biasi.

"The Wizard," he repeats.

"Legally, what's your name?" asks Biasi.

"The Wizard," The Wizard giggles gleefully and his pointed shoulders bob around his ears.

Lash pulls the chair that had been occupied by George Sam and he first checks his boots, then props them up in the seat of the chair. He readjusts his cowboy hat and he asks, "Well, what does it say on your driver's license?"

"Of course you would regard that as the one piece of a man's true identity — the state-issued driver's license. If that is your criteria for identification purposes, then, yes, as a matter of fact, it's true...it's 'The Wizard.'"

The cowboy hat turns a little as a cocker spaniel's head might turn when hearing a cat's meow from a television.

"The spot on your driver's license that says, 'name.' In that spot, on your license, it says, 'The Wizard.' Is that what you're saying?"

"That's what I'm saying," The Wizard chirps.

"So what do we call you — 'The' for short?" pokes Lash.

"I guess I'd prefer that over 'Mr. Wizard.' "

"That's been taken," barks Hershell. "What was the name that your mother gave you?"

"It is interesting that you would use *that* criteria for securing identification..." The Wizard notes.

"What's the name on your birth certificate?" asks Chadwick.

"What's the name on the pass you got from the state hospital?" asks Biasi.

The Wizard smiles and his small, toothy smile is clever and playful. "Your questions, as usual, reveal more about yourselves than they do about me..."

Biasi's short-tempered pirate eyes swashbuckle a glare at The Wizard. "Let's try this...what name would you like on your *tombstone*?"

The Wizard's beaming smile is reduced to a pale pucker.

"My name, as if that tells you anthing at all about me, is, legally, The Wizard. T.H.E. — Terence Hildebrand Eaton."

"Sounds rich," sniffs Hershell with distrust.

"My point exactly!" flares The Wizard. "I could have said 'Jackson Brown Washington' and you would have thought something different! You form impressions — often inaccurate — from whatever name I chose to call myself. So my name is my life; it is me. Your name is the only thing you truly own!"

"Your family was, then..."

"Comfortable," The Wizard quickly fills in.

Lash grimaces and waves his ostrich feather eyelashes in dismay. "Why is it," he asks, "that the rich don't just *say* they're *rich*? They have to say 'comfortable' or some other cockamamy word?"

"Because," The Wizard addresses his student, "the term 'rich' has far reaching implications, the least of which is economic. What *is* in a name? A hell of a lot, I can tell you. Change your name and you change your life. Kipling said that words are the most powerful drugs. I believe that to be true. Especially with names. So we must be very careful with words. And many times, not use them at all."

"Well, we're in a crunch here, Wiz," needles Biasi. "We need words here tonight because some of us can't decipher vibrations, OK?"

"Ninety three percent of the words in the English language have more than one meaning," lectures The Wizard. "How are we supposed to know which meaning? And only 20% of our communication is the actual words that we use. The other 80% is split up between body language and paralanguage."

"What the devil," asks Biasi, "is paralanguage?"

"That's voice inflection, tone of voice — delivery. For instance, consider the following sentence and listen to what happens when I change just the emphasis of certain words. It changes the meaning. Here goes:

> "*I* never said he stole the book.
> I *never* said he stole the book.
> I never *said* he stole the book.
> I never said *he* stole the book.
> I never said he *stole* the book.
> I never said he stole the *book*."

As The Wizard waves his hands in holy-man gestures, the sides of his caftan billow wing-like. His face looks like Silly Putty that some mischievous child has put a hook into and pulled at the nose. The result is a thin, chinless face with a beak that precedes him. The Wizard is 37. The army of hairs on his head has become a simple security force, the platoon of them running down his neck and tied with a red elastic. His eyes, a deep and reassuring dark brown, and his constantly giggling voice are what make him "wizardly." It is a good and natural "here I am" sort of face, a court jester face, a wise East Indian face, a delicate face, a really marvelous multi-life face.

"The ridiculous thing about communication is...the illusion that it has been accomplished," says The Wizard. "The odds of anyone communicating accurately any*thing* to any*body* are next to impossible. You, Chadwick, you wouldn't invest in such odds in your business. And yet, we all go about our daily lives banking on the impossible — communication."

"I can see where you and Travis would hit it off," notes Hershell. "You both have that moronic fascination with communication."

The Wizard's hands come to rest, crossed in front of his black bamboo print. His nose tilts up.

"What the hell is a Wizard anyway?" asks Lash. "What do you *do*?"

The Wizard's black eyebrows dance up and down as if pulled by strings. He begins his bouncing again, the thin feet massaging the Oriental carpet.

"Technically, a wizard is one who mystifies and/or confuses. Another definition is simply: a very clever or skillful person," responds The Wizard.

"How well does it pay?" asks Lash. "'Cause all in all, I'd have to say that if confusion is your game, you're pretty good at it, having told us practically nothing so far."

"Yeah," jeers Biasi, "what's a typical wizard's day like anyway?"

"By definition," giggles The Wizard, "it is impossible for a wizard to have a typical day."

Chadwick stands and unbuttons his suit jacket. "A little coffee, gentlemen? We may be sorry that we started with this one. Tell me, Wizard, assuming that you did not enter our atmosphere via Shirley MacLaine Airlines, can you give us some idea of where you were born...?"

"Or hatched?" asks Biasi.

Chadwick pours two cups of coffee and hands one to Biasi. Biasi waves the brew away and reaches for a stray champagne bottle. He ignores his champagne glass and instead, pours the bottle's contents into his empty drinking goblet, a much larger container. Part of his gulp splashes out on his beard and bubbles there.

"Oh, you want the material plane details of my present incarnation!" exclaims The Wizard.

"We want English," drawls Hershell.

The Wizard moves from his place at the table to where Timothy had been sitting, at the head of the oval. He places his long fingers on the back of the chair and he addresses the chandelier.

"I come from a land far, far away...Nova Scotia," he says, trance-like. "My father must have qualified for cancer research because he was the original Canadian rat. Mother, American, not a rat. He abandoned us...the us included my younger brother...and we left Nova Scotia when I was three. Moved to California and my mother worked as a set designer for Disney. Kept us in Disney passes for the next 15 years; I've personally ridden Magic Mountain 47 times. To my mother, everything was a set. The street, my school playground, our living room...everything was a set and therefore, not completely real. I always wondered if maybe the cold of Canada froze patches of her mind where reality was supposed to be. So she had the perfect job... working for Disney. The danger in having a mind is that you may lose it..."

Chapter 25

The illusion of logic is logic.
                                    — Homer Groening

An exasparated six year old boy crawled out of a split in a plaster of Paris tree trunk. He rolled his eyes and brushed the morning from his flannel Mickey Mouse pajamas, Pluto running circles around his tush. He was not outdoors. Morning at the Eaton house. Los Angeles, California, 1954.

"Come on, Harley," he called to his brother.

"I can't find my glasses!" he heard his brother's irritated cry.

"Look under Donald Duck!" the boy yelled back.

"Which one?" his brother called through the tree stump that was the entrance to the boys' bedroom.

"The one that's an alarm clock! Jeez, Harley, shake it, will ya?"

A four year old moppet with Dumbo-shaped ears crawled out of the split in the tree, glasses askew, and together they carefully picked their way down the hallway. Fake cobblestones littered the hall floor and the going was tough for two barefoot boys. "We couldn't have normal carpet like everybody else," groused the six year old.

A clownish face appeared from an arched doorway, big red lips grinning over large white teeth. It was Mrs. Eaton.

"Hi, Mom," said the taller boy, "sign my report card yet?"

"What, no kiss?" she asked, feigning a frown.

The older boy executed a perfect raspberry in his mother's direction, cursed the stones half embedded in the floor and said, "I haven't got time to have my face steam cleaned this morning, thanks, anyway. Hey, you're not trying to cook again, are you?" The younger boy reached for his brother's hand and pulled him.

"Aw, Mom. . . ."

The mother stood over a five foot tall metal replica of a mountain, glazed with blue and white paint. The side of the mountain folded out revealing a Hotpoint range. Black smoke billowed from the "Matterhorn."

"What *was* it?" asked her oldest boy.

"Pancakes," she whimpered, a Goofy asbestos mitt on her left hand and a Minnie spatula in her right.

"I just thought you kids could use a hot meal, you know?"

The boy padded over to his mother and tugged at her red Minnie apron.

"Mom, it's Southern California, we don't need a hot meal. What I need is to have my report card signed. What'ya do with it?"

"I think I left it in Pluto's doghouse," she said, waving Goofy in the smoke.

The little boy started to walk away but his brother held fast to his leg.

"It's OK, Harley, there's milk and Sugar Pops. Go to the bathroom and I'll catch up with ya, OK?"

The younger boy sucked his thumb and examined his brother and the large red-haired woman towering above him. "Goofy fly?" he asked, watching the padded mitt.

The exasparated six year old looked at the blackened Matterhorn and then to his ditzy mother. "Yeah, that's it," he said, "Goofy fly." He stomped wearily into another room and disappeared under a wooden sign, "Pluto." Next to a couch made from the trunk of a '39 Buick was a desk made from the nose of a '39 Buick. He looked in the area between where the radiator and the fuel filter might have been, had the Buick been a real car.

"Ma! I can't find it!" he screamed.

"Check the glove box!" she harped back.

The boy rolled his eyes and slapped his hand to his forehead. "Oh, no," he said, "anything but the glove box. . ."

The boy pulled a Snow White key ring from a drawer in the grill of the '39 Buick and walked around the desk to the dashboard. He unlocked the little door and cautiously pulled it open. Little rubber dwarfs tumbled out on the floor.

"Ah," he said when he found the report card, still unsigned, under Captain Hook and Peter Pan.

"Dammit, Mom, you've got to sign this thing!" he yelled, pawing further into the glove box for a pen.

His mother, smoke-choked eyes tearing up and watering her black mascara, stood, still Goofy-pawed, in Pluto's doorway. She had been mistaken for a popular female impersonator on several embarrassing public occasions.

"I do?" she asked.

The boy sighed and handed her the Tinker Bell pen. "Can you just do something normal. . . sign it! Pretend it's a 3-day pass."

Chapter 26

*'Be yourself' is about the worst advice you
can give to some people.*

— *Mark Twain*

"**I** did what any normal, rational, rebellious kid would do,"
The Wizard explains, his hands now defiantly on his hips.
"I became a nerd and studied math."

"God, sounds like a fun way to grow up to me..." says Lash.

"Yeah, well, you've heard of people who bring the job home with
them every night? Well..." The Wizard's right hand wags back and
forth, "so-so."

"Anyway, I graduated from high school when I was 16...that was
the same year my mom won an Academy Award for set design...and I
had my bachelor's degree in math by the time I was 19. Everybody else
was studying theatre arts at USC, so I had my master's in math when I
was 22. Having been suckled on illusion, I opted for reality...or what I
thought was reality."

"What happened to your brother?" asks Hershell.

"He overdosed on cotton candy, threw up on Winnie the Pooh and
spent two years in a private mental hospital...got out and became a
child psychologist. Lives in L.A. Drives a custom-made Lincoln with a
Mickey Mouse clock in the dashboard. If he ever finds a woman with
large black ears and puffy white hands and the libido of a mink, he'll
probably get married."

"Granola Land," remarks Biasi, shaking his pirate head.

"Huh?" They all turn to the architect.

"L.A. is Granola Land. Haven't heard that before? Land of
fruits, nuts and flakes..."

The Wizard laughs gleefully and begins bouncing again. "Yes!
And it pays really well, too."

"I'd rather take a beating than take my truck into downtown
L.A." says Lash, nodding his head.

"So what can you do with a degree in math?" asks Hershell.

"Oh, a bunch of things," replies The Wizard, "none of which I wanted to do. It was about 1970 then and I got involved with Trans-cendental Meditation, TM. I went to India and studied with the Mahar-ishi himself: travelled to Europe as a teacher. That's what I did for years...taught TM. Taught thousands. I was hired, eventually, by a progressive American furniture company to teach TM to its employees all over the U.S. I've stayed in more hotel rooms than the Gideon Bible.''

"And I thought I'd racked up some miles," says Lash.

"I had so many frequent flyer points, they offered to give me Ozark Airlines.''

"So what happened next?" asked Biasi. "You went into aviation or what?''

The Wizard's face turns from delight to somber. His boney should-ers poke at the silk fabric and he sighs audibly.

"Just for the hell of it, I decided to hitchhike to Canada from L.A. in some misguided effort to find my father. I found Oregon instead. Which has become my Father-Land. I got involved with TM a little bit in Portland, but mainly what I did was teach statistical analysis for Marylhurst College, a Catholic girls college...until 1974. The school closed and then reopened as a co-ed professionals' college, you know, a place for people who've been out in the work world and want to go back and get a degree, like, *real* people. After years of trying to com-municate with students, I gave up and studied communication science at Santa Cruz. I became a wizard.''

"How does one *become* a wizard?" asks Biasi, skeptically.

" 'Wizard' is the title given to someone who has demonstrated abilities in neuro-linguistic programming. To an uninformed person, the techniques appear to be magical and they are...quite powerful. I integrated my math culture with the TM training and spiced the whole mess up with NLP and voila! I became a Wizard with a capital W. I took it into areas that no one else was going. I mirrored the behavior of a parrot once and the damned thing followed me around for hours. I saved a little girl's life once...car accident. Used the same techniques and got the bleeding stopped. There's all sorts of applications but the one I discovered most useful had to do with *intra*personal communication...overcoming self-defeating behaviors by negotiating with unconscious beings within the individual. I did some remarkable workshops, gave some speeches...but it seems this is not the perfect time for this information to be on Planet Earth...yet.''

"Do you come with English subtitles?" Lash asks.

The Wizard stretches his arms full length and takes on the appear-ance of a large, flat movie screen full of bamboo. He bounces a couple of times and then sits in his chair. He leans on his elbows and looks di-rectly at Lash.

"OK, you've got something about yourself that you don't like. Don't tell me what it is...but there is something in your behavior that you do, that you wish you didn't do. Might be smoking, or eating cho-lesterol or filing your taxes late or remembering to have something fixed. . .there is something that you say that you want and then *you go about making sure it doesn't happen.*"

"OK, right, I've got something," says Lash, listening intently. Three other heads around the table nod.

"What would you say if I told you that I could change that behavi-or for you in 15 minutes? *And* I wouldn't even have to know what the behavior is?"

"I'd call you a wizard. . ." says Lash.

"I rest my case," says The Wizard. "I am not an extraordinary person. I'm an ordinary person who has learned some extraordinary things."

"So you still teach?" asks Chadwick, taking notes on his pad.

"Nope," says The Wizard, leaning full back in his chair and cross-ing his arms defiantly.

" 'Pearls before swine,' " he says. "I decided to 'go within.' About that time my mother died and had the good sense to leave me half her mouse money. My brother bought a yacht and named it 'Money Mouse'. . .I bought a house in Dufur, Oregon. I've been holed up there ever since."

"What in God's green earth do you do in Dufur, Oregon?" asks Biasi. "I know where that is!"

"Where is it?" asks Lash.

"Well," says Biasi, "there's a sign on the highway that reads: Wel-come to Dufur, set your watch back 50 years."

The Wizard seems stuck in his chair, his toes flip-flipping under the table. "I meditate, I write, I take long walks in wheat fields and I am creating a new language. A language that expands the consciousness. I don't try to communicate with the outside world anymore. I will answer questions from people but I won't make a concerted effort to speak. I have had no visitors for the past year. That's when Travis stopped com-ing. I'd talk to Travis."

"So. . ." says Hershell, "no one gets in to see The Wizard. Not no one. Not no how."

Chapter 27

*The longest journey begins by getting
dressed.*

— Zen Master

Or undressed.

— T. Duncan

A yellow newsletter turned in her hand. She checked her
watch, the number over the auditorium door and the date
— April 24, 1981. She walked into the little theatre and stepped down
the incline to a spot three seats from the front row on the aisle. She
opened a small notebook and started to write. The theatre was empty
except for a pale Musak wheezing in the overhead speakers high above
her head.

The lights from the stage colored her skin with ivory. The felt tip in
her hand flew easily across her pages and she occasionally touched an
auburn curl in thought. She wrote and read her work for several minutes, stretched in her theatre seat and as she brought her left arm down
over the aisle-way, she became aware of a presence next to her. She
spied him as one would a new electronic gadget in a discount store. He
sat on the step next to her... dry, wispy brown hair, a nose that preced-
ed him by several inches, wearing tan pants and a simple cotton shirt.
They talked.

After a few minutes, she turned in her seat and he rested his forearms on his knees. They continued their talk. In a while, she grasped the
theatre seat arm with her hands and leaned over it towards him. He
rocked back and forth on his thin tush and wobbled his head in agreement. They talked on. The Muzak was easily forgotten in the lively
conversation that left both of them grinning excitedly, their faces just
inches apart. Finally she noticed the Mickey Mouse watch on his wrist
and said, "Oh, my God... it's been an hour! I was supposed to attend a
lecture... here!"

They looked around the room as if they had been dropped into the
middle of Pittsburg. They both seemed to notice the theatre for the first

time and no one else was in it.

"Well, you have been," he said. "I'm the speaker...and it appears that you're the only one who came."

"*You're* the *speaker*?" she asked, holding her pen upright as if it were an exclamation point.

"Eaton," he said, extending a long, thin hand.

"Duncan," she responded, the handshake more a pact than a greeting.

She checked the fat hands on Mickey again. "Let's go for some coffee, want to? There's a little coffee shop down the street..."

They walked out of the Willamette Center's theatre complex and onto Second Avenue, continually under construction and they walked north towards the Riverside Hotel. Jackhammers split the morning peace and fine dust choked the air. The sexy hard-hatted men in the street noticed her but did not whistle. They noticed the gaunt fellow with her and their eyebrows came together disapprovingly and they wagged their metal hats. Her attention was focused intently on the long, expressive fingers that played keyboard in the air to his cosmic sonata.

"And what about those poor kids?" he asked.

"What poor kids?" she asked back.

"The slow kids. Seems kinda cruel to me. People don't need to know that they aren't too bright..."

"What *are* you talking about?"

"See that sign over there? 'SLOW CHILDREN.' "

"Oh, for God's sake."

"Oh, it's all right...because they all manage to grow up and get jobs."

"How do you know that?"

" 'SLOW MEN WORKING.' "

Travis' mouth puckered like she had a sour ball in it, she laughed and rubbed her grey eyes with the back of her delicate, ivory fingers.

"And what about the sign in this grocery store: New potatoes! You want to buy *old* or *used* potatoes? How about 'low mileage spuds.' 'One owner russets.' What do you think?"

"I think you're quite nuts!"

"Who is crazier — me for talking or you for listening? But, really, I'm making a point about communication here. Think about it. When people have a fire, they call a 'fireman.' Well, we don't need no *fire*-man, man! We already *got* a fire! Send over an *anti*-fire man!"

She was choking with laughter and street dust.

"One of these days, I am going to start work on creating a new language. Many words will be spelled differently in order to access the unconscious and rearrange reality. Emotion, for instance, is actually energy *in motion,* so it will be hyphenated 'E-MOTION.'"

"OK, give me another example..."

"Heeling...that is, H-E-E-L-I-N-G, like heeling a dog means 'to discipline.' To heel an urge for example, would be to curb it or put it under disciplinary action. Tell it what to do.

"Well, when people or organizations have a sickness — mental, physical or emotional or spiritual — they require a healing, H-E-A-L-I-N-G. Go to a doctor and he puts you on a strict diet for healing your ulcers and instructs you to write down everything that you eat, tells you when to do what. When you want to 'heal' something, trying 'heeling' something in your life. When something needs to be 'healed,' it's because something needs to be 'heeled.' Got it?"

"Amazing! Yeah, I got it. Communication is in a disastrous state, you're right."

"There is no right or wrong," he protested. "Those words would be eliminated."

"I beg your pardon?" she said.

"For every right you can give me, I can give you a culture that calls it wrong. And for every wrong that you give me, I can give you a system that calls it right. If *one* of us on this planet had *all* the evidence, then maybe all of us would believe the same thing. Eliminate the concept of 'right and wrong,' Duncan, and you'll like your world more."

"Well, I'll try it..."

"Don't TRY! DO! The word 'try' is eliminated too! You increase your chance of failure to 83% when you use the word 'try.'"

"I agree. That's a truth. But there is no such thing as 'truth.' Only perspective. I want to say that I think your perspective is 'right on!' I can see where it would get to be difficult communicating with you."

"That which you resist will persist."

"Then I plan on resisting you for awhile because I want you to persist. Just keep talking."

"Does our thinking form our language? Or does our language form our thinking? The Eskimo has 27 words that all mean 'snow.' Yiddish has delightful words that don't translate easily to English. Words like 'chutzpah.'"

"Chutzpah?"

"Yeah, you know, 'chutzpah,' " he emphasized, shrugging his thin shoulders and waving his palms upward, his weathervane nose moving south-southwest. She gently shook her head.

"OK, 'chutzpah' is when you murder your parents and then throw yourself on the mercy of the court on accounta you're now an orphan..."

She nodded til the soft waves in her hair lifted a small dust storm above her head. A sunbeam shot over the top of Cal's Bookstore and zipped across her hair lighting the fine street dust like smoke.

They walked through the parking garage and into the elevator that rose to the lobby level and to the hotel's coffee shop.

"So what do you do...when you're not giving speeches?" she asked, being careful not to mention the empty auditorium.

"I'm a..."

She distinctly heard him say CAR MECHANIC.

"But it says here in this newsletter..." she began.

He took the newsletter, pulled the pen from her notebook and wrote across the top of the paper: KARMIC-ANTIC.

"Oh!" she exclaimed.

"How many?" the hotel coffee shop hostess asked in her aged monotone.

"Two," said Travis, "for me and Mr. Goodwrench, here."

A waitress filled water glasses at a table surrounded by a fuzzy mauve circular booth. A beige and silver wallpaper graphic raced across the wall behind it and silk daisies popped from a milkware vase. Travis slipped into the booth and the velvet upholstery grabbed at her dress, pulling it to mid-thigh.

"So you work with past life regressions?" she asked him.

"No..." he answered, bumping the table and spilling ice water onto the paper place mats. "Present karma only...that's quite enough."

"You know," she said excitedly, "things are really coming around when country western music talks about *karma,* for heaven's sake! I couldn't believe it when I heard it! I mean when Willie Nelson sings about a 'little old-fashioned karma comin' down,' you know the New Age has finally arrived."

"It'll be the next blue light special at K-Mart," he remarked, sarcastically.

A waitress hovered. "Coffee," said Travis. "Stash tea," said her gaucky companion. "You buying?" he asked. "Yes, sure," she answered. "Two eggs, toast, hash browns...gravy on the hash browns, side of sausage..." he said.

"Jeez, when did you eat last?" she asked.

"Probably two days ago. I've got a complete photo dark room for sale. Want to buy it?"

"Sure," she said. "Now to what end do you make antics with karma?"

"I see the hope of human-kind," he began, his hands resuming their orchestration on the table top, "in communication...*intra*personal communication. It is a faster and more efficient way of dealing with inner conflict, psychosis, neurosis, behavior modification — all sorts of things — it is the *life* that brings good things to *life.*"

Travis' grey eyes were transfixed on the odd face with the hypnotic voice and the waving hands. He, forever the teacher, made students of all listeners whether they chose to sign up for class or not.

"I am multi-disciplined. I believe that if all you have is a hammer, then you tend to see all problems as nails. Well, I have hammers, screw drivers, wrenches...a whole tool kit full of methods to use. And I use them as they are appropriate. Karmic-antic sounds like 'car mechanic' and that isn't too far off from what I do. I am a mechanic — only the cars that I work on are the vehicles of your mind.''

"Mine certainly gets wrenched from time to time..." observed Travis pouring cream in her coffee.

"Spoon?" he offered.

"Never stir it," she answered.

"Never?"

"Never," she stated. "Does this mechanic-ing that you do...does it pay?"

"Enough to keep me in incense and gasoline for my Volkswagen. Pays extremely well spiritually. But that wasn't your question, was it?"

"I don't really care," said Travis, "But I couldn't help notice that you didn't have a dramatic following."

"Hmmmmmm," said the thin lips as toast crumbs avalanched down his chin. "Expanding anything can be a painful process... expanding this building would be difficult. But expanding a person's mind is even more difficult. Expansion is the primary motivating factor in the Spiritual Warrior."

"So you're the opposite of a shrink!" she exclaimed, happily.

"Exactly!" he giggled, waving a forkful of gravy until a blob of it splattered near the salt shaker, missing the daisies by millimeters. "I expand, I don't shrink!"

"Don't you find it rather remarkable that I should be the only one to show up at your lecture this morning?" she asked, delighted that he had turned out to be so entertaining.

"No, the people who were supposed to be there, were there," he said. "It is always that way. We are all in our perfect space in our perfect time. And the Universe is unfolding as it should."

"Still..a coincidence..."

"Coincidence," said The Wizard, "is God's way of remaining anonymous."

Chapter 28

One thing worse than being alone —
wishing you were.
                                        — Bob Steele

" hen Travis was convinced of my 'wizard-ness,' she
made my first caftan for me...I had seen it in a
meditation. It was silver satin with a little rainbow on the front of it.
She thought it was important to bring meditation images into reality...
that there was some power in that. I really had to talk her out of having
her mantra done in neon."

"Travis gave you your first dress?" asks Lash. "And you say she
was a *friend* of yours?"

The others snicker and get the joke. The Wizard, however, preys
on words like a robin preys on worms.

" 'Friend' is a word that expands and contracts depending on
who's using it," says The Wizard sadly.

"If you have all this great information," begins Biasi, "and if
Travis said you're a wizard, that's good enough for me...but why
aren't you out using it? Why aren't you out enlightening the masses?"

"The mind that most needs enlightenment is the one that thinks
that human beings need to be enlightened. People are getting what they
want,"he answers.

"Or what they deserve," says Chadwick.

"Eew," grimaces Biasi, "I don't want what I deserve. I want
mercy."

The coffee brews noisily on a side table next to the great dining
table. The Wizard walks to it and pours a cup...it is like seeing Jesus
Christ use a Coke machine...a modern, and somehow, unholy act.

"An Inuit shaman once said, 'True wisdom is always to be found
far away from people, out in the great solitude. Solitude opens the
human mind.' And I observed: 'Sink and you shall find,' " explains
The Wizard.

Hershell's wiry eyebrows shoot up and he nods his Cro-Magnon
head in agreement. " 'Solitude is the school of genius,' " he quotes,

"Edward Gibbon."

"In the great expanse of wheat around Dufur," begins The Wizard again, "a funny thing happens as you look across the vastness. You become the act of vision. You record the scene but you are not *of* the scene. Without a reflection...from a window or from water...you would have no proof of your existence at all. For a time, I will need this to develop what I have inside me."

"What's inside?" Biasi asks, becoming mystified with the mystic.

"I don't know what it is yet. The language I am supposed to develop, I suspect. I hunger for it. I know that there is a guidance factor, a homing device inside that directs my course to a destination I don't know. Look, I'm really not a space case...this is communication science. And my teaching is lost currently on those who want a quick fix and want to transfer their power to me. The world does not need another messiah. We've heard enough. Enough has been *said*, anyway. As much as I would like the people of Earth to learn, I no longer feel compelled to teach. I hunger for my own discoveries; then I can re-enter and share."

The Wizard walks back to his place at the table, sets his coffee cup down and straightens his back, the caftan caressing him gently.

"Wizard," starts Lash very softly. "I know the feeling...of looking out across a plain or a desert or a forest and becoming kind of... detached...or maybe more attached, I don't know which, but it's like I have to see the shadow of my truck just to remind myself that I'm there and not just a camera floating invisible on the highway. It's weird. But it's peaceful. Once in a blue moon, I get that way. I can't hear the truck ...or feel it...I hardly know she's there."

"I sometimes get that way when I design," says Biasi. "I get so into the drawing that I feel like I'm watching my hands create...and that I'm not really doing it, I'm just watching it happen."

The Wizard's high cheekbones radiate a pink light and his tiny mouth smiles an enigmatic smile.

"That's called 'witnessing,' " explains The Wizard.

"Ah," says Biasi, "a perfect word for it. Yes, that's just what it feels like. When things get that way, I know that the design will go well ...and I know something else...I know that the client will like it. That's the most amazing part."

"We've all had times," puts in Chadwick, "when we have driven down a highway for 20 miles and then suddenly thought, God, I can't remember anything about those last 20 miles. Is that what you mean?"

"That's the beginning of it," says The Wizard. "When you become aware of the 20 miles, then you're back into it. If you were to continue, as Lash here does, you would experience the 'witnessing' that he has described...and Biasi too. Physically what's happening is, your brain wave pattern is slowing down."

There is a short silence in the dining room as the individual thoughts catch up to The Wizard's teaching voice.

"Suppose that's what the old guy is doing in Wallace, Idaho?" asks Biasi.

"Yeah," agrees Hershell, "he's probably sitting there in his cabin witnessing books being written."

"It also sounds like," The Wizard speaks louder, "he's got the bucks to keep it all going too. I, unfortunately, do not. If I don't create some wealth and abundance pretty soon, I am going to have to re-enter the material world without my knowledge complete. My inheritance is running out. My time in the vastness is running out. And I am close but I am not *in* my discovery."

The Wizard's voice is more stern now. There is an edge to his words. He knows his hunger and he knows what will satisfy him. He doesn't know yet what his destiny is; he just knows that it is significant.

"So I'd be curious about what you've learned..." Hershell quietly thinks aloud.

"Life," begins The Wizard, then he stops. "Ah, LIFE!" He looks at each of their faces as if for confirmation that he continue. "Please, go on," encourages Chadwick. Lash has leaned forward and rests his beard in his hands, fixed on The Wizard. They are an "audience." The Wizard seems to be reluctantly breaking some internal policy.

"Life," he says again, "is like Disneyland."

Lash's eyebrows pop like toast from a toaster and his pretty brown eyes are fanned by his long lashes. Hershell lets out a little snort. Biasi smiles. Chadwick lifts his coffee cup in salute. "Go on," he says.

"We enter this life and we chose what 'Land' we want to be in," says The Wizard, using his hands to divide up the invisible land in front of himself.

"We chose Fantasyland or Corporateland — they're right next door to each other — or Alcoholism-land, for instance. And we play by the rules in that 'Land.' When I ask, 'What is the name of the Land you chose to visit while you're on Planet Earth?' you might say... 'Security-Land.' Now, if you chose Security-Land, the rules that you live by are to create a safe place for yourself and *you'll make decisions based on being safe.* And your idea of a good time is to ride the rides with the least amount of stress.

"Now, you can choose Adventureland and inside Adventureland is Learning and Growing... some people choose to spend their entire lives in the pursuit of knowledge and enlightenment. They get what they want too, but they will base their decisions on what is new to them. This is a rocky, difficult land and people frequently injure each other. But it's all OK since they've paid their money and they chose to be in Adventureland.

"Then there's Got-Bucks-Land and the motto here is: 'He who dies with the most toys wins.' This is an overcrowded area of the park and there are long lines waiting to get in. It appears that people who spend their lives in this Land always seem to leave feeling like they've missed something...a ride didn't go well, didn't give them a big enough thrill or a long enough thrill.

"Then there is Avoidance-Land. This is really a very funny part of the park because it was so simple to create it and the people in it just love it. In Avoidance-Land, the folks spend all their time trying to avoid things...like taxes, and commitment, and intimacy, and deep thinking, and movement of any kind. They put in their time, they have their fun, but when it's time to go, they look around and say, 'Is that all there is?'

"Now all of this would work out to be just swell if it weren't for just one little thing. There is no map at the entrance and none of the Lands are marked. So what happens is, everybody is in a theme park with each other and they are tramping over each other attempting to make whatever Land they're in, whatever Land it is that they think it should be.

"If it were organized, then it would be great because all the people interested in playing WAR, for instance, could go to War-Land and not bother the people who are not interested in war. War isn't bad, it's just that many people do not want to play that game. And that does irritate the people who *do* want to play.

"Life is a personal event. That's what I'm saying. People choose what they want to experience, they pay their ticket and they play in the park. A few, damned few, have figured what part of the park they're in and *based on the results they're getting,* they either stay where they are or they move. To put it another way, gentlemen, everyone is dealt a hand in this card game of Life...but not everyone is going to play their hand the same way. At any time you can choose to hold 'em or fold 'em. Some of us get 'good' hands and some of us get 'lousy hands.' What matters is what we do with it. And *that is all.*"

" 'It's not what happens to me, but how I handle it that determines my well-being,' " quotes Biasi in a monotone trance.

"B.F. Skinner?" asks The Wizard.

"Travis Duncan," answers Biasi.

Chapter 29

Either get what you want or just get old.
— *Billy Joel*

"Gentlemen, and I use the term loosely," begins Hershell, hoisting himself to standing, "when I entered this life in a California hospital room, I was asked to say something.

"If I hadn't said something, the doctor would have wolloped my ass until I *had* said something.

"This evening reminds me of that event. Of course, what I said then wasn't coherent or particularly useful and this evening's turn to speak may be a repeat of that performance."

Hershell's snow shoe-sized feet draw long skid marks in the thick, creme-colored Oriental carpet as he shuffles towards the coffee pot. His saggy eyelids look like fresh cement squeezed through heavy bricks on a rainy day. His eyebrows pull at the aging cement and reveal slightly clouded eyes of blue-grey. Occasionally the clouds drift away from the grey and his old eyes flash with indignation or humor which usually occur simultaneously.

"So you're going next?" asks Chadwick.

"Sure, I'm going next," bellows Hershell. "I'm bored. Already! I'm not saying you guys are dull exactly. . . but if there were 100 of you, we'd still have to send out for charisma."

Hershell turns back to the coffee urn and splatters a cup for himself, leaving the drips soaking in the white linen. His cup rattles on the saucer as if he were riding a West Virginia train. He lifts the delicate silver cream pitcher and splashes the Half and Half in the direction of the cup. Mercifully he doesn't take sugar. Hershell lifts his left foot to take a step as if the train has lurched into the station and the movement empties two-thirds of the coffee onto his shoe.

Hershell, unaware of the flopping coffee, starts and hesitates on his way back to his place at the table. He lowers his flat bottom onto the padded dining chair, pulls his baggy tan trousers up at the knees and clamps two old fingers onto the round handle of the cup. Just as he is about to take a sip, he halts, looks into the cup and his eyebrows shoot northward. He studies the inside of the cup and looks around the table at the others.

"I thought I went for coffee," he mutters.

There are scattered snickers and Lash, who has turned and sprawled in his chair, chomps his toothpick.

"You did. But that was a half hour ago. Here, I'll get ya a hot cup."

Lash takes Hershell's cup, fills it at the coffee urn, pours another cup for himself and returns to his spot next to Hershell.

"You really own a nudist camp?" asks Lash.

Hershell slurps lovingly at his coffee, holding the china cup with two hands. He stops abruptly, raises his head slightly, says "yes" and returns to his concentrated sipping.

"Why?" asks Biasi, finally.

Hershell slams his cup into its saucer. Every question is an interruption, a mosquito in his tent.

"I'm allergic to laudry detergent," he snaps.

Lash chomps on his toothpick and massages his own cup of black coffee. "Can't kid me," he says. "You're the original dirty old man."

"Shows what you know," answers Hershell flippantly. "The human form is far more provocative with cloth...or sequins or feathers or jewels or even paint on it...everyone knows that. Nudism is hardly the preferred choice of one seeking a stimulant. A nude human is like seeing your truck in primer — not exactly a turn on."

"But you got dressed to come here..." Chadwick notes.

"Nudists are nudists, not crackpots. Wear clothes when clothes are needed. I visited a nudist resort once in Maryland that posted a sign: CLOTHED FOR THE WINTER. When it turns cold...if your sunburn doesn't keep you warm, then you put on...ugh!...clothes. Our visitors will sometimes wear clothes at first, for maybe 10 minutes. Then they get so embarrassed by looking different, they give it up. Mostly, however, our residents are retired people who own property there. We're a little community and visitors are mostly relatives of the residents."

"I've always wondered..." starts Biasi.

Hershell rivets a glare at the architect. Whatever is coming, Hershell has heard it before. "Yes," he states flatly, no questioning tone to his voice. Biasi presses on.

"Where does a nudist keep his change?"

"In a piggy bank. How the hell should I know? There's not much to *buy* in my little burg. People just sign for stuff — like at the snack bar. It's a very simple life. People are honest. It's pretty hard to 'put on'...with nothing on. Everything you need is just there for the delight in using it. The pool. The tennis courts. Women just love nudism, you know. No clothes to wash or iron or fold or pack. And we could put Samsonite right out of business."

Eight eyeballs had dilated with disbelief when Hershell started to speak. Now they relax. Curiosity sniffs the air.

"You're not kidding about this, are you?" asks Chadwick. "You really do run a nudist colony..."

Hershell stands up, hand on his hips.

"When I tell the truth, nobody believes me. That's been the story of my whole life. OK, try this...I'm a retired insurance salesman and I just flew in from a round of golf in Maui. Now, can your yuppie mentality grasp that a little better? Do you find that a little more acceptable? So what do you want? The truth of my life — which will be about as palatable as swallowing a Brillo pad — or some cute little story that will go down easily?"

Two seconds...maybe three...of silence.

"Well, which will it be, *gentlemen*? I haven't got all night! I'm old, ya know! If you want my story then I'd better go next...I may not make it through the telling of *your* lives. It's been enough living through my own!"

Hershell nears MGM lion level as he waves his arms and seeks a vote. The billowing Hawaiian palm trees in his shirt quake violently. As they begin to settle, Hershell takes notice of them, one particularly large cocoanut palm leaning on his chest. With thumbs and index fingers he lifts his shirt at about nipple level and holds the quaking palm tree up to them.

"Think about it, gentlemen. Would anybody who *likes clothes* buy this shirt?"

Chapter 30

*It's never too late to have a happy
childhood.*

— Tom Robbins

"Why'd you become a lawyer," asks Biasi, "if you
never practiced law?"

"The answer to that question," begins Hershell, immensely
pleased with an intelligent question, "lies in the sordid past of the State
of California, a history as murky as the La Brea Tar Pits...and perhaps just as sticky. I knew Los Angeles when you could ride across it on
a bicycle."

Hershell's tone is reminiscent of a camp fire ghost story yarn
spinner. The late hour has mellowed Hershell and his audience of four
would-be millionaires.

"Adventurers, explorers, opportunists, criminals, sea captains, vi-
sionaries and penny ante crooks — wild people all intent on doing as
they damned well pleased — invaded California 150 years ago. My father was all of these things. A sea captain by trade, who hated the sea,
he had no intention of returning to Ireland and whatever Blarney rock
he had crawled out from under. Many of these early California opportunists took to marrying Indian women who had land claims.

"Motivation for marriage has been a distorted custom in California for generations. It is our heritage."

Hershell swirls the coffee in his cup thoughtfully and then downs
the last of it, the gulp audible from across the room.

"Anyway, some of these marriages for the acquisition of land
turned out to be some pretty fine matches. Because these land claims
were such a botched mess and boundaries were described according to a
rock here and twenty paces from there, everybody ended up in court
sooner or later. There were great legal contests over ownership. A family could own a third of what is now Santa Barbara and because of the
legal spaghetti, they could be paupers while waiting to cash in on a land
deal. It was a strange bind and the legal battles went on for years sometimes, waiting for the circuit court judges to ride the circuit. The only

ones who seemed to be getting rich, the only ones seeing any cash flow, were the lawyers. My parents explained very early on that lawyering was the only sure pay off.''

Lash re-tips his cowboy hat. "So your mother was an Indian?''

Hershell nods. "Almost 100%. And my father, anxious to avoid another sea voyage, married into wealth — on paper only — and spent his life pinching pennies and waiting for the legal system to unsnarl itself and declare him a land baron. He had all the humor of Sitting Bull with hemorrhoids. My mother, on the other hand, had all the light-hearted charm and enthusiasm of a good Irish drunk. It was as if they traded scripts. Marriage does that to people, on occasion.''

Biasi listens intently and nods his agreement. Hershell has touched a nerve in the architect, who pushes his chair out, stands and begins to pace. "Just tired of sitting,'' he explains with a wave of his hand. "Continue.'' He walks the length of the dining room.

"I'll tell you one short story about my father and you'll understand what I grew up with,'' says Hershell, his saggy eyes clearing for a faint sparkle.

Chapter 31

*For in its innermost depths, youth is
lonelier than old age.*
                                        — Anne Frank

W indows shuddered like Minnesota cheerleaders in a Christmas parade when Engine 1206 hurtled its way past a wooden house in the tiny community of San Cinto. Sandy dirt puffed angrily into a cloud that enveloped the two-story unpainted desert home. A large picture frame hit the wide floor molding, unable to withstand one more visit by the Southern Pacific monster that visited twice daily on the track just a few yards away. A dark haired woman in a cotton print dress picked up the picture, a sailing ship on the high seas, now finally scuttled to the floor, ice bits of glass surrounding it. San Jacinto Valley, California, 1906.

"Oh, well," she said, merrily, "now, without the glass, I can see the picture better."

Braids framed her round, happy face and she swept the broken glass with a homemade broom while she hummed. Some people hum while they work. Mrs. Kaye worked while she hummed. She finally saw her young son who hadn't yet let go of the kitchen door jab.

"Did old 1206 'bout knock you flat that time?" she asked him.

The little boy nodded without answering and started to put his thumb in his mouth but the security digit was coated with dust and was no longer an attractive pacifier.

"You go on, Baby-Cakes, and read your book in there with Daddy," his mother said.

"Aw, Mom," he whined, "do I have to? Nobody else my age knows how to *read*."

The dark woman scooped up the last bit of glass. When she spoke, her voice was so musical that it was as if she hadn't stopped humming in order to speak.

"You are not 'nobody else,' " she said and then kissed the top of his head on her way through the kitchen door, "and you never will be. . ."

"OK, I'll read," he said, having lost this argument several hundred times, "but do I have to do it in there...with him?"

"Baby-Cakes, come on," his mother crooned with complete surpise. "Your daddy loves you, sweetheart."

"Yeah?" the four year old said. "How can you tell?"

Mrs. Kaye's secret to her own personal serenity was to answer questions that only had happy answers. She could become "appropriately deaf" as she did twice a day when the Southern Pacific rattled the nails literally out of her house. She brushed her son's hair with her hand and smoothed the Size 4 Fiesta Bowl hair cut.

"Going to have to use a bigger bowl next time we cut your hair," she said, lovingly. "You're gettin' so *big*."

It confused the boy that his mother took pride in his growth while his father seemed to take it as a personal financial insult. Big meant shoes that weren't yet worn out, were outgrown. Big meant the crib would have to be replaced when, if the boy hadn't grown, it could have just been repainted. Big meant that much closer to cavities, school books and college.

Baby-Cakes took the small book from his mother's hand and reluctantly walked to the dim living room where a low watt bulb flickered on the desk. His father sat in a straight back chair, creaking from time to time, as he scratched figures onto a page near the light.

"Come sit over here...next to me," his father said as the boy shuffled into the room. His eyes and ears perked at his father's invitation. He was being asked to join his dad so that they could sit and read and write together. It was man-stuff, important, adult-stuff. Maybe he could ask his father a question about a new word. Or maybe, just maybe, his father might ask him something. About anything. Just something. He eagerly took his place in the overstuffed horsehair chair next to his father's desk. The naked little light bulb cast a creamy light on the pages of his first grade primer.

"There," said his father, "now we don't have to turn on another light."

Chapter 32

Old age and treachery will overcome youth and skill.

"When I turned 18, my father presented me with an invoice," Hershell was saying as he flipped a silver spoon on the linen tablecloth, the heavy wax candles dripping quietly in the Pittock Mansion night.

"For 18 years he recorded how much I had cost them, made precise entries into his ledger and on my eighteenth birthday he gave me a bill for $16,638.37. Remember this was 1920 and I could not fathom that amount of money. Money is a curious thing...any amount that you *don't* have — $50 or $500,000 — seems to be a mountain.

"A friend of mine wanted to go to San Francisco and he wanted me to go along. I didn't have the money for the boat fare. My passage was $21.00 and I didn't have even that much money at the time. I borrowed some money from a lady friend and bought a raffle ticket. It paid off about three hours later and less than an hour after that, I was on my way to San Francisco. I got off the boat and started up Market Street looking for work with my friend. I went into an office building and up to the second floor where there was a sign posted: Southern Pacific. I spent the next forty years there."

"Ever see the girl again?" asks Lash.

"Nope. Never did." Hershell's large head tips forward and his voice softens. "She was a pretty little thing. Probably married a gas station attendant and had eight kids. Well, life's a joke. It's like that. All because of a raffle ticket, I get to sail away and she gets to do whatever happened to her. And ultimately we all end up sitting around a dining table trying to figure out riddles..."

Hershell reaches across the table and takes Biasi's water glass. He sips it and then downs it, little clear ice cubes and all. Biasi ignores the old man's theft.

"So what did you do for Southern Pacific?"

"Made 'em more money than anyone else ever did. I processed

claims. Probably met only one honest man in 40 years of doing it.''

"Who was that?'' Chadwick asks.

"Had one old farmer who claimed to have an ordinary cow. Wanted us to pay on a claim. And I said to him, 'You're the first guy to make a claim that didn't have a prize, championship, gold medal, state fair winning cow...you sure this is just an ordinary cow?' 'Yep,' he says, 'it's an ordinary cow.' So we paid the claim. By the time I retired, I was on the board. I've been retired for 20 years.''

"You were an attorney?''

"Back in those days you didn't have to go to law school...all you had to do to be a lawyer was pass the bar exam. I did that so I'd always have something to fall back on. You know, the same kind of thinking that made women take shorthand in the 50's.''

"You'll excuse me,'' says Biasi, "if I can't quite fathom you inside a corporation...''

"Oh, I had a turning point...'' answers Hershell. "I looked around the board room one day, like I told Chadwick, and it occurred to me plain as a cuss word in church...*the best dressed ones died first!*''

"So you went home, took off your clothes and the rest is history...?'' Biasi surmises.

"Sort of...''

"And your change has obviously brought you longevity...''

" 'Obviously,' hell,'' says Lash. "How do we know that he isn't really a 27-year old who's just been livin' hard?''

"You *don't* know!'' puffed Hershell. "This is what knowing Travis will do to a man!''

"Speaking of Travis...'' says The Wizard. "You must have known her a long time ago...''

Hershell's wiry eyebrows shoot for the ceiling again.

"What makes you say that?''

"Well,'' Biasi says, "Twenty years ago, you were 63, right?''

"Oh, you mean that I must have been a much younger man in order to have done her any good, huh?'' bellows Hershell.

Four palms hit four foreheads. Four groans.

"Jeez, Hershell!''

"Under 'curmudgeon' in the dictionary, there's a picture of Hershell,'' observes Chadwick.

Air escapes from Hershell's flapping lips making a horse-like snort.

"Cantankerous-ness is an acquired art, taking nearly a century to develop into a daily routine, a habit. I wasn't born obnoxious! I did not pop from the womb with a barb on my lips! I spent many years, as you all are, languishing in the disease of Nice-Guy-itis. It's a progressive illness and often terminal. I spent many years fighting acquiescence. Many years. More than I care to recognize or admit. My fiesty state is a purposeful science, carefully constructed and practiced until it has become unconsciously a competence of mine. Don't you know that people build up 'walls,' or emotional defenses — *especially men* — to protect themselves? It isn't surprising that at the same time, we build up walls in our arteries. Why do you think it's called *'heart attack'*?"

The four younger men sit in a fascinated silence.

"Now why would your heart attack you?"

Still silence.

"Why would *anybody* attack you?"

Eight eyes stare at Hershell, ponder quickly but realize that it leads only to his answer.

"Your goddamned heart attacks you because you haven't been true to it!" Hershell roars at his students.

Chapter 33

*The reasonable person adapts him/herself
to the world. The unreasonable one per-
sists in trying to adapt the world to him/
herself. Therefore, all progress depends on
the unreasonable person.*
— *George B. Shaw*

"And has anything changed since your last visit?" the
cheery receptionist behind the computer said to her
computer screen.

"Well, yes and no," said Hershell, rubbing his rubbery chin. "The
air jets aren't working in the hot tub, the city won't grant us a food license, the water pump just went out on my Vega and my cat barfed in
my sock drawer...other than that, not much has been going on..."

The cherry-cheeked receptionist's cheeks sank like an overcooked
pie. "That's not what I mean and you know it, Mr. Kaye."

Hershell shrugged.

"You want me to bleed for you, then you gotta bleed for me."

She spun in her perky little desk chair and ripped the computer
sheet from the printer. "Just take it down the hall."

Hershell leaned far over the receptionist's office blockade and
pushed his face close to hers. "You're the only one who can tell me
where to go, you know that, don't you, you wonder-wench?"

The receptionist pointed and screeched, *"Next!"*

Hershell padded down a white hallway to the Red Cross room
marked "Donors Waiting." He sat in a plastic chair and scribbled on
his carbon pack form that was clipped to a clear plastic clipboard. He
had difficulty with the clipboard because he was left-handed. His tongue pressed through his teeth as he concentrated on the questions about
the last time he'd been tattoo'd, been to Haiti, had sex with another
man, seen his dentist or been pregnant. Hershell marked through the
boxes with disgust.

He signed the bottom of the form and approached the high white
bar at the nurses' station. He waited while they searched his carbon

form and attached OK slips to a clear plastic bag with clear plastic tubes hanging from it.

"Ooooooh!" said one of the nursing staff behind the counter, "you have a pin coming today, Mr. Kaye."

"I know, makes it easier to get the blood out..." he quipped.

The nurse pinned a little plastic blood drop pin to Hershell's collar. "That makes 3 gallons for you as of this time, Mr. Kaye-that's-wonderful-of-you!"

Hershell winced. "I just want to give blood today," said Hershell, "not run for public office."

Hershell felt a heat radiating to his left. He turned, expecting to see a large sunburned person. Instead, he saw a pink face held together with dark auburn curls. The soft, big curls reminded him of a mix of cocker spaniel and Irish Setter. They seemed to press her pink-ivory cheeks together and form a perfectly straight nose. The heavy, lazy lashes blinked once and when her eyelids slowly came up a flash of grey met his dumb, blank look.

He recovered in an instant.

"We have the same blood type!" he said, glancing at her form and hoping her blood type was A positive.

In a voice that reminded him of a discount store check out clerk, she said, "Well, then, if something violent and awful should happen to you, maybe you'll be lucky enough to get some of my blood."

It was clear that an unusual set of circumstances would have to occur before he would get anything else from her either.

"Ms. Duncan, drink your 7-Up and go up the stairs," said the nurse behind the counter. "And here's yours, Mr. Kaye."

Hershell took his plastic bag with the plastic tubes dangling from it. Then he took her bag and handed it to her. "May I?" he said.

The laser grey eyes carved a "NO" in his chest. "We're giving blood, not going to the theatre," she said. She took the clear plastic bag from his hand.

"Is that any way to talk about our first date?" he asked.

He hadn't seen anything but her spotlight eyes and that crown of Ruben hair. She had already turned around and he watched her white sweatsuit as she climbed the stairs. The sweat pants were obviously a man's XL and her body rumbled around in them like kittens in a sack. Hershell grimaced, imagining that she had accidently put on her husband's pants that morning. Husband. A ring. A ring? Hershell took to the stairs.

"Come here often?" he asked merrily.

"Are you nuts?" she shot back. "This is a blood bank. You can't come here any more than every 56 days."

Hershell put his head down and whispered, "Coming every 56 days ...that's not good...not good for your health, I think."

She didn't hear him and probably would have taken a pint of his blood herself if she had.

There was a large amethyst on her finger where a wedding ring could have been. Hershell sat next to her in the waiting area. If life were a souffle, he thought to himself, she'd be the egg whites.

A few minutes passed in silence and the silence grew a guilt on her.

"So why do you give blood?" she asked.

"'Cause I won't give 'em my money," he answered.

"There's no age limit for giving blood, I guess."

Hershell took the sting.

"Actually, I'm 83," he said.

"You *are*!" she exclaimed, truly surprised. "You must be in great health. You look wonderful." ("For 83" implied.)

Hershell's bushy eyebrows drooped and he took on a basset hound look to her Irish Setter.

"I lied. I'm really 71. I just wanted to hear you say how great I looked."

The black in the center of her electric grey eyes grew like black balloons at an Over-The-Hill Party.

"There are three things that don't have a prayer," she said. "An atheist, the national budget and *you*."

Think, Hershell said to himself. The woman has a heart or else she wouldn't be at the Red Cross giving blood.

"Hell of a place to meet someone, eh?" he began. "But can you think of a better place? Do you give blood if you're sick? NO! Do you give blood if you're depressed? NO! Do you give blood if you're mad or stingy or self-centered? NO! Soooo...to meet healthy, happy people, go to the Red Cross and open a vein."

She very slowly turned to him and looked full into his eyes with all the enthusiasm of studying a piece of wadded up toilet paper and she said, "I'll keep that in mind the next time I want to meet someone."

The finality of her flat "someone" was a clear message that Hershell was not that someone. Hershell finally sat quietly holding his empty blood bag in his hands. Pretty soon the bag would be full of his warm red, healthy, American blood and he would hold it as if it were his heart and the Red Cross would take it away.

Maybe she was politically minded...

"What do you think of Red China?" he asked.

"Looks great on a white tablecloth," she answered.

She leaned forward to tie a tennis shoe lace that had pulled itself apart. Across the expanse of her bulky sweatshirt read: DON'T DIE WONDERING. She tied a double knot in the shoelace as if to teach it a lesson and then leaned back into her chair.

"Your sweatshirt?" he asked.

She zapped a sideways glance at him. "Yeah..."

"A gift, perhaps?"

"Noooo..." Two little lines appeared in the furrow of her brow as a question mark formed on her face.

"How do you know you're loved?" he asked, his voice now confident and a sparkle coming to his old eyes.

"What?" she nibbled his line.

"What does it look like? What does it sound like? How do you know you're loved? What gives you the impression that someone loves you?" His words poured out like an inspired tent preacher.

" 'Cause if you don't know, if you can't answer that for yourself, then you're being led by the nose through life by forces within yourself that you don't even know about. And don't tell me that you know that you're loved when you hear the words 'I love you' either!"

She pulled back and looked at him, the laser in her eyes turning from piercing to warming.

"Why not?"

"There may have been a time...maybe in the back seat of a '55 Chevy, when you heard the words, 'I love you,'...but you knew they didn't mean it."

Her right shoulder tipped slightly forward seductively and she added, "Or care."

"Then there may have been another time in your life when the person never said it...maybe a grandfather...he never said the words, but you *knew* you were loved...so it's not hearing the words 'I love you.' What is it for you? How do you know you're loved? Because you'll go to *whatever it is* for you like a moth to a flame. Aren't you even curious what it might be?"

She looked at him. She didn't speak. She looked at the fuzzy curls on the top of his head. She looked at his bushy eyebrows and his funny, rubbery face. He had shut up and now only grinned. It was a cartoon smile, like one she'd seen drawn on Snoopy.

"You some kind of authority?" she asked.

"I'm not young enough to know it all," he said.

She took the sting.

"Besides..." he added and then unbuttoned his blue shirt and pulled it open, Superman-style, to show her the type on his T-shirt. In bold letters across his ample chest were the words: QUESTION AUTHORITY.

The wide auburn curls moved gently as she nodded her head approvingly, her ivory skin gave way to pink, her grey eyes went more to green and a mega-kilowatt smile crossed her great face. He took a moment to mentally photograph that first smile before he could go on.

"Not that saying the words isn't a way of expressing a love," he continued. "George Elliot said, 'I like not only to be loved, but to be told that I am loved; the realm of silence is large enough beyond the grave.' "

Suddenly he was precious to her and the fact that he wasn't young meant that he was closer to "going," like a good bargain on sale.

"I'm the only one left like me," he said into her spotlight gaze.

A nurse in white pants stood in front of her, hand extended for her plastic bag. "Your turn," she said, interrupting the sound track in her mind. She handed the bag to the nurse without taking her eyes off Hershell. And he, immensely pleased with himself, said, "Can I buy you a cup of coffee after?"

Mesmerized, she answered, "The coffee's free."

"As our thoughts should be," he said, softly.

Chapter 34

*You're only young once, but you can stay
immature indefinitely.*

— *Anonymous*

" I wanted her to remember me, so I gave her my three gallon blood pin," Hershell says, "even though she was a quart low."

Then he leans back with a great "Ha!" and laughs a fantastic laugh. "A quart low!" he says again and laughs at his joke.

There are groans and grimaces around the table.

"Travis was addicted to learning," begins Hershell again when his body finishes the laugh and winds down to a chuckle. "Anything to *learn* something."

"She was a good student," puts in The Wizard, resting his slight chin on his boney index finger and watching the dining room's ceiling. "But rigorous honesty...she was a great deal more than a student. She was canvas or a clear window."

"For a wizard, you're no dummy," admits Hershell.

"Travis had a great capacity for taking in all kinds of information, didn't she?" asks Chadwick.

"Travis had a great capacity for trash, yes," observes Hershell. "The philosophical Statue of Liberty. Bring me your tired, your ragged ...philosophies. Travis was like that. Bring in any old perspective and she'd just take it in. She didn't seem to have an editing system that would reject an idea. And she would integrate the most opposite insights in the world. The miracle was that she could take conflicting trash and make very pretty sense of it. She seemed to think that everything had *some* validity if you just looked long enough. She was exasperating that way. She was exasperating to *herself.*"

"Hershell, you've just said the first thing that has made any sense to me this whole evening," says Chadwick. "When I look around the room and try to make sense of this little group of ours, it is like studying a cryptograph. Find the repeated similarities. Well, there just haven't been any. Or any that I could see up until now. Given what you just observed about Travis...one could have predicted a varied group like we are. It would not only make sense, it would *have* to be this way! Do you see that there is only one architect? Only one wizard? Only one military man? That's because she only needed one of each of us!"

"You mean, what we have in common is that we're all different?" asks Lash.

"Edwin already guessed that..." mentions Biasi.

"No," says Hershell, "what Chadwick is saying is that Travis chose us with intent, purposely sought us out to fill some sort of interviewing assignment...like a 'Man on the Street' sort of thing...choosing us specifically and with calculation."

Lash's eyes glance rapidly back and forth across the table. "You mean, like ordering from a menu?" Suddenly his specialness is threatened. "You mean, like she needed a trucker so she just went and found one?"

"Not exactly," says Hershell, patting the back of Lash's hand with his wrinkled and bent paw.

"I don't think we were chosen by profession..." hazards Biasi.

"Chadwick, you yourself may be ultra purposeful...to plot such an assignment...but nobody in real life could have been *that* purposeful," says The Wizard.

Hershell is slumped in his chair, his large shoes anchoring him in place like insert tabs. His chin sits on his chest and his pudgy fingers are interlaced across his tummy.

"I agree," says Hershell, "but she could have been purposeful in another way. She didn't duplicate *philosophies*. There is no reason to if you're a Student of the Universe. And if you chose to learn your Life's lessons through your lovers, then it follows that they will be of different professions. They will also appear to have nothing in common. Otherwise, you're just learning the same lesson over and over again."

"Why *were* we chosen?" asks Biasi.

A five-second silence.

"Because we each had something different to teach," says The Wizard. "What Hershell just told us...about how he finally got through to Travis, think about it. He didn't entice her with money and remember, this was before she had much of it. He didn't use flattery, a fairly useless commodity for a Spiritual Warrior like Travis. And, forgive me, Hershell, a 71-year old man isn't going to use brawn and a tan to attract a 25-year old woman."

"Notice something else..." adds Chadwick. " 'Don't die wondering.' That's what her sweatshirt read, right? Travis was motivated by curiosity. And Hershell appealed to her curiosity."

" 'The cure for boredom is curiosity. There is no cure for curiosity.' " Lash speaks as if he were in a trance. He stares at a pool of white candle wax that has made its journey down the long taper, over the ridges in the silver candlestick and finally onto the cloth of the table.

"Where did you hear that?" asks Biasi.

Without taking his eyes from the tiny growing pool of wax, Lash says, "Travis used to say that all the time..."

A light and gentle sadness filters into the room when they hear "used to." "Travis used to." Travis used to. It was past tense. What "Travis used to" she would no longer do. It is as if this has just occurred to them.

For awhile no one wants to talk. Five minds go into five separate worlds as if they have temporarily left the room to go find personal solitude for a moment. For just a brief station break, the wonderful sum of $23 million is ignored and a big, fat memory sadness occupies the space inside their heads. Finally, mercifully, Hershell sneezes. It is a great AH-Choo that could fill a convention hall without the use of a microphone, a schnozzle-clearing, chest-racking, ear-popping, throat-ripping sneeze that rattles windows in the Pittock Mansion.

Violent sound waves blast through the dining room and move the crystal in the chandelier. When they stop, Lash asks, "Are you all right?"

Hershell sniffles and then straightens himself in his chair. Chadwick suspects that Hershell sneezed on purpose. Biasi suspects that Hershell sneezed just to disturb Biasi's deliciously morose artistic thoughts. The Wizard suspects that Hershell just sneezed.

"So what finally happened with you and Travis?" asks Chadwick.

"She loved the story about my hat," Hershell answered quickly. "The president of Southern Pacific wore a hat and all the vice-presidents wore hats. Everyone expected that when I became a vice-president, why, I'd get a hat. Well, I've always had lots of hair on my head and I've never worn a hat."

" 'Beware of all enterprises that require new clothes,' " Biasi quotes Thoreau.

"Precisely," nods Hershell. "Went out for lunch for a monthly meeting of the upper management and well, I didn't have a hat. Get a hat, the president's secretary said. I was the only one without a hat. Finally the vice-president of finance sat me down and said to get a hat. President isn't pleased and wants to know where your hat is. Don't have one. Get a hat. On and on."

"So did you?" asks Chadwick.

"Oh, I got a hat," says Hershell, simply. "I put it on my expense account...along with my UGN contribution."

The others cackle and snicker.

"If they thought that I needed a hat to do my job, what else could I do? I'd have to take their word for it. But that didn't mean that I had to pay for it. I don't imagine a hat made me a better thinker...but it seemed to calm everybody down so maybe *they* could think a little better."

"People are weird," says The Wizard, shaking his head.

"If there be any doubt of that, all one needs to do is look at this evening..." grouses Biasi.

"What about Travis..." asks Lash again. "Can you think of anything more about Travis that might help..."

"Have any of you noticed," Hershell addresses them playfully, "that most people keep learning the same lessons over and over again in Life...like the woman who keeps marrying alcoholics? I believe that we are doomed to have the same lessons repeated over and over again to us until we learn the lesson. The thing that was different about Travis was — she was aware of the Lesson Plan and needed the lesson taught only once."

"What did you teach her?" asked Chadwick.

"That presumes that I 'taught' her anything," mutters Hershell, painfully aware of the tenuous position of any teacher. "To be taught, one learns. For me to tell you precisely what she learned or wanted to learn, I'd have to get inside her head. And if I thought that I could do that with any precision, I wouldn't be sitting here wasting a good night's sleep on this puzzle. But I can tell you what we talked about..."

Hershell moves his rump toward the wall and rests on his right hip. He looks as uncomfortable as a llama in a lawn chair.

"We talked about The Corporation. She was most interested in the political intrigue, the relationships of men in organizations. And I say 'men' because there were no women there at the time. We would occasionally play chess and discuss the behavior of men in corporate life... the predictability of the moves and the games played. When we began, I could kill her in chess. Eventually though..."

Hershell lapses into a memory that brings a grimace to his face.

"Well, do you know how embarrassing it is to be check mated by someone 46 years your junior? That was another thing about Travis... she didn't have the built-in female decency to allow me a win now and then. She didn't seem to know what other women know. That's why I liked her, dammit."

Hershell's lower lip slides out like a rubbery shelf and he focuses on nothing in particular.

"Anything else?" Biasi breaks the reverie.

"Travis would come to visit from time to time. She'd be very quiet and spend most of the time in the shade...as if her energy source wasn't from the sun. Her hair, you know, she'd burn like a cinder. We'd carry on great philosophical discussions in the hot tub, frequently lasting most of the night. Sometimes others would be around. We'd let them join in the conversation but whether they stayed or left didn't seem to make much difference...we just kept hashing life's mysteries. We'd argue over certain points...she infuriated me, causing me to talk all night...but even when we were in agreement, we were so animated and so...just plain loud and enthusiastic...people thought that we were arguing."

Hershell slowly and deliberately straightens in his chair and expands his chest. With great dignity he surveys his tiny audience. "Travis called me the Cosmic Jab in the Ass," he says proudly, his official title now made public. "And I think I taught her... 'Be anything, just don't be boring.' A difficult lesson for a youngster of 25 but as The Wizard has pointed out, she was an apt student."

Chadwick raises a finger. "You obviously got your lesson taught, Hershell, or we wouldn't be in this dilemma tonight. She couldn't have just left us each some money?"

"Boring, boring, boring," chants Hershell. "Lucky I got to her before you did."

Hershell sits very upright now and proud, an old tan king in a wild palm print.

"Then one day, I get this telegram. It is so unusual to get telegrams. That's such an old-fashioned communication. So like her. I can still recite to you *verbatim,* what it said: 'I have finally decided to take your advice, Hershell, and put it where the sun don't shine. I'm moving to Portland, Oregon. Love, Travis.' "

Chapter 35

Entrepreneurship is the last refuge of the troublemaking individual.
— *James Glassman*

"OK, Chadwick, you're up."

"Travis was responsible for staging my assassination ...that's how we met...seven years ago," begins Chadwick.

The four would-be millionaires expect something similar to a stock report from Chadwick...a story as perfectly pressed and aligned as his underwear...a description well-tailored and appropriate to the occasion...something starched and crisp and tidy and complete and even buttoned-down.

Chadwick pulls a silver lighter from inside his suit jacket pocket. The lighter is thin, barely a quarter of an inch thick and the corners are rounded, an antique. There is no inscription on the smooth, silver surface. He pulls the cap from the lighter with a little "ping." From his side pocket he draws a pack of Marlboro cigarettes and he lights one by flipping his thumb over the metal wheel on the lighter. A puffy trickle of smoke comes from his nostrils. The jaws under his smooth, shaved face work themselves in an isometric frenzy. He props his elbows on the table's edge, cups the cigarette and keeps it close to his lips.

"You all may have been a lot of things to Travis, but I'll wager that I'm the only one who was a target. And by being a target, she saved my life...in a way...."

"Would you find it insulting," says Biasi, politely, "if I told you that you make less sense than The Wizard?"

"OK," says Chadwick, a major puff ball of smoke surrounding his hands. "Then ask questions."

The Wizard, seated to Chadwick's immediate right, reaches for the silver lighter, now out there on the table. Chadwick adjusts his thin, rimless glasses but expresses no objection. The Wizard studies the lighter and presses it to his palms.

"Travis gave you this lighter, didn't she?" asks The Wizard.

Chadwick's teeth touch just the tip of his thumb as he watches The

Wizard. "Yes," he says.

"You must have been married when you knew Travis..." ventures The Wizard.

"Right again," says Chadwick, unflinching.

Lash is sprawled on the table, his butt resting on the edge of his chair. He looks over the table flowers and past the candles at The Wizard. "How did you know that?" he asks.

The Wizard holds the lighter up for all to see, between his thumb and forefinger. It's an elegant, simple silver piece about an inch and a half long.

"There's no inscription," points out The Wizard. "This is the kind of item you'd buy just to put an inscription on...but there is none. And it isn't the sort of thing a man would buy for himself. No inscription speaks louder than words."

Chadwick's shoulders drop, his elbows come off the table and he takes his lighter back. "The Wizard is right on all counts," he says. The lighter is returned to his left breast pocket.

"It's not what is, gentlemen, it is what it appears to be."

"Come again?" says Lash.

"It doesn't make any difference what is, only what it appears to be." Chadwick seems to be quoting from an ancient text. He takes a breath from his cigarette and ponders his wide, polished thumbnail.

"You can feel and think a certain way but unless that is communicated, it just doesn't matter. By the same token, what is communicated may be closer to the truth anyway, you just don't know it. It makes absolutely no difference what is real...only what appears to be real. That's business."

"The illusion of power is power," says The Wizard.

Chadwick gives a short snicker and nods in agreement.

"Can anybody make sense of what these two are sayin'?" asks Lash, turning towards Hershell. Hershell makes a noise something like a belching turtle.

"The point I'm trying to make here is that I can tell you what appeared to be...about Travis, I mean...and you will think that you understand. However, it wasn't that. I've thought about it many times and it just wasn't that simple. Am I making sense so far?"

"Keep going," encourages Hershell. "This is either getting closer to the bone or it is the biggest bunch of horse pucky...either way, it's entertainment."

Chadwick takes a deep breath.

"First you're going to tell us what it wasn't, is that right?" asks Lash.

"That part you'll think is the truth because that's just what it appeared to be. On the surface, just looking at the facts, it sounds like a classical case of adultery. And maybe it was. That's what I mean. What I communicate may be what is real and what I *think* may be the illusion."

"Don't part with your illusions," advises The Wizard.

Chadwick stands up at his place at the table and pulls his jacket from his shoulders. He hangs his suit jacket on the back of his chair being careful to flatten the lapels and adjust the shoulders until they align perfectly with the chair's back. He flips the catch on his cuff link and pulls it from his shirt sleeve hole. "No," he says to The Wizard, "these weren't a gift from Travis." He pulls the other cuff link from his sleeve and the gold bits go into his pants pocket. He begins to roll the cuffs of his white Oxford shirt.

"Travis had a fear of flying, so we flew a lot. There was plenty of flying around, crossing oceans to see each other, finding hideaway restaurants on three continents, living with a travel alarm. Love means never having to unpack your suitcase. Travis thrived on it. She was obsessive about adventures. And I could participate in a royal transcontinental escapade. She was on a first name basis with a dozen sky caps in a half dozen countries...even knew some of their kids' names. She knew how to say 'How much is?' in ten different languages. And for someone who claimed to have math anxiety, Travis could figure the rate of exchange in her head. And she did finally get over her fear of flying..."

A percentage of a smile crosses Chadwick's small mouth.

"What in God's green earth do you do to do all that flying?" asks Lash. "You with the airlines?"

Chadwick's mouth goes to a full grin and he laughs so vigorously that he snorts. "If I cashed in all my frequent flyer chits," says Chadwick, "they'd have to give me a 747."

Chadwick nips at his Marlboro and takes a sip of his coffee. He delights in the mixture. "Ah, coffee!" he exclaims, "the great glue of business deals, the elixir of closings, the stimulant that launches a thousand daily schemes."

Chadwick closes his eyes and leans his head back. Without returning his head to an upright position, he slowly opens his eyes just a slit and adds, "I move money, that's what I do."

"Well, that's sufficiently vague," grumbles Hershell.

"I thought you said that you did land development..." prods Biasi, perhaps feeling a business opportunity himself.

"I do land deals..." offers Chadwick.

"Real estate," suggests Lash.

"No..."

"All right," storms Hershell. "We don't need to play 20 questions with this. It probably isn't all that important and God knows it's probably boring as hell anyway. What is a bit more interesting is what you said about assassination. What was that about?"

Chadwick tips his cigarette ash neatly in the small, square crystal ash tray directly in front of him. Without his jacket on, it is evident that the short man is powerfully built. His petite body is well-proportioned and he fills the shoulders of his executive shirt. The fabric around his biceps is stretched tight. His eyebrows arch slightly and his voice goes down to just above a whisper. It is as if he is about to go over the plans for breaking into the national vault.

"It's all an illusion. And it's all a game. And I don't mean that in a negative sense necessarily. There are people who don't know there's a game going on. There's people who know there is a game going on. And there's people who have known it for so long, that they've forgotten there's a game going on.

"And make no mistake! It is serious business...this business of business. You can get assassinated — if you're big enough, powerful enough and dumb enough."

"Assassinated?" Lash asks.

"I mean politically assassinated. 'Relieved of your command,' the military calls it. Know that whatever they're telling you, they're not telling you the whole truth. And if they *knew* the whole truth, they wouldn't tell it.

"Strategy is essential in order to just maintain in The Game, much less succeed. Whatever 'succeed' means. To be cunning and not to appear cunning is also a requirement. Jeez. Talking like this reminds me of talking with Travis in the old days...."

Bluish smoke mercifully drifts away from the table and out to the foyer where the words don't drift.

"In fact, at one point, Travis and I were going to write a book together. 'The Gunslinger's Guide to Business.' We compared the characters of Dodge City to characters that you meet and deal with in business. There are gunslingers...the professional gunfighters...and young upstarts who try to outgun them. There are marshalls and side-kick deputies...every organization has a heavy gun with a sidekick. And there are the townspeople who just want to live in peace. There are bar girls and then there's Miss Kitty, a really wise and powerful woman in the organization who knows where all the bodies are buried. There's Boot Hill...that's the memory of those who have met their ends, died on the job or in their beds...people who have retired or been fired, who left their marks.

"The whole playing field of an organization can be easily compared to old Dodge City. And, of course, once you identify the different characters, including yourself, it's a simple matter to predict outcomes and play your part."

Hershell snorts and twists in his chair. He says, "You know, sometimes I think that the real reason people work is for the social interaction. It isn't really *primarily* for the paycheck...that's just a happy by-product. The real reason people work is for the gossip, the scenes, the fights, the stress, the comedy, the comraderie...it's a daily soap opera. So whatever happened to the book idea?"

Chadwick uncupped his hands and gave a little shrug. "Travis said that the best literature was in the heads of people too active and too undisciplined to write books. Her theory was that the only things we get to read, of course, are those things written...and the people who are banging at the keys writing things are those people who are writing instead of living. I'm sure that I don't have to remind any of you which activity Travis preferred. The only thing that Travis ever wrote, to my knowledge, was post cards, usually postmarked in airports. It is a sobering thought, however, to think that the best, the very best that we have to read is substandard compared to what is in some people's heads. I couldn't really argue with her on this point. So the 'Gunslinger's Guide to Business' was shot down, so to speak."

"And so back to your story..." prods Hershell.

"Yes, well, I spent my time in someone else's corporation. I played out the Super Star on someone else's 50-story Manhattan playing field. I put together industrial development deals for public utilities, port authorities and local governments. What many people don't realize is that there is a tremendous amount of property that is owned by power companies, ports...agencies that are finally beginning to develop property and compete with private developers. They have an edge with bond sales and in's to markets — this isn't discussed much; it's old news. I was working for a public-type agency, the head of their industrial parks division, when I, well..."

Chadwick purses his lips and looks for his champagne glass. Biasi has taken it and drained it. Chadwick sips his cold coffee instead.

"I had things going in the right direction. Things were starting to move. We had some Europeans interested in us. Lots of Japanese interest. Then there was a bad investment. Ground was broken on this thing ...I'm sure the law suits are still going on. Anyway, I always thought that they were looking for a scapegoat for that deal. But for whatever reason...remember, it's never for what they say that it is...I was high enough up in the organization that they just couldn't walk in and fire me. I suppose that the advantage of being a peon is, people are more honest to you. They can say, 'You're fired.' But when you're high enough up, plots are required."

"So you were politically done in?" asks Hershell.

"Yeah, and I gotta tell ya, in such an ingenious way...the knife goes in so clean, you don't even feel it. But we have Travis and ourselves to thank for that."

Lash has been barely following Chadwick's story. "Wait a minute," he says, lifting his right index finger. "You took a fall for something that wasn't your fault and got fired? What does Travis have to do with that?"

"I wasn't fired. I resigned. It's a long story and I'll explain it briefly. Sometimes, when a corporation has a problem, they hire a consultant. You know what a consultant is — that's somebody who takes out *your* watch to tell *you* what time it is...only sometimes they take your watch and give you the weather report. And then they keep the watch."

His cigarette ash shoots 40 m.p.h. into the ash tray.

"Now consultants get hired for all sorts of things...untangle a data processing system, teach healthy lifestyles, run better meetings, give better performance reviews. There are more bandaids than there are wounds in the corporation. But when they've really got a sticky personnel problem, or they think that's what they've got, a real high-priced pro is brought in. And frequently there's a management retreat. They'll go off to some woodsy little place, perfect for a murder. And through a series of mind-bending games, appearing to be innocent enough, the very serious business of business takes place.

"I concentrated on profit. I did not concentrate on being Mr. Congeniality to do it. It wasn't possible to do both. And I'd had some great successes. Documented. That's why I say, if you're big enough and powerful enough and dumb enough, you might qualify for an assassination. It's really quite a compliment that someone would go to so much trouble."

Chadwick is cheerful. His sweet mouth smiles gently, his pale blue eyes seem to sparkle and his eyebrows are telling you a happy story. His hands, cupped near his chin, are relaxed balancing his shortened cigarette. But there is something...perhaps the tenseness in the muscles in his back, the too-square shoulders, those lips capable of a calibrated smile, that give the impression that he wants to tell you that your new puppy has just been run over by a Mack truck.

"I'm on the plane ready to fly back, after it's all over, and next to me on the plane is..." he spreads his hands, "Travis Duncan."

Chadwick's tush rocks from side to side in his chair as his body remembers, stirred just by the sound of the name.

"I thought I had seen her before and I asked, 'Aren't you a member of the Lake Hanover Resort staff?' and she says no. I thought I had seen her there. Well, she'd been there all right. Behind the scenes working for the consultant that facilitated the management retreat. Well, on the plane she was having trouble...pale as a ghost and leaving fingernail marks in the upholstery.

"When I told her who I was, she reacted in an odd way; she said that I was 'better looking' than she expected. When I asked her about that, she just said that I was a better looking seat mate than she expected to have on a plane. Well, it was probably a year later when she told me about her involvement in that management retreat. You see, Travis worked for all kinds of management consultants, behind the scenes. She was a stage director that was never seen. Others took the glory but others took the heat too. Credit and blame smell the same."

Chadwick smushes his cigarette, folds his arms across his chest and leans forward toward Hershell.

"I suspect that some of your infinite wisdom found its way into

Travis' bag of tricks." He sits up and eyes The Wizard. "And you as well, Wiz."

Hershell is deep in thought; he hasn't moved for several minutes and his Rushmore face is caught in intensity.

"So what happened after that?" asks Hershell in a quiet whisper.

"I went to work for the biggest sonuvabitch I've ever known," Chadwick roars, leaning back in his chair and stretching his short arms over his head. "Myself!"

"And you're better off for it?" hazards Hershell.

"Never better," chirps Chadwick. "It was a life-saving maneuver. I put what I knew on a global scale and now I move money. The politics of business are still there but I don't have to attend meetings in my own organization with my back towards the wall."

"Wait til you hear about the politics of *architecture...*" adds Biasi.

"I know some of that scene, Biasi," says Chadwick, "and the simple fact is, when you have men, you have politics."

"What about women?" asks The Wizard.

"There's three different kinds of politics," answers Hershell. "There's the political dynamic that occurs between men, there's a separate politic with women and there's another one...between men and women. Chose your game, gentlemen." Hershell shrugs.

"Tell me something, Chadwick," ventures Biasi, "did you ever resent Travis for that caper?"

Chadwick reaches for another cigarette.

"If she hadn't been hired to help stage that assassination, I never would have met her," says Chadwick, "and I would have missed out on the Love Affair of the Century. OK, maybe Affair of the Decade. Besides, there's probably nothing I admire more than engineering."

"I notice your tailor graduated from MIT," cracks Biasi.

"Thank you," says Chadwick.

Biasi rolls his eyes and rests his head in his hands.

"Travis was an engineer, a flawless strategist. She was *good* at what she did. *I'm* good at what *I* do...and I don't think I'd have made the big move or be this far along in my career if it *hadn't been for Travis.*"

The silver lighter sings its "ping" again and Chadwick talks with the Marlboro between his lips.

"Haven't any of you observed by now that sometimes what we think is a tragedy...well, in time, we end up saying, 'You know, that was the best thing that ever happened to me.' I like to think about Jason Robards. He had a terrible car accident and went through the windshield of his car. Ended up in the hospital with his famous face all cut up. But...now he has this accident, he's in the hospital, he gets off the sauce, (he'd been quite a drinker, I guess) gets his face rebuilt even better than before and goes back to serious acting. In one interview he said that that accident was the best thing that could have happened. Now I can guarantee you that when he was flying through the windshield of that car, he wasn't thinking, 'Wow, this is the best thing that's ever happened to me!' "

Chadwick puffed sharply on his cigarette.

"No, my friend, if the Devil himself had staged that event, I would be blessing *him* to this day!"

"You know," says Hershell, "you've just compared knowing Travis to having a car wreck. Just an observation."

"I'd say that's a chillingly accurate comparison," adds Biasi. He turns in his chair and, hand on hip, he asks, "Travis knew you were married?"

The fine muscular line of Chadwick's jawbone works itself. "Not that it's any of your business...but my wife and I never agreed to a monogymous relationship. Travis and I had discussions about this. But I can go into that later..." He stretched again and said playfully, "Don't you want to know about my childhood?"

Chapter 36

Aten year old black boy in a stained flannel parka stooped to pick up a long cigarette butt, crushed into the sidewalk. His friend, a ten year old white boy, tackled him, wrestling the tobacco stub from his mouth while shrieking, "Dibs! I saw it first!" They tumbled together across the sidewalk and into a low level snowbank. Two women, walking home from work, stepped over the brawling youngsters. "Hey! She don't got no underpants on!" shouted the black boy. They stopped tussling and chanted wildly after the two women. "She don't got no underpants on! She don't got no underpants on!" The women rolled their eyes and pretended to ignore the taunt by checking the Holiday Sale sign in Greenfelt's shoe store window. Christmas in New York City 1957.

Unable to horrify the two women, the boys threw snowballs. Greenfelt came out of his store, shook a broom at the boys, tipped his black tam to his two potential customers and returned to his store, yelling at his help. "Get the snow shovelled off the walk and we won't have such trouble," he wailed.

"It's not the snow that makes the trouble," one woman said to the other.

The two boys ran to the alley across the street from Greenfelt's and they found matches to light the cigarette. There was only enough tobacco and paper to allow for two drags, one for each boy.

"You know, days a war on...gonna be a rumble between the kids on Sixth Street and the kids on Eighth Street!"

"What are they gonna use for ammunition?" asked the white boy.

"The kids from Seventh Street!" The black boy laughed a long time at his joke.

The white boy sat down on the street where the snow had been cleared and sighed, "You know, there's not much to do around here in the winter time..."

"Sure, they is," said his friend, trying unsuccessfully to eek one more draw from the cigarette butt. "Plenty. Shoot Christmas lights out with a BB gun. Start chimney fires on the roof. Great snow ball fights. And it gets dark early so we can get Chadwick every night if we want."

The grey, dreary street turned blue in the twilight and began to squirm with black silhouette figures finding their apartments.

"He be goin' for his mom's *New York Times* right about *now*!" predicted the black boy.

The two disappeared further down the alley and made a left hand turn. The path, very deep between two four-story buildings, was dark as night. They slipped to the entrance of the narrow passageway and had a short wait for the predictable event. Chadwick Ollander and his mother's *New York Times* appeared and were plucked from the street disappearing into the alley, carried like a Macy's Christmas parade balloon person. Lucky for little Chadwick that the two boys could not afford decent mittens...or the beating would have lasted longer. The black boy rubbed his knuckles and stood above his prey, the newspaper billowing around them like disturbed seagulls in the cold draft of the alley.

Chadwick, older by two years, lay crumpled before his classmates, blood dribbling from his nose and onto his lip. "It isn't fair!" he protested.

"*What* isn't fair?" taunted the white boy.

"You guys got me tonight. It's not your turn. Today's Tuesday."

The black boy laughed his best Tough Guy Laugh and ripped the knitted ski cap from Chadwick's head, taking several strands of hair with it. Chadwick knew better than to cry out in pain.

"See you later, asshole," the white boy said, giving Chadwick's thigh an extra kick.

The two boys ran out of the alley and into the blue grey light of the street. Chadwick tried to catch the flying pages of the *New York Times* but too many of them had already taken flight. He propped himself up against the brick wall and assessed the damage. He was conscious and could still walk. There had been times when even that wasn't true.

Chadwick had considered it a major victory when he had broken the four foot mark on the height chart at school. It was a milestone; his growth was painfully slow. But hitting the mark wasn't enough, it hadn't come fast enough for him to match, much less best the would-be Joe Louis's that occupied his neighborhood. Still...one wondered why Mrs. Ollander didn't have her paper delivered...

Chadwick limped to the opening of the alley and found that the pain in his leg wasn't really that bad after all and he could walk down the street without drawing attention. His nylon parka would not absorb the blood and his little gloves were vinyl, made to look like leather. The finger of blood stayed on his lip. A patch of pink about the size of a fist was turning blue near his eye. Chadwick walked to the Sunshine Grocery & Deli, where he had just purchased the newspaper. He picked up another bulky issue of the *Times* and cursed the Christmas ads.

The Christmas holidays had brought old man Guido's daughter home to help out at the Sunshine Grocery & Deli. She was recently widowed and Guido knew that she would draw business — the women to press her for details of her husband's unusual death and the men who would come and press against her if they could. Carmella had been raised and married in the neighborhood, left and returned...with no bambino and her uniformed spouse in a box, missing his sexual organs. Carmella had been in flight to join her husband in Japan when the event of his death occurred, an irate Tokyo woman disturbed at Carmella's existence and impending arrival. Polite military procedures had only advised Carmella of her widowhood; it was left to her local funeral director, a friend of her papa's to give her the details.

She had left the old neighborhood to be a Navy wife. That fact alone had made her both an adventuress and also kind of a traitor. Guido was relieved to have his only daughter married before she sprouted with a child before his eyes. Men seemed to give her power but she never seemed to observe it. Now, she was back, still beautiful, still unplucked, a suggestion of Italian tragedy about her and she had just spied Chadwick coming in the door of the Sunshine Grocery & Deli.

"Oh, my God, what's happened to you?" exclaimed the young, black haired widow behind the counter, clapping her hands to her face when she saw him.

Chadwick only wanted to pay for the newspaper. Instead, he was half carried up a flight of wooden stairs to Carmella's room over the store. The sympathies poured out in a mixture of Italian and English. Carmella was unaware of the regularity of Chadwick's predicament. Chadwick was in no mood to argue with anyone. She bathed his face with a washcloth that smelled like lilacs. She pulled his parka off to check for broken bones. She put milk in a pan to warm on her hot plate.

But when she cradled his bruised head between her cashmere-covered breasts, Chadwick rejected the notion of delivering his mother's newspaper on time. Somehow the daily news, however important, didn't seem so important anymore. The bravado he felt, trying to persuade Carmella that he was really all right, that went out the window...somewhere on the ledge where Carmella kept her milk cold. When Chadwick could hear the soft pounding of Carmella's heart right through her white sweater and when he smelled her heat mixed with the goat hair fibers and when he touched her breast as if to steady himself, Carmella sighed the deepest, greatest, sweetest, most tragic sigh of her life. Chadwick touched her other breast, just gently placed his hand under the fullness of it. Carmella let her head drop back and she pulled him closer to her.

"Poor little boy, poor little boy," Carmella crooned softly, kissing the top of his head. Carmella rocked them both back and forth, repeating her words of solace. Chadwick nuzzled deeper and deeper into Carmella's fluffy bosom. He shivered with excitement.

"Oh, you're cold..." she whispered, rubbing his arms and shoulders and pulling her sweater up to wrap it around him. "Such a sweet, little boy," she sang, as Chadwick's face was pressed into her skin. He repositioned his hands again around her breasts, feeling the lace of her bra and inhaling deeply.

"Are you feeling better?" she asked, stroking his hair.

Knowing that any man in the neighborhood — from Greenfelt to Old Man DeFiori, from Cappy the Cop to young Manning Foster, even Chadwick's father — would have given anything to be in his position, Chadwick searched for a pathetic, little boy voice. He found it. "Just a little better," he choked.

In the weeks that followed, Carmella restored Chadwick from a dozen beatings, even if Chadwick had to pay his classmates to rough him up. It was Chadwick, of course, who was providing solace to Carmella. And Carmella, who might have been self-conscious with adult men, found it easy to teach Chadwick the essential details required to make a woman very, very happy.

Guido hired Chadwick to deliver groceries after school and on Saturdays. Guido noticed the sweet harmony that seemed to prevail in his store but he didn't understand its source and didn't want to. His female customers were especially happy with the delivery service and although Chadwick seemed to be awfully slow about his rounds, there were virtually no complaints.

Later Chadwick served as altar boy at the wedding mass for Carmella's second marriage. Father Schudsick was blessing the rings when he thought he saw his veteran altar boy wink at the bride and he almost caught Carmella wink back. Father Schudsick looked hard at Chadwick, his best altar boy, draped in a starched white cotton cassock. His little smile was that of an angel...he could have been a model for one of the cherubs hanging off the statue of the Virgin Mary. Father Schudsick continued to bless the rings. Later, however, during the recessional, Father noticed several of the parish women give little waves to Chadwick as the wedding party moved down the center aisle of the church.

Guido, who wasn't losing a daughter but gaining a son to help out with the Sunshine Grocery & Deli, was too delighted to notice the attention paid to his delivery boy.

Chapter 37

First Rule of Holes: If you are in one, stop digging.

— Denis Healey

"So you see," says Chadwick to his comrades at the Pittock Mansion, "New York City is a wonderful place for a kid to grow up...once you know the system."

"Ah, the system..." agrees Biasi.

"Part of the system is that any natural attribute, for instance, *my size,* will be both an asset and a liability depending on how I use it. Gee, I'm glad I learned that early on. It's not what happens to me, or to any of us but what system we create to deal with things that determines our success."

"And I'll bet that you're the one who said, 'Success is not a secret; it's a system,' " says Lash.

Chadwick tilts his head like an elfin Santa Claus. "I suppose I said that," chips Chadwick. "It sounds like something I'd say. I do believe it."

Lash tugs at his wallet stuck in the hip pocket of his jeans. He unfolds the leather and produces a business-size card with a typeset line on it: SUCCESS IS NOT A SECRET; IT'S A SYSTEM. "Travis used to hand these out to anybody who'd take 'em."

Even Chadwick cannot contain the increments of his smile when he reads the card. The vein in his neck throbs against his shirt collar. The starched line of Oxford cloth across his back shivers slightly.

"She listened," he says simply.

"So how do you go about creating a 'system'?" asks Biasi. "If coming up with a system is the answer, then how do you *do* that?"

"I couldn't tell you how you'd do it," replies Chadwick, "I can only tell you how I do it. It's called Tunnel Number 4."

The Wizard plays with a spoon on the tablecloth. He has sectioned a tributary of melted wax from a pool into his spoon. The white creamy wax has filled the bowl of one spoon and The Wizard has placed another spoon under it to catch the next drop. As the evening progresses, he will construct a wax and spoon sculpture.

The delicate balancing of spoons and wax annoys Lash, who says, "Don't they make dripless candles? If they don't, they should."

"But that would spoil the fun," says The Wizard.

"Exactly the point," says Chadwick.

"So tell us about Tunnel Number 4," hurries Hershell.

"An interesting study was done at the University of Michigan a few years ago," begins Chadwick. "They built a maze with four tunnels and they put a piece of cheese down at the end of Tunnel Number 4. Put a mouse in the maze...and eventually the mouse found the cheese. They kept doing this over and over again and finally the mouse learned to go down Tunnel Numnber 4 the minute that it was placed in the maze. Got it so far?"

"What are we, dolts or something? Yeah, we got it," grouses Biasi.

"Then they built a bigger maze, an identical maze but big enough for a person and they put a $50 bill down the end of Tunnel Number 4. Now eventually the human being learns to go down Tunnel Number 4 in order to get the reward. In fact, the good news is, the human being learns to go down Tunnel Number 4 in less time than the mouse. So far, so good.

"*Then,*" Chadwick says, holding his hands out as if to catch a basketball, "they move the reward in both mazes down *Tunnel Number 1.* Now...who do you think gets to the reward first?"

"The mouse," says Hershell.

"The mouse," says The Wizard.

"The mouse," says Lash.

"The mouse," says Biasi.

"You're absolutely right," whispers Chadwick and then he almost hisses, "and that's what human beings do. They keep going down Tunnel Number 4 even when there's nothing down there. They keep doing the same damned things over and over again and hoping for a different result. It's amazing!

"The most profound truth of my life has been the realization that in order to succeed, I must *stop doing what doesn't work.* Whatever is working for you, keep doing it. But what isn't working, cut it out. Simple. But it's the simple things in life that elude us.

"I pay attention and try to figure out what's working. Or more importantly, what isn't working. If I want to lose a few pounds, I have to stop doing what isn't working...namely Italian sausage sandwiches, my own personal favorite. And watching television doesn't get my business plan written. If it isn't working, I quit."

"So, what made you quit on Travis?" asks Biasi, frustrated with Chadwick's perfect logic.

"I didn't quit on Travis," Chadwick shoots back angrily, surprising the group. "I think she quit on me."

Chapter 38

*A poll taken of Frenchmen, asking what
they did after making love, brought this
response:
10% said they made love again;
15% said they smoked a cigarette;
75% said they went home to their wives.*
                              — London Daily Mail

Creamy, peach-colored lipstick from a tube smeared its way
across the bulge of her lower lip. The sensuous curve of her
upper lip tightened and the stick of peach goo left its frosty pink mark.
She watched the application in the mirror of her powder compact.

"I should have found one of those 1940's compacts for you,"
Chadwick suggested, watching her touch the powder puff to her nose.
"I should have done that for this event."

Chadwick adjusted the foot pad on the floor of the 1928 Rolls
Royce. The driver, in front of the glass partition, could not hear the
conversation.

"You mean like the ones in the old movies?" she asked.

"Yeah," he respnded. "One of those powder compacts with a
curved top on it and a place for engraving."

Travis snapped the plastic lid on her 1983 compact. "And what,
pray tell, would you engrave on it?" she asked, sarcastically, arching
one eyebrow. The horns honking on Broadway drowned her comment.
She was grateful that he hadn't heard her. "You look great in a tux,"
she said. "Of course, Charlie McCarthy looked great in a tux."

The vintage Rolls stopped in front of the search lights, the crowd
and the cameras. The driver popped open the back door and Chadwick
stepped out, turned fast enough to set his tails flying as he held his
white-gloved hand out to his lady. Flashbulbs zapped light that was
caught by her white satin and zapped back. She started to step from the
rented Rolls when he pressed her hand hard and she looked into his blue
eyes.

"Lady, you have never looked more radiant than you do right at this moment.''

She looked up at the crowd and more flashes peppered the night. "They think I'm someone famous," she whispered. "This is only supposed to be a building dedication. . ."

Her dress alone could have made her famous. In an obscure antique store, Travis had found a 1920's Jean Harlow-style white satin evening dress just in time for the glitzy dedication opening of the Broadway office complex. The theme was "Puttin' On The Ritz" and the closely held tickets were trophies to those who watch, read and appear on the society pages of the newspaper. Party goers were encouraged to attend as their "favorite silver screen movie star."

Travis did not understand what "cut on the bias" meant, but the dress took whatever form was under it. The thin white satin gave off silver streaks of light as she walked, leaving none of her muscle tone to the imagination. Fifty white fabric-covered buttons pearled down her back and a cluster of rhinestones held the belt around her waist. If Travis had chosen to join the society wars, this dress was napalm. Her dark red hair was pulled fiercely back and held in a tight little chignon guarded by two fresh white gardenias. When the dancing began, the warmth from her hair encouraged the fragrance to waft around her.

Travis had never attended a celebrity-studded, media-mongering, see-and-be-seen, full blown society event. She was never ill at ease while the music was playing, however, and the music played nearly all night. Chadwick, complete with mother-of-pearl shirt studs, grey leather spats and black satin cummerbund had pulled out all the stops for the evening, including renting the antique Rolls for their impressive arrival.

Chadwick knew what to do with a woman's body on a dance floor. There wasn't a hoofer in the place who could best him. Travis was a hesitant partner at first, but gradually learned the subtle direction given by his grip and the angle of his shoulders. The orchestra flooded the room with 1920's and 30's music while the cut mirror ball flickered reflections on the crowd of nearly a thousand people. Several times the dancers cleared an area and let the two show what a truly great dress can do in the arms of a scaled-down Fred Astaire.

Chadwick was no society star. He had the tickets because he had engineered the financing of the building that involved a swap for land in Kansas City and an industrial park in Iowa. So no one knew these newcomers who could move their feet as quickly and easily as a butterfly doing reconnaisance on a good garden. Eventually the orchestra was playing just for them, after Chadwick requested "Cheek to Cheek." By now, Travis could bend and float and twirl and step, be lifted and held, guided and cuddled to Chadwick's never failing beat. If there had been a contest, there would have been no contest.

When the orchestra's horns began the familiar introduction, Chadwick pulled her hand and brought her to him on the dance floor. The final dance was "Puttin' On The Ritz" and Chadwick started with a small corner near the orchestra's stage and gradually moved into the center as fewer couples stayed on the dance floor.

Chadwick was a master of precision and grace, two qualities his business client had already noted in the making of the Broadway office deal. On the dance floor, he took absolute command. Travis would have been upstaged by his footwork, except for the fact that she had the dress. The dress itself seemed to possess the magic of another time, remembering within itself the glorious dance moves of a past era.

Chadwick gave coded messages to her back with his fingers. She pulled away at just the right instances and returned passionately to his side in the next beat. Her white satin pumps stepped perfectly with his black patent leather and not a toe was touched incorrectly. Best of all, they looked at each other when they danced. They smiled, heads up, eyes inviting the next move and no words spoken. It appeared as effortless and delightful as any two paired on a dance floor.

When the end of the rhythm was coming, Chadwick set her in a series of twirls. The front of the dress lay tight against her body and the drape in the back fluttered like a great white wing. She prepared herself for a flamboyant finish, knowing that he was playing to the crowd and he did not disappoint her. She had already accepted the fact that she would bend as completely as possible, trusting that he would be able to hold her. She made a good effort to forget that they weighed approximately the same.

The horns grew louder knowing this would be their last blow of the evening. The orchestra leader, anxious to leave them on the wildest possible note, kept the rhythm with prize fighting gestures. In the last two measures of the music, Chadwick lifted Travis off the ground and brought her down into his arms and over backwards. Her back curved in a delicate arch and her head missed the floor by an inch. Chadwick held her in the final pose but brought his mouth up close to the gardenia in her hair.

"Will you wear this dress when you marry me?" he asked.

Chapter 39

Marriage is an institution and I'm not
ready for an institution yet.
— *Mae West*

"What did she say," whispers Lash, "when you asked her?"

Chadwick comes out of his private reverie and looks vaguely in the direction of the question.

" 'Yes.' She said, 'yes.' "

There is great movement around the table. The Wizard's eyebrows go up and stay up. Hershell sits up and puts his hands to his sides. Lash pulls himself up from being draped on the table. Biasi refolds his arms and lets a thin whistle leak from his pursed lips.

"Ah, well," says Chadwick, sensing the shock, "that was long ago. If I had met Travis when we were young and married her, she would have missed knowing all of you!"

From the other side of the table, Lash does not restrain the obvious comeback, "Don't count on it."

Chadwick tips the ash from the end of his cigarette when there is no ash to fall.

"She used to tell me," his soft, gentle voice goes on, "that there was a drug in Wheat Thins...and that if you eat enough Wheat Thins you think that you're having an affair with Travis Duncan. God, I used to polish off a case of those things in a month."

Hershell brings his fist to the table top. "Dammit, man! What happened?"

"Sometimes the magic works," replies Chadwick, "and sometimes it doesn't."

"Not good enough," threatens Biasi, gripping Chadwick's wrist in his bear paw.

Chadwick studies the architect's grip, then looks long into Biasi's eyes. Biasi removes his hand.

"I knew Travis for five years," explains Chadwick, beginning very slowly. "And all those years, she wrestled with my married condition.

As I said earlier, my wife and I never agreed to a monogymous relationship and in fact, it was a marriage of convenience for her. We lived together sporadically.

"Travis never mentioned marriage except to downgrade it as an institution. She had no intention of changing her marital status and I probably don't have to remind any of you about her opinions on the subject. Anyway, I know that it bothered her that I was married but she had no counter argument to mine.

"Until one day..." Chadwick says with his voice nearly cracking. He scrapes his thumbnail on the edge of his lighter and studies his hands.

"She announced that it didn't matter what agreement I had with my wife. She said that marriage was a public agreement about a private relationship and that you could rewrite marriage vows til the cows come home, but in the eyes of those around you, marriage meant that you were expected to behave in a certain way. If you didn't want to behave in accordance to what the world knows as 'marriage' then you shouldn't sign up to call yourself a married person. Therefore, my behavior as a married man being unacceptable to the married condition, I was breaking a vow even though, to my eyes, it was one that I hadn't made. What she was saying was, you can't rewrite a norm to fit yourself. And, of course, during the sixties and seventies we were rewriting everything for ourselves. Flower child though she was, Travis finally concluded that there are some institutions bigger than individuals and that certain things cannot be rewritten. Suddenly, I was *very* married in her eyes and that was it.

"Fidelity is what is expected if you're married. To act in any other way is to *not act like* a married person. All my great logic was lost after five years. It all hinged on whether the individual has a right to rewrite the rules of society."

Hershell rubs his eyes and scratches his head.

"And Travis, more than anyone I ever knew," Hershell says, "rewrote the rules. That's amazing. It's fascinating to hear all this...to discover that even old Travis found something she'd bow to. You sound just a trifle bitter, Chadwick. Is that possible?"

"Part of the situation was totally my fault. I was not consistent about my beliefs and behavior. When I was reluctant to introduce Travis to a client — while we were dining at an intimate restaurant — I, myself, was affected by old rules. I wasn't true to one standard. Once Travis realized that, she was gone."

Chadwick's shoulders drop two inches and he pulls his thin glasses from his face. Suddenly he looks very tired. He holds the bridge of his nose between his thumb and forefinger, his head down.

"Here's a supposition for you..." he drawls wearily, "try this one on for size since we're taking some of our valuable time to guess about Travis's life and intentions.

"What are you feeling right now? And I don't mean you should answer that for me or for anyone else in the room. But take a second and get a reading on your emotional state as it is right now or how it's been throughout the evening. What do you feel? Jealousy? Embarrassment? Anger? Frustration? Grief? Sadness? Loss? Or, maybe intrigue by the puzzle of it all? Manipulated? Pissed?"

"That's the one," says Biasi.

"I'd just like to propose," Chadwick proposes, "that whatever it is that you're feeling, Travis, at some point in *your* relationship with her, felt that same feeling. Biasi, you're pissed. I'll wager that Travis spent a portion of her life being pissed at you. For myself, I am getting some idea of the philosophical box I put her in. Because that's how *I* feel right now..."

Lash stands up, presses his hands to his back and begins to pace. "I've felt all kinds of things tonight," he says. "Anger? Not really. Jealousy? Certainly. My moods on all this keep changing. Just when someone hits a certain chord, I start gettin' hurt inside...and then someone says something funny...and it kinda goes away. Anybody else need to take a pee? Whooow..."

"Yes!" Chadwick stands up. "I've got one last comment to make. Success takes hard work. Enjoying it takes talent. I can enjoy it. Travis knew that...and I'm sure she invited me here because she expects me to win."

Biasi turns on his hip and narrows his glare on Chadwick. "You know, I was just startin' to like you, you asshole, and now I'm back to wanting to reach down your throat and pull your heart out."

Chadwick raises his eyebrows slightly and asks politely, "I have that effect on people. Would you care for more champagne?"

Chapter 40

The way to a man's heart is through his stomach.

— Anonymous

"Y'suppose those caterers left anything behind?" ponders Lash, peering out into the foyer.

Hershell jumps to his feet with such energy that the others forget he's 83 years old. "Let's form a scouting party!"

Biasi looks with disdain at the old man. "How could you even think of food after all that cheesecake you ate?"

"So what are you? My mother?" Hershell rubs the palm trees that surround his belly.

"I'm hungry too," says The Wizard. "There's nothing here but coffee. I'm about coffee'd out. Any more coffee and I'll begin to think *I'm* mountain grown."

"Yeah," says Lash, a lilt in his voice, "but are ya good to the last drop?"

"We could order a pizza..."

"If we could find a phone..."

"We need a liquor store that delivers," votes Biasi. "By God, that's what I need...a drink. I didn't know I was going to be here this long."

Lash and Hershell check the foyer and the hall. No sign of food, drink, phone or life.

"Are we allowed to leave and go get provisions?"

"There was nothin' in the will about starvin' all night."

"Anybody else getting hungry?"

"I'm fine," says Chadwick, lighting another cigarette. "I don't need anything to eat."

"That's 'cause you're eatin' those cigarettes," cracks The Wizard. "Here, give me one...."

"What?"

"You smoke?"

"I'm a wizard. I'm not God."

"So who's going to go to the store? Anybody know this area well enough to find an all-night grocery store?"

"Liquor store."

"Need some chips."

"I could use a burger..."

"Red meat isn't real good for your arteries, you know."

"Killing animals for food...that's really not necessary, you know."

"Yeah, well, the burgers at MacDonald's are from cows that committed suicide."

"I suppose you think that the salmon we had for dinner died of old age."

"Look, I'm going into town and find something to eat. You guys want anything or not?"

"You can't do that."

"Why not?"

"Because if one goes, we all have to go...otherwise somebody could say something that might be a clue. It wouldn't be fair if..."

"Well, you're not all going to fit into my Jaguar."

"We're not going to fit in my Volkswagen."

"I came in a cab."

"So did I."

"Well, that leaves the Kenworth."

"Better blow out the candles. We don't want this place to burn down while we're out feeding our faces."

"God, I'm hungry. My stomach thinks my throat's been cut."

"Yeah, I could eat the south end of a northbound horse."

"Enough, already! Come on, Chadwick, if one goes, we all go. Put out that cigarette! No smokin' in the truck."

"We really going to go in that thing?"

"Man, that 'thing' will take you anywhere you want to go..."

"How did we get in here anyway? Where's the front door?"

"It's right here."

"Fix the latch so it doesn't lock us out."

"Jeez. How can you stand walkin' around in bare feet?"

"I prefer to be bared of foot so that the energy field of the planet to my body is not interrupted by a layer of leather."

"Boy, give me the leather any day. And Goodyear rubber too. And I'll communicate with the Universe just *fine*."

Chapter 41

*If the situation is hopeless, we have
nothing to worry about.*
                              — *John Cage*

"**L**ook, if I get the twenty-three million dollars, I'll hire a
limousine for our next meeting!" barks Lash over the
complaints about his truck.

Five silhouetted figures gather in front of the high snout of the red
Kenworth. Their voices carry in the still, black October night. The lights
of the Pittock Mansion are too far away to help. They give all the ap-
pearances of five college boys out for a Halloween prank.

"Look, dammit, you step on my feet one more time, you're not
going to live to see 84."

"How do we get into this thing, anyway?"

"Let me think about this," says Lash, scratching his chin. "OK,
Hershell, you're gonna ride shotgun. You three guys can ride in the
sleeper. Yeah, that'll work. OK, Wizard, ladies first. Get your butt up
there."

An anemic interior truck light casts a yellow glaze but not enough
light for a novice to find the first two steps into the truck. A challenge
for anyone in a dress, The Wizard fumbles his way in the dark and
lands on top of the gear shift. "Give me a minute!" he yells. Flopping
around like a skinny, just-caught fish, he finds the bedroom of the cab
and sits, then gathers his caftan around him and gropes for a safe place
to put his feet.

"Biasi, you'd better go next," frets Lash. "Just go over the seat
and turn left. There's a bed back there in the sleeper. You sit on that."

Biasi finds the first step, misses the second, recovers by getting a
toehold in front of the shotgun seat, loses his balance and sits in the
seat.

"Outa the chair, Biasi; Hershell's goin' there!"

"Would you give me a break! I can't find any place to put my
feet!"

The Wizard grins from the back bedroom. "Quit complaining,"

he says, "or we'll have to use your Jaguar."

Biasi's size 13 barely makes it over the shifter and into the back area. His large ass sticks out into the cab and he looks like the Hamm's bear trying to fit in a box. "Move over, Wizard!"

"I'm over as far as I can get!"

Chadwick climbs both steps, sits in the seat, pulls his short legs around, plants his feet behind the shifter and brings himself Tarzan-style into the Kenworth's bedroom. "Isn't this cozy?" he says. "Shut up," gnashes Biasi. "Travis couldn't have known somebody with a station wagon?"

"Or a van?"

"Yeah, a van. That would've been nice."

"Well, why don't you think of that next time you have an affair with somebody who's going to inherit a fortune, OK?"

Lash is having no luck getting Hershell to see the truck's steps. "Hey, come on, you guys, give me a hand out here!"

There is an applause from the three in the back of the Kenworth.

"I'm not kidding. . . ." Lash sings.

Hershell gets one foot in the first step and Lash puts his shoulder in the old man's armpit to steady him. He lifts his other foot and wobbles. Lash spreads his own feet to balance his weight and Hershell. The old man grabs the door and puts a hand onto Lash's head, pushing the cowboy hat down over his ears.

With a great "oomph!" Hershell is maneuvered into the Kenworth passenger position like a sack of wet cement. Lash pulls at his hat until his head pops free, rebuilds the crown and takes his fist to the truck's door. There's a slam and Lash grumbles, "Goddamn greenhorns." He circles the snout of Red Bessie, his cowboy boots clump-clumping on the asphalt. "We've hauled some useless freight before, but this really tears it."

Lash springs into the drivers' seat as if he levitated to get there. Lash's thumb hits a button and 400 horses scream out of the Caterpillar 3406B engine. The vibration rocks the truck cab and Hershell reaches for a door handle. There's a metal "pop" and the dashboard dials light up, a city of information. Lash shivers and rubs his arms.

"Hey, guys, there's a jacket back there, can you hand it to me?"

The three, packed like kids on a crowded school bus, squirm and strain to see in the halo of the cab's light.

"Here it is. The Wizard's sitting on it."

Lash groans. "Thanks anyway. Leave it back there. I'll take it to the laundry later."

"Jeez-US!" snaps Hershell. "Would you mellow out? Here, hand me that jacket."

Hershell takes the red baseball jacket and thrusts it at Lash.

"It's probably got kooties all over it," whines Lash.

"Grow up. Shut up. Zip this up. And move out!"

Lash takes the jacket, leans forward in his little space and shoves his fists through the arms of the jacket, finds the zipper catch and pulls the tab up to his chin. There is silence.

"I'm waiting for the air pressure to build up for the brakes," says Lash, eyeing the gauges.

The engine changes pitch and the vibration seems to go from outside the truck to inside the truck. Lash works his arms and legs in a kind of ballet and the semi starts to move. The headlights flash a beacon of light around the Pittock's parking lot, hit a grace note on the mansion itself and then point down the narrow drive that leads to the street.

"God, this is great! I've never been in a big rig like this before," says Biasi.

"Me either!" says Chadwick.

Red Bessie makes the first sharp turn and her inhabitants bounce six inches upwards.

"Is it always like this?" asks Hershell, amazed to feel his own bulk floating in the seat.

"She'd settle down if we had a load on," explains Lash.

"Well, I can't imagine going very far bouncing like this...tough on your back. I didn't realize..."

"That's quite a chair you got!" yells Biasi from the back.

Lash is seated in a cushy throne with a high back, fuzzy arm rests and a sculpted seat. "Chair cost over $2,000," says Lash, proudly.

"Goddam, that's a lot," winces Biasi.

"Not when you gotta live in it," answers Lash, pulling on the jiggling steering wheel and making Red Bessie sashay down the twisting road.

A slip of a moon spreads a neon glow over the damp black asphalt. It outlines the pines in the west hills of Portland and crowns the tiny lights in the city below. The town sleeps in a black quiet while five would-be millionaires go for burgers and booze in a red Kenworth. The downshifting of gears splits the sleepy autumn stillness.

"Are we there yet?"

Chapter 42

Never bet on anything that talks.
— Damon Runyan

The woman tending the counter at the all-night Kash 'n' Karry shouts an obscenity as Hershell swings through the glass door. Startled, Hershell searches the store. The sports commentary for a wrestling match can be heard overhead and the woman is peeved at her choice, a Gary the Grinder, for missing a potentially painful hold. A small black and white TV is mounted to the wall near the ceiling and two beefy nearly nude men sweat it out for the screams of the fans, one of whom will be running the check stand for a soon-to-be-millionaire. Rhonda (the plastic name tag indicates) pounds the case containing the fried chicken and jojo's as she watches the Grinder hit the mat.

"I like a woman with spunk," states Hershell, eyeing the clerk.

Lash observes the biceps on Rhonda, a woman his mother's age, and he says, "Hershell, she could tear you a new asshole."

Rhonda jumps slightly at the unlikely sight of five customers in the Kash and Karry all at once. Her hand immediately goes to the stack of paper bags under the counter where she keeps a loaded pistol. "It doesn't have to be Saturday night to make use of a Saturday night special," is Rhonda's theory.

"Help you *gentlemen*?" The "gentlemen" part is venom on her lips and she straightens slightly to pull her two ample breasts apart to make her T-shirt more readable. A California state flag is stretched, as if two motorcycle helmets support it, and the words "Don't Tread On Me" are clear.

"Just came in for a little food, ma'm," smiles Lash, with a little wave of his hand, sensing trouble. "Gee, the jojo's look good..."

Rhonda's hand comes up to the counter and she looks Lash over. "They're a might cold," she says, "but the grease is good." Lash turns and Rhonda spies his little, hard-packed tush. "Comes with free dip..." she adds quickly.

Chadwick and Biasi nod toward Rhonda and her hand moves two inches back towards the paper bags. When she sees The Wizard, who has an annoying habit of bouncing when he isn't actually walking, her eyes narrow and her grimace moves to the lefthand side of her face.

"What are you supposed to be?" she asks.

"I'm a karmic antic," grins The Wizard.

Lash, a veteran of all-night diners, truck stops, Minit Marts and gas stations, quickly shoots a glare at The Wizard. "Don't start that," he warns. He turns to Rhonda and with his warmest smile he waves his long, long lashes and says, "Don't mind him, ma'm, he's just a little fruitcake, you know?"

Rhonda stares at Lash's lashes. She really stares. "Oh, sure, no problem. I saw that muu muu in Penney's last week and I almost bought it myself."

Lash cannot resist the temptation to play with Rhonda. "Well, ma'm, I know it'd look a lot better on you than it does on him." He lets the fronds on his eyelids move slowly to his cheeks and back up again.

Chadwick tugs on Lash's plaid sleeve. "Do you mind? We've got a business meeting that we're trying to conduct, if you remember?"

Lash pushes his cowboy hat back on his head and asks Rhonda, "Ma'm, could you point me in the direction of the beer?"

"That way," she points, never interrupting her stare.

Chadwick and Biasi argue over the demerits of the wine selection. The Wizard frowns at the puny vegetables. Lash pulls a sixpack of Henry Weinhard from the cooler. Hershell orders the jojo's.

"How about some fresh fruit?" asks The Wizard.

"You're already with us whether we like it or not," retorts Lash.

Biasi punches a bag of cheese-flavored popcorn under his arm like a football. "There's no hard liquor," he grouses.

"So be a wino for a night," advises Chadwick.

They watch Lash as he plucks a can of jalapeno bean dip from the rack to go with his Doritos.

"Give us all a break, will ya? We've still got to live together until dawn...know what I mean?" says Biasi.

Hershell watches as Rhonda tongs the battered and deep fried slices of potato. "That enough?" she asks. "Give me two orders," he says, "and don't forget the dip."

"Oh, yeah," she says, irritated that Hershell had remembered her offer.

"You know, not many women can wear their hair that color," tries Hershell.

Rhonda moves her bleached blond hair from side to side. "Oh, yeah?" she responds. "I've only had this for a couple of months now..."

"Very becoming," lies Hershell, hoping for an extra jojo and he gets it.

"Well, you know, ever since my fourth grandchild, you get... well...(sigh) a little tired of goin' to the wrestling matches by yourself. . ."

Chadwick searches the crackers section until he finds two boxes of Wheat Thins. Biasi puts a quart jug of Carlo Rossi White on the counter. Lash pulls pepperoni from the glass jar next to the cash register.

"Anybody got a knife?" hollers The Wizard from the far side of the store.

Rhonda stops and her eyes narrow again. Four men stand in front of her across the counter. She drops the tongs and her hand reaches towards the paper bags.

"What do you need a knife for?" shouts Lash, knowing Rhonda's Plan A. He can almost smell gunfire.

"Apples and cheese!"

"I've got a pocket knife in the truck! Come on!" He shrugs towards Rhonda, hoping she'll know they are all unarmed.

Chadwick holds a bottle of Oregon Reisling up to Biasi. "How about this? Shall we risk it?"

Biasi winces. "I'm a man who is about to become a millionaire," says Biasi. "We'll take both and throw away what we don't want." Chadwick takes the barb. "That's most generous," he says sarcastically.

Rhonda shoves the white paper tubs of jojo's in a deli sack and begins to ring up the goods. "This separate or all together?"

"I want some apples, too," says Hershell and he totters off down an aisle between the Pampers and the Kitty Litter.

"Better make that separate," says Lash apologetically.

"No problem," says Rhonda warmly.

Chadwick nudges Lash and whispers under his breath, "Is there some reason you develop a Southern accent when you talk to women?"

"Like you said earlier, Chadwick, do what works for ya," Lash whispers back.

The cash register ka-chings and dollars and coins are exchanged. The green fluorescents in the all-night store bathe them all in a Martian light. The candy mints, *People Magazine* and an MS donor jar make their last minute bids for money.

"I'd give twenty bucks for a bottle of bad rum right now," Biasi complains.

"This all for you?" Rhonda asks Chadwick.

"Yes," he answers.

"Little guy like you gonna eat all these Wheat Thins himself?" she teases.

"Every last one," says Chadwick, "and then I'm gonna wash it all down with Dom Perignon as soon as I find some."

"The yuppie spring water's in the back next to the diet drinks," Rhonda barks.

"Dom Perignon is *champagne*," corrects Chadwick, not willing to humor the clerk.

"And I'm Rhonda Fleming," says Rhonda. "Beaverton Fire Department to you."

Hershell has bounded up and quickly says, "I *thought* you looked familiar!"

Rhonda smirks at the old man. "You get your fruit?" she asks.

"He's right here," answers Hershell, jabbing his thumb towards The Wizard.

Rhonda sighs and rings up Hershell's purchases.

"Any lotto tickets for you guys tonight?" Rhonda asks.

There is a two second silence and then a great explosion of laughter. Rhonda jumps back from the counter, distancing herself from the unlikely collection of strangers, unnerved by their outburst of laughing.

Lash smiles a warm and sensuous smile at Rhonda and gives her his most glorious wave with his eyes. "Lady, there isn't a man among us tonight who thinks he needs a lottery ticket..."

"Just out of curiosity," says Chadwick, "how much is the winning pot worth this week?"

"Seven million dollars!" says Rhonda.

They all laugh again.

"Ah, a mere pittance!" snorts Chadwick, wiping his eye under his glasses.

"I don't know what's so damned funny," fumes Rhonda. "Ain't nobody thinks seven million dollars is very funny."

"You're right," says Biasi, anxious to get to his wine by moving the group along. "Four of these jokers could use a lottery ticket. We just don't know which four. It's a long story. And if this night ever ends, one of us will come back here and buy you..." He notices the tangled human scene on the television overhead. "...one of us will buy you a wrestler!"

The Wizard has used his caftan to carry his groceries and he begins putting his array on the counter. Apples, cheddar, oil-free popcorn, pears and a cabbage wobbles around on the counter top.

"What is this...the last of Adelle Davis' estate?" asks Lash, frowning at the cabbage.

The Wizard tears a leaf and plucks it in his mouth, chewing loudly. "Good for your colon," he munches.

Lash fingers the cabbage like a basketball. "Yeah, well, if I only eat half...is it good for my semi-colon?"

Rhonda rings up the last of it. "That does it, you guys are out of here," she says.

The five head toward the door, Biasi bringing up the rear.

"Say, you!" calls Rhonda.

Biasi stops. He reluctantly turns to the tough, blond woman. "Yes?"

"You serious about wanting that rum?" she asks.

Biasi's eyes dilate quickly and he sets his wine jug on the counter.

"Are the Kennedys gun shy?" he demands. "Twenty bucks!"

Rhonda steps from behind the counter and moves to the ice cream cooler. She shoves Heath bars and Fudgcicles aside and pulls up a stubby clear bottle of 86 proof rum.

"I keep a little around for sippin'," she explains.

"Yeah, snake bites, I know."

"But as you can see, it's nearly a full bottle."

Biasi holds back his delight at seeing the rum before his eyes. The others are hollering at him from the truck.

"You been drinkin' straight out of the bottle?" he asks, suspiciously.

"No, no," she insists. "I been usin' a little cup from the Slushy machine!"

"You didn't put your mouth on the bottle, did you?" Biasi interrogates.

"Holy Christ, what do you think I am, some sort of heathen?" she just about screams.

"I don't know..." haggles Biasi, rubbing his chin. "Fifteen dollars?"

Rhonda squints at Biasi. Ice drips from the wet sides of the rum bottle. She looks hard at Biasi's face and the tiny broken veins in his nose.

"You need this bottle, Fred," growls Rhonda. "The price is twenty bucks."

Biasi pulls a crumpled bill from his pants pockets that never made it to his wallet. He puts the bill on the counter, plucks the small bottle from Rhonda's hand and shoves it in his sack.

When he joins the group at Red Bessie's side door, he pushes his sack towards Chadwick. Chadwick holds the bag while Biasi produces the rum, uncaps it and takes a swallow.

"You'll ruin your appetite for the Reisling," observes Chadwick.

"Don't count on it," comments The Wizard, watching Biasi's face as the sweat pops on his forehead.

"Wizard! Wake up!" orders Lash. "Remember? You in first!"

With the light from the Kash and Karry, The Wizard finds his way to his place in the sleeper of the cab. A docile Biasi deftly follows and Chadwick hands sacks of groceries to them. Lash removes his cowboy hat and throws it over to his seat before bracing himself to help lift Hershell up into the cab.

"Do you think maybe Rhonda was coming on to me?" Hershell asks.

Lash grimaces and rolls his eyes. "Hershell, Walt Disney could have used your imagination..."

Chapter 43

When viewed against the background of problems that face mankind, what we do is so relatively meaningless, that we might as well try to be extraordinary.

— Anonymous

The quintet in the formal dining room of the Pittock Mansion fills the air with the Melody of the Midnight Snack. Crinkly plastic bags rip, tops pop, apples tumble, bottles gurgle, coffee perks, brown bags rattle, jaws munch and lips smack: the Nocturne of Nachos, the Fugue of Fast Food.

"I propose a toast!" a grateful Biasi says to his champagne glass full of rum.

They all stand. "A toast!" they agree. Lash has his beer, The Wizard has his Evian, Chadwick and Hershell have shared the Oregon Reisling.

After an awkward silence, Biasi asks, "What shall we toast to?"

Hershell takes a step forward. "We should have a toast to Travis Duncan!"

"Ah, of course!" they agree.

"How about," interjects Chadwick, "the *fraternity* of Travis Duncan? She brought us together. Do you realize what a select group we are?"

"Ah, yes, the Chosen Ones, that's us!" cheers Biasi.

"The Brotherhood of the Bucks, that's us," says Lash, lifting his beer can.

"Travis brought us together, maybe..." says Hershell, "but it is the money that's keeping us together."

"Hershell's right. Do you think we'd be spending the whole night together if it weren't for the money?" asks Biasi.

"I don't know," says Lash, "I'm beginning to get used to you guys."

"Right," says The Wizard sarcastically. "Tomorrow I'm going to tell everyone that I spent the night with you..."

"You do," fumes Lash, "and you'll have that beak pointin' out of the other side of your head!"

"Gentlemen, GENTLEMEN," says Hershell, reaching for Lash's wrist. "Whether you like it or not, we are a strange sort of fraternity. Even the colonel who is missing in action at this moment is one of us. But we're here and we've made it this far. I propose a toast. To the Fraternity of Travis Duncan — good health, long life and prosperity to us all!"

"That was diplomatic. . . ." says Chadwick.

Glasses, can and plastic bottle all go up in the air. There are five "ah's" and containers hit the table top. They take their same seats. Men do that. The chair at the head of the table is empty; Timothy had sat there. The Wizard camps just to the left and an empty chair separates him from Chadwick; the vacant seat marks the missing Col. Williams. Biasi anchors the opposite or foot end of the oval table next to Chadwick. To Biasi's left is the slumping Hershell who keeps Lash within arm's reach, like a protective father. Lash has two empty chairs between himself and The Wizard. He has turned George Sam's chair towards him and frequently rests his cowboy boots in the attorney's vacated spot.

"My dear brothers," says Chadwick, "we are in the middle of this problem."

"How do you figure that?" asks Biasi.

"Because it's dark at both ends," replies Chadwick, swirling his wine in his glass, playfully.

"Come on Biasi," says Hershell, "let's hear your story."

"Yeah, let's hear it before you get so loaded on Rhonda's Rum that you can't remember your life," chides Lash. Hershell frowns at the little trucker. "Just kidding," says Lash apologetically.

"Men are never more serious than when they're joking," states Hershell. "Go on, Biasi."

"Actually," interjects Chadwick, "I could introduce Mr. Biasi. I know something of his work. He's fairly famous, if you follow art and architecture. . . ."

Biasi, slightly wounded by Lash's observation because it was quite accurate, is recovering in Chadwick's glowing interruption.

"I attended a gallery opening a couple of years ago, I think it was . . ." Chadwick goes on, "of Holbrook Biasi watercolors and a collection of his architectural drawings. They were masterpieces. Truly, Biasi, I mean it.

"This man—" Chadwick continues, aiming a thumb at the swelling pirate to his left, "can take your breath away with a stroke from a pink paint brush and then on the next wall over is a drawing, so detailed, so precise, so. . .so. . .strong and sure. I can't tell you."

"I could use you in my marketing department if you're ready for a career change," suggests Biasi, breaking his embarrassment with a try at humor.

"I could see a wealth of contradictions in your work, Biasi. I've been looking forward to your story."

"What I can say about my life is," Biasi begins slowly, his head slightly down, eyeing his glass, "if it's true you learn from adversity, then I must be the smartest son of a bitch around." He shakes his pewter-hued curls.

"You also have the reputation of being the Peck's Bad Boy of Architecture. How true is that?" asks Chadwick.

"True enough. It's been the 'pain of my opinions.' I never mastered the art of subtlety when it came to my mouth. It's cost me."

Biasi is quite tall: six feet four. A man of impatient gestures, he seems taller. His soft navy blue turtleneck sweater folds just under his ears. Grey is overtaking his curly hair and his manicured beard. No two clumps of hair grow in the same direction on his head, giving him a wild and "dark artist" look. He can't help the direction of his hair and this gives the impression that he can't help much else in his life either. His clear green eyes, grown dull with alcohol, need only the sight of a curved hip in a skirt to rekindle their megawatt light. He saves his smiles, preferring to brood, but when they come, it is the charismatic big grin of a delighted Franklin Delano Roosevelt. His moods and his inability to hide them with his face, make him flash color like a changing stoplight.

"Sometimes I hate architecture," Biasi begins his rant, lighting the fuse to his kilowatt temper. "We foist impossible monuments on people to live in, work in, even die in. And you know how *people* judge architecture? It's the old lady in the records department of a building who wants to work without a draft. She wants a comfortable temperature or by God, the architect is going to *pay*...with his balls.

"And politics? You speak of *politics*? The Politics of Architecture are the worst! And never ending! If it weren't for that part of it, I could exist a happy man!

"Did you know..." Biasi leaves his seat, "that the builders of the Rialto Bridge in Venice *turned down* a proposal by Michaelangelo? MICHAELANGELO? And these same men, the selection committee for the Rialto Bridge, had children and these children had children... and with each generation they inbred and became more and more tasteless and stupid. And these offspring, they are the purchasers of architecture today in the United States. *These* are my clients!"

Biasi orchestrates his tirade with a conductor's hand movements which have just ended in a crescendo in the air. There is strength in the muscles of his hands as if his opinions come right out through his fingers. A light in him changes.

"You know what I love most about my work...?" His voice has dipped into a softness. "I love life most when I walk around a construction site for one of my buildings..." His fingers grip the air. "...and the workers are there doing their work and enjoying it. It is the carpenter whistling as he works the wood that will be my design made real. When the craftsmen *also* love what I have done, then it means more to me than all the architectural boards, school boards, boards of directors, city boards, boards of boards — all that, all those frightened bureaucrats nodding some sort of agreement that turns to lies halfway through a project. All that falls away when I see a man working in bronze or brick or steel or wood, doing a part of a design that I started on the back of a cocktail napkin.''

Biasi stops his pacing and notices a part of the chandelier.

"That's heady stuff," comments Hershell, genuinely impressed with the raving pirate standing above him.

"Look at that," admires Biasi, pointing at the chandelier. "There's a cable holding that thing to the ceiling. You can't even see it. That light fixture must weigh close to 500 pounds. And there are supports in the ceiling. Somebody planned all this ahead of time. They don't *do* work like this anymore. There's nothing in the crafting of this magnificent mansion that is done *anymore*. Remarkable.''

Biasi lumbers past Lash's chair, the second chair with Lash's feet in it and on to Timothy's designated chair. The brooding architect slumps in the banker's chair.

"You know," he continues to lecture, "things are so fast and so temporary today...that a friend of mine, an architect, watched them tear down a building he had designed only 20 years ago. That hasn't happened to me. Yet.''

Biasi slumps further in his chair, throwing his arms out across the table.

"Nowadays, in a building's budget, there's a fund set aside just for the litigation.''

Lash pulls his feet off George Sam's chair and sets his bag of Doritos on the table. He sits up and begins to rub the top of his thighs with his hands.

"So why'd you become an architect?" asks Lash, hoping to find a better mood for the large man.

Biasi perks, straightening his back and grateful for a question. "I believe that an architect should be like a method actor. Take the role of a person who will have to be in that space. What do they need? I designed a hospital wing once for handicapped kids. What a challenge! I got down on the floor and lived with those kids for three days. I *do not* go near a drawing board without living in the space. Here is the land! the client says. I go live on it or in it! I've been known to camp out in a tent in downtown Toronto until I could feel that land speak to me. I want to see it in the dawn's light and the dusk. I want to be in the space when it rains, when the sun is high and shadows are short, when it's pitch black and surrounded by the city's crawling alleys.

"Architecture does not exist in a vacuum! It must become part of what is there even when what is there will be gone some day. And what about the space *around* the building! Sometimes, what is most important is where the buildings are not...the so-called 'negative' space! Who will be there? What do they need? What do you want them to do? What do you want them to feel?

"If I were king tomorrow," Biasi bellows, "I would make it *illegal* for an architect to practice in this country without first seeing Europe. There is no spot in America that can equal the charm of a simple Paris street.

"Our urban downtown areas in this country only serve to isolate people from each other. The spaces are not conducive to life and they don't promote immediate death, just a long, slow one."

Hershell reaches for Biasi's champagne glass, still half full of rum, and passes it across the table to him. "Thank you," Biasi says, his eyes flashing lightning bolts. He drains the glass in one large swallow and the lightning in his eyes becomes a simple desk lamp.

"Space can determine how people will act in it...don't you see? If you want people to be violent and coarse, an architect can design the space that will make that kind of behavior happen!"

He stares into the empty glass.

"We get what we deserve," he says, flatly. "We get the kind of government we deserve, the kind of air and water we deserve. We get the kind of architecture that we deserve."

The curly head hangs a degree lower.

"I don't understand it," he sighs.

"Well," says Lash, still anxious to inflict a merrier mood, "how's your love life?"

"I'm on my third marriage and after tonight, that one will be down the tube," groans Biasi.

Chadwick blows a little whistle.

"Look, goddammit!" shouts Biasi, "I'm an architect. Not a marriage counsellor! You can judge me on what I do well, OK?"

Chadwick holds up his hands. "No judgement made!"

"Judgements rob us of happiness," interjects Hershell.

"But we all make judgements! We have to!" argues Biasi. "It is required of human beings to make judgements!"

"Each opinion," explains Hershell, patiently, "each judgement is a bar on your cage. Yes, we all have to make judgements *but* the trick is to have the bars on your cage far enough apart so that you can still get out!"

Biasi reaches for Lash's Doritos bag. He spins it and reaches a hand in for a fistful of corn chips.

"Travis used to say things like that to me," sighs Biasi, shoving the triangular chips in his mouth and leaving salt crumbs in his beard.

"I'm married now. I was married when I knew her. I'm always married. I don't know how to be anything else but married. I must like it; I've done so much of it. Married all three of them twice. But only been divorced twice. Twice? Just twice? Yeah, just twice, I think..."

Lash leans slightly forward. "What?"

Hershell tugs at Lash's flannel sleeve. "Don't ask," he advises.

"So what kind of things do you design?" asks The Wizard, tearing another giant leaf from his cabbage.

"Government buildings, bank towers, homes, hotels, memorials, college dormitories, pump houses, schools, a church, medical building ...even a park. That was a joke. I just said, 'Plant trees.' I did a library in Toronto, a parking structure in Tokyo, apartment buildings in Hawaii. I don't know. A lot of projects. I lecture from time to time. I watch my son play soccer. I write checks to my ex-wives. I drink with my friends. I paint. I fight with bureaucrats — I'd like to take contracts out on most of them. I sketch incessantly. I babysit my partner who is making me bankrupt. Mostly I just work. Or try to work. Architecture is a lot like acting. It's getting to be very competitive; everybody thinks they can do it; and it's very easy to get typecast into a style role. The one thing that I can say about my work is that I am proud of all of it. I did not compromise my design sense; I offered no standard design solutions. I satisfied the client, but I satisfied myself too. And more importantly, I satisfied the people who use the space. That's the most any designer, in any field, can say."

His audience applauds. It is the greatest applause an audience of four can give, which sounds pretty wimpy, but it is the best they can do. Biasi looks exhausted. The applause moves him and he sits up. Chadwick brings Biasi a cup of freshly brewed coffee.

"Thank you. Thank you," Biasi acknowledges the Fraternity.

Chadwick folds his arms and stands near Biasi.

"Biasi, you're not that old. How were you awarded all that work? How did you get such a reputation in such a relatively short span of time? How old are you anyway?" Chadwick asks.

"I'm 45. I know, I know, I look older. How'd I get to this point? Well, I started early. I've always been an architect. My mother said that I constructed things in my crib, for Christ's sake..."

Biasi giggles and gives a presidential parade smile as he remembers...

Chapter 44

*The artist is not free to do what he wants
to do; the artist is free to do what he has
to do.*
— *James Baldwin*

A cold chill nibbled at the boy's nose, the only part of him not covered. He frowned in his sleep and buried his shoulder further into the straw and down bed. After a while he sniffed and rolled onto his back, blinking at the flecks sticking to his eyelashes. A quiet reassured him that the rest of the family still slept. A tiny window threw a dim winter light across the grey blankets covering him. He looked down the length of his body and across the blankets were white stripes. He pulled his head up to get a better look at the stripes that were not there the night before. The white lines, evenly spaced across his bed blankets, were snow that had fallen through the wooden slats from the roof above. Bonneville, Oregon, 1948.

His hands and feet grew colder as he lay there and remembered his chore: start the first fire of the morning. The thought of his staying in bed never occurred to him, so thorough were his father's orders. The straw and down crackled slightly when he sat up. He slept in his clothes so he only needed to grab his boots, which he did as he swung down out of his attic loft, tiptoed through his sisters' bedroom and down the creakless wooden stairs to the central heating system for the cabin — a monstrous black stove the size of a Clydesdale.

He hated wet wood more than anything, even the cold. He blessed the woodshed at the end of the porch; there were no snow stripes on the logs or kindling. He could barely see in the dark of the cabin but he didn't want to take the time to light a lamp. Warmth was more important. Pleasing his father was even more important.

Fat-sticked matches lighted instantly when struck on the red and white Diamond box. The boy learned to master the flame, starting a perfect fire with only two pages of the Sears, Roebuck catalogue. He was trying for one page, but only a slow-burning slick page would do. Those were best for lighting the fire since they weren't prized pages for the outhouse. When the thin cedar kindling caught fire and popped at him, he bolted for the door to relieve himself in the snow, making yellow circles. A skinny German shepherd wagged its whole body in morning greeting and rubbed against his leg, spoiling his yellow design.

By the time he checked the fire again, it was hungry for bigger pieces of wood, right on schedule. Feeding a fire, it was called, and aptly so since the one inside the big stove would have a voracious appetite for wood. It was awful how fast it could consume a log. It would fry cedar and pine so quickly that he only used these woods for kindling. Maple or elm was better and the best, the thing that would appease the fire most, was alder. Alder was heavy and dense, hard to cut, impossible to split and heavy to stack. He cursed the alders in the summer. But he blessed the dense alder after he'd made the fire come to life and his father wasn't up yet.

He would try his hand at making the coffee again this morning. He couldn't seem to get it right...the way his mother made it. It would make his father so happy if he could just make coffee the way his mother used to. There hadn't been a good cup of coffee brewed in the house since she died, two months before Christmas.

The miracle was that she had lived that long. Uncle Val, his father's brother who had always lived with them, used to delight in telling the story of Holbrook's birth and the attempt to make it to a hospital in Portland, fifty miles away. Eight years ago, it was, he thought, watching the fire crawl around on the fresh log. Eight years ago, today. The fire warmed his face as he stared into it, a little sleepy, a little fixated.

When he was born there was nothing but the old highway — a twisted, cliff-hanging road that followed the Oregon Cascades and stopped at all the waterfalls. That night the headlights went out on the Model T as his father, his mother and Val were attempting to cross the Columbia Gorge mountains. Val lit a lantern and rode on the hood of the car while his brother drove as fast as he dared over the hairpin turns. After that night, Deirdre avoided most car travel for the rest of her life. Holbrook was delivered into a blanket somewhere in the Cascades with Deirdre pressing her back against a tree.

Val, the boistrous, never-serious, happy Val would tell the story every birthday for Holbrook. But not this year.

He sighed and looked around the main room of the cabin. It hadn't changed much since his mother died; he was grateful for that. His whining sisters had given up complaining, that was nice. Val stopped most of his practical jokes, that was almost nice. Holbrook would have welcomed a prank — socks tied in knots on the clothes line, a garter snake in your bed, a wisecrack about your hair cut.

Holbrook had helped build the cabin. Without the use of power tools, Holbrook had been taught how to work the wood, measure twice and cut once. He learned how to bend metal, split stone, lay brick and mend pipe. The acreage on the stony Oregon hillside seemed never at a loss for a lesson. Holbrook and his sisters did not hear an unkind word from their proud father. It was an angry mystery to Holbrook why his mother had left them.

"Only seven years old and so talented," his mother would say, looking at his drawings.

But not talented enough to make coffee, the boy criticized himself.

"You can make anything!" she said, when he built the miniature furniture for his sisters' dolls. "Why don't you build them a house?" she suggested.

Holbrook pumped water from the red hand pump into the grey metal coffee pot. "Make anything but coffee," he said to himself.

"Holbrook, there's beauty everywhere," his mother had said. "You just have to be quiet enough to see it and hear it."

Holbrook scooped coffee grounds. Some grounds scattered on the kitchen's counter. He brushed them to the floor.

"Never sloppy," she had said.

Holbrook mopped the grounds with a damp rag until he had them all. He slammed the coffee pot on top of the squat black stove. If his mother had still been alive, she would have been up and about by now.

"Skin has a bad memory," Mrs. Biasi would tell her son. "Your nose can remember the smell of pine. It won't forget my cinnamon cakes. And your eyes can recall the path to the river from here: they don't forget. Your ears, they can remember things too. You can hear the sound of yourself chopping wood even when you're laying in your bed at night. But your skin has a poor memory. It forgets the pain of a knife cut after its healed. And it also forgets the touch of your sweet face on my hand. That's why I have to touch you so often, Holbrook. My skin has a bad memory."

"Hmmmmmm! That coffee smells good!" Holbrook was startled by his father's loud voice. Mr. Biasi hadn't spoken above a whisper all winter. Boots ka-lump-lumped down the stairs. A lantern light wobbled against the cabin walls as Mr. Biasi descended. Holbrook felt a panic inside himself; he wanted to go check on the dog or the chickens or the woodshed.

Holbrook just stood, struck by his father's voice. The elder Biasi took three steps across the kitchen and put his finger through the handle of the chipped metal cup. He set the lantern on top of the great black stove and he poured the coffee. A little billow of steam made a nice cloud above the cup.

Mr. Biasi bellowed to the ceiling, "Ya'll git up! This ain't Sunday, Val! You girls! This ain't the Ritz! You'll not be gittin' room service from me and Holbrook!"

The boy stood at attention. "Me and Holbrook." It was music. "Me and Holbrook."

Mr. Biasi pursed his lips and took a careful sip of the hot, hot coffee. His eyes winced at the burning brew and the left shoulder strap of his overalls fell to his arm.

"Goddamned, if this ain't the *best* cup of coffee I've ever tasted!" he roared. "Val! Ya gotta come down and have some of this coffee before I drink it all!"

Holbrook had never seen his father yell before. It was frightening but his father was smiling. And he liked the coffee. He *liked* the coffee!

Mr. Biasi's calloused hands reached for his son.

"Happy Birthday," he said.

Chapter 45

*Having everything can sometimes make
you stop wanting anything.*
                        — Jane Wagner

"My dad never had a sou," says Biasi, mesmerized by his own story. "And he had such a fine life."

The audience of four is struck with the tenderness of Biasi's memoir.

"You've come a long way, Biasi," admires The Wizard, who grips the architect's shoulder as he stands to get more coffee.

"You know, you're right, Wizard. About meditation. I used to meditate. Things were better. I don't remember that I stopped. I just haven't any more. I should start doing that again.

"And you, Chadwick, I've been thinking about something you said..."

"Me?" startles Chadwick. "I'm flattered." He really is.

"You said that it takes talent to enjoy success. You are obviously more talented than I am."

There is a short silence. Chadwick does not know how to respond. Hershell cracks his teeth on Corn Nuts and Lash takes another swig of beer.

"I suspect that you traded your mantra for muscatel," says The Wizard, pouring two cups of coffee and returning one to Biasi. The architect either doesn't hear or ignores the remark.

Hershell paws in his bag of Corn Nuts searching for the well done ones. "Biasi," ventures Hershell, "do you have some sort of problem with besting your father?"

Biasi dribbles the last of the rum into his hot coffee.

"There's a war goin' on inside you, my friend," observes Lash.

Biasi rests his furry chin on his cupped hand, his elbow on the table. He rubs his eyes and sighs.

"I think I was embarrassed to have him come to openings and dedications. You know, the greatest gift and the greatest insult you can give a father is your success. He always *seemed* proud of me...and yet...I don't know. It's like, if everybody in the family is fat and you're fat and you don't want to be fat anymore...and...and you take the weight off, the message to the rest of the family is: 'You're wrong, fat's not the thing to be.' On the one hand, we're expected to excel and on the other hand we're not supposed to 'get above our raisin.' Most of the time for most of the male population, it's just easier not to try...and a lot of guys just don't. I can understand it.''

Hershell sits up and reaches for his wine. He takes a sip. "Excellent choice of reisling, Chadwick. It was a vintage week,'' says Hershell.

"Biasi, truth be told, I wrestled with my past in competition with my future...for a time there, too. I noticed it about the first time I went to buy a Cadillac. I found that I wanted the dealership to remove the emblems so that the car would look like a Buick. I wanted the Cadillac but I didn't want anybody to see me in it! It is absurd to work so hard to achieve something and then have some voice inside your head ashamed of it all.''

Biasi looks up through his curls at the old man.

"I know what that's like. The voices inside my head...argh! I wake up in the morning. The jury's in...and I'm guilty.''

Biasi looks old and hurt and tired.

"But I thought I had it licked. That's what the Jaguar was supposed to do for me. You have no idea what an adjustment I had to make...that car is a statement that I wanted to make to myself about what I've accomplished.'' Biasi begins to sound fierce again.

Lash, cowboy hat pushed back on his head, eyes on Biasi, says, "It ain't workin' for ya, partner.''

"It's pretty hard to create abundance for yourself when somebody on the inside wants to live without indoor plumbing,'' says The Wizard.

"In all our misery, we are comfortable,'' adds Chadwick.

"What the hell is that supposed to mean?'' asks Biasi.

"It means just what you said. We may be miserable being poor or being fat or being *whatever,* but we keep doin' it to ourselves because there is an element of comfort to it. We are comfortable with the old set of problems. We know them...really know them. We just don't want a new set of problems. So we get stuck in a comfort zone and, like you have so brilliantly pointed out, it's easier not to try...or, like Hershell has so creatively suggested, change the emblems on the car! Hershell, I have to give you credit, that's really quite creative!''

"And stupid,'' snorts the old man.

"There's just one thing that doesn't make it simple. It would be easy to just stick with the old status quo *unless* you can't help responding to an inner passion for greatness...'' Chadwick lets his voice trail off.

"I lack the courage,'' says Biasi, "to be a nobody.''

Hershell pelts Biasi with Corn Nuts. The Wizard wads up wilted cabbage leaves and throws them at the architect. The fraternity boos the speaker.

"And boo's to the booze too," comments The Wizard, quietly.

There is another silence. This time it is Lash who grows impatient.

"This ain't no encounter group," he says. "Let's get on with this barn dance."

Biasi grins and then starts to laugh. He slaps the top of the table so hard that the candles quake. He roars with laughter, the tension falling from his face.

"Barns!" he hollers. "Let me tell you about Travis and *barns*!"

Chapter 46

We may lose and we may win,
But we will never be here again.
So open up, I'm climbin' in.
— The Eagles

"You know what the difference is between men and women?" she asked, gazing up through the yellow maple leaves at the crisp, blue Toronto sky.

Her fingers played mindlessly with the salt and pepper curls nestled at her breast bone. The faint perfumey smell of champagne came from his lips.

"No, but I have a feeling you're going to tell me."

Travis' hand drifted down to his ears and she curled his beard around her forefinger.

"Women say, 'If he'd just fix something around here, change a light bulb, *anything!*' And men say, 'If she'd just make love to me, just *once in awhile*!' That's the difference."

"Suppose men and women will ever get it together?" he asked, then yawned.

"I dunno...but a man could do real well with a box full of light bulbs."

Wind pushed her soft curls in front of her face and she tossed her head.

"Well, pretend I'm General Electric," he said, pulling himself on top of her.

He pulled her wild hair back. "You're everything wonderful about autumn," he whispered, looking squarely into her eyes.

As she always did, she returned the look. "Chromium Oxide Green," he said to her.

"Beg pardon?" she asked.

"Your eyes," he answered in a far away tone. "Chromium Oxide Green, three parts, with one part Payne's Grey, four parts Titanium White and sometimes a little Cerulean Blue."

"Oh..." she smiled, cocked her head under his hand and warmed him deliciously with her eyes. No one noticed her eyes, studied her eyes with such enthusiasm as Biasi.

He nuzzled her neck, their curls mixing together.

"What are you going to build here?" she asked, resting her arms around his shoulders. Biasi was spending three days on a hillside near a barn and a greenhouse, getting to know the space before beginning his drawings.

"A performing arts center will be here," he answered.

"Right here? Right here on this spot?" she wanted to know.

Biasi rolled off of her and onto the red plaid blanket. He squinted into the Canadian sun and studied the position of the old barn and the rickety greenhouse. He chewed his lip a bit as he thought, turning his gaze left and right. He twisted and looked over her head at the grassy incline above them. His blue pup tent with orange rain cover was settled in the shade of the barn just a few feet away.

"No, probably where the barn is now."

The college had the land for nearly thirty years and now the Board of Commissioners was ready to expand the campus into the old pasture. The barn lost its function when the farm estate of Riley Penn was bequeathed to the college. The landscaping department had built a greenhouse near the barn and kept petunia and geranium startings in it. Tools, lawn mowers, small evergreen seedlings and hoses were stashed in the dirt splashed greenhouse. The sun-bleached barn leaned dramatically away from the direction of the wind, which always blew and was puffing even now.

"How do you decide what's going to be here?" she asked.

"I don't decide," he answered. "The Board decides. The land decides. The money decides. I only make the minor decisions...like brick and steel and height and length and glass and bathrooms."

"Yes, but how do you know where to begin?" she insisted.

"I'll know after I've been here and listened long enough. Usually about three days...if I'm not interrupted..." He grabbed her waist and kissed her flat firm tummy. "With you and your incessant questions as a delicious distraction, I expect to be here in this field about six months."

She swatted his head. "Don't you wish," she teased.

"So how long are you going to be here?" he asked.

"Truth be known," she began, wistfully eyeing the cadmium yellow maple leaves bobbing and weaving above her head, "I could have handled this research on the telephone, probably. But I had to meet this handsome and passionate architect, you see..."

He half rolled on her again and kissed her several times, as if he might be leaving to catch a ship soon.

"If this were wartime," he asked, "would you wait for me?"

"Of course," she lied.

"You lie!" he exclaimed.

"You bullshit," she countered.

"I want you," he demanded.

"You'll 'have' me," she stated.

Biasi rolled his head. "No, no, you gave in too easy," he whined.

"You want games? The soccer field is that way."

"No, it isn't. It's that way. You have no sense of direction."

"Au contraire! I have an excellent sense of direction."

"Been in Canada two days and already you speak French. Better not let the college president hear you. . . He's no frog, you know."

"Frogs, frogs! You have to kiss a lot of 'em before you find a prince. I kissed you and you're still a frog."

"I mean it. Watch yourself here or you'll lose your pass to the library. You'll be thrown out."

"If anybody's going to be thrown out, it'll be you. . for molesting women in the college pasture under the guise of architectural soothsaying."

He held her down and kissed her hard. His head popped up like a duck from an underwater swim. He stared at her. She offered no resistance. Then she simply moved him away with no more effort than moving a blanket. She stood up and pulled at her navy blue sweater, then readjusted her bra. She winced in the bright sun and with hands on hips, studied the barn and the greenhouse.

"So how do you do this? How do you design in 3-D?"

Biasi pouted and reached for his paper cup and the champagne bottle. He sat up, crossed his legs, poured the Asti Spumanti and said, "It wouldn't do any good to explain it to you. Women have no depth perception."

She whirled on him. "You know *why*?" she demanded.

He only squinted, trying to see her standing above him, the sun barely behind her. "No, why?"

"Because," she spat at him, "we women have been told all our lives that *this*" she held her fingers three and a half inches apart, "is six inches!"

"Very creative," he said, sarcastically.

"I'll show you creative," she said, returning to her good mood once she'd matched his point. "I'll help you with your project here."

"Oh, yeah," he said, unimpressed and licking a droplet of champagne dribbling down the side of the paper cup.

"There's supposed to be a theatre here, right?" she began. "Well, let's use the space as if the thing is already built. And when we do that, you'll come up with the design."

Biasi scratched his short beard and was preparing a shut down response, but the idea began to intrigue him.

"Say that again?" he asked.

She dropped onto the edge of the plaid blanket, just touching her knees to his.

"It's like this...there's supposed to be a theatre here. So if we act as if it is already here, which it is — everything that ever has been or ever will be *exists* right here — then you'll start to see the theatre already finished. You'll know what it's made out of and where the bathrooms are and where the stage is and all that. It'll save you hours at the drawing board. And you'll only have to propose it to the board once because your first design will be the accepted design. It'll work! This is an opportunity!"

If he had had a scissors, he would have cut her sweater off of her. The champagne fizzed in his mouth and he swallowed, feeling the warmth brewing now inside even as the lowering sun cooled the air on the hillside.

" 'All the answers you seek are within.' Remember? You told me that. Come on! This is an opportunity! Road test your philosophy."

Was she ever more radiant? he asked himself. Her auburn hair covered her eyes and half of her face. God, I hope so, he answered himself.

"How do you know when opportunity knocks, Biasi?" she asked. She was harder to take when she got excited about an idea. She was starting to get excited. He wanted her excited about other matters.

"How?" he played along.

"Open the door every time you hear something!" she insisted, punching him gently in the chest with her two hands.

"How can you tell whether it's a door or a window?" he asked.

"You just try walking," she demanded, "and if you get your knee caps clobbered, it's a window. Now come on! You know this will work!"

She pulled at his sweatshirt and he stood up, looking towards the barn. He looked up and down the hillside, stared at the maple quite awhile and he reached for her hand. "When the construction is finished, this maple will still be here," he declared. He let the Canadian wind fill his nose and throat and lungs.

"This might work..." he said, his enthusiasm growing. The light made an amber halo around her hair. A thin sunbeam took the color from her pale eyes and left them an irridescent grey.

"Creativity is not restricted to the arts, Biasi. Creativity is an approach to living life...you know that. You live it! You are it! Creativity is a way of seeing and listening to the world..."

Biasi heard his mother's voice in stereo with hers. He shuddered.

"I think that what really causes creativity to happen is when we're ready to drop being embarrassed," she went on rapidly, taking deeper breaths. He thought she was about to run down the hillside or do a cartwheel.

"How about the guy who went over the high jump bar backward? He must have felt pretty foolish doing it for the first time! Spectators must have thought he was pretty foolish, too, until someone checked the measurement and said, 'Wow! He went higher than anybody!' "

She turned his hand up, palm out in front of his chest and took his other hand, did the same. She held her palms up to his, stopping a quarter of an inch from actually touching.

"Biasi, your paintings are like whores wrapped in pastel lace. How can you be so powerful and so fragile at the same time?"

Blood began to throb up Biasi's neck into his brain. His breath faltered and he lunged at her, gripping her hands and smashing the space between them. His eyes locked into hers. She stood defiantly, pressing her fingers into the backs of his hands.

"We are all passionate—" he breathed, "somewhere, on some level. We are trained out of it, talked out of it, bred out of it, cheated out of it — but it's never really gone. Your Creative Self *knows*."

The green was gone from her eyes. A luminous pearl color remained, the eyes of a wise blind man. His chest began to hurt, he wanted her so much. She gripped his hands harder.

"Exactly! So what's *here*?" she hissed, bringing her face close to his.

Part of him wanted to collapse into her arms and just be comforted for twenty years. Part of him felt angry and challenged, almost psychically outmatched. He wouldn't, couldn't, stop the performance in her eyes.

"There's a theatre here," he said, slowly. "It's over there. You're standing next to the Riley Penn Performing Arts Center sign."

"Is there a play going on?" she asked.

"A rehearsal. . . a final rehearsal," he answered in a voice so definite that he wondered if he had actually said it.

Sunlight was hitting squarely on the most weathered side of the barn. A door creaked gently and bang-banged against a pine wall. The two-story structure dwarfed the greenhouse. In thirty years it had been a refuge for only field mice and swallows. Piles of musty hay still filled the loft and the main floor where the stable had been.

"What's the name of the play?" she asked him, pulling from his subconscious as if she were tearing sheets from an internal teletype machine.

His eyes flashed lust and victory when he realized the title of the play. He pulled her grip out to their sides, hunched his shoulders, drawing her nearer as he pinned her hands behind her.

"*The Taming of the Shrew,*" he muttered through clenched teeth.

Her eyes widened, she whimpered and struggled against his grip. "*Let me go,*" she said, "Act Two, Scene One."

"*No, not a whit,*" he responded, picking up his cue perfectly.

" *'Twas told me you were rough, and coy, and sullen,*
And now I find the report a very liar:
For thou art pleasant, gamesome, passing courteous. . ."

He released his grip as he raised one pirate eyebrow, gleefully challenging her. She raced for the greenhouse door, flipped the old rusty latch and slipped inside. He seemed almost right behind her as she slammed the solid wooden door, safe behind it. A rough wooden table wobbled at her unexpected entrance. She dragged it in front of the door, knocking a trowel and two pots to the gravel floor. She turned, sat on the table top to weight her protection and she folded her arms, a victorious look on her face.

"*Good morrow Kate, for that's your name I hear!*" he shouted, coming through the door at the opposite end of the greenhouse.

She jumped to the ground, positioned herself on the other side of a wide wooden seedling bench. She threw a gardener's stiff mummified glove at him.

"*Well have you heard, but something hard of hearing:*
They call me Katharine, that do talk of me," she recited.

She threw another glove that popped him in the forehead.

"What's here?" she asked.

"The practice rooms for the music department and the dressing rooms for the theatre," he answered, motioning around the greenhouse.

"*You lie in faith!*" he screams at her, taking his position on the other side of the wide bench.

"*For you are call'd plain Kate,*
And bonny Kate, and sometimes Kate the curst:
But Kate, the prettiest Kate in Christendom!
Myself am moved to woo thee for my wife!"

She started her way around the bench, keeping an eye on him and an eye on the opened door behind him.

"*Let him that mov'd you hither*
Remove you hence!" she warned, venomously.

She moved to the left, gripping the edging on the bench. He moved to the right, knocking old dead seedling pots over. He reached for her arm, lost his balance and plopped flat on the dirt and gravel floor.

"*Nay then,*
Do what thou canst, I will not go to-day,
No, nor to-morrow, not till I please myself
The door is open sir, there lies your way . . ." she sang in a haughty voice as she made a try for the door.

He stood and hurled a seedling pot that splattered on the brace above the door way, sending pieces of brick-colored flower pot onto her head. She turned, shaking the broken bits and spitting red dust. "Where am I now?" she asked.

"You're in the ladies restroom," he answered.

"How many stalls?" she asked.

"Three," he said.

"Not nearly enough!" she countered. "Make it five."

He grimaced, nodded his head from side to side and looked at his feet, his hands on his hips.

"You're probably right," he said.

"*O Kate content thee, prithee be not angry.*"

She ruffled her hair with her hands and eyed him as if he were a clerk who just announced a price check.

"*I will be angry, what hast thou to do?*" she bellowed at him.

A shelf full of pots presented itself next to the door and she picked up the ammunition.

"*For I am born to tame you Kate,*" he said as he ducked the first pot.

"*And bring you from a wild Kate to a Kate comformable!*" He hid behind the seedling bench. Still hiding he called out, "*I must, and will have Katharine to my wife!*"

Pots crashed through the glass roof of the greenhouse; they popped like popcorn from a hot air popper. Bits of dusty glass rained inside the dilapidated building. Shelves full of rusty tools toppled over and made holes in the glass walls. She ran from the greenhouse, slamming the door behind her. What was left of the glass, dropped to the ground. He crawled from beneath the protection of the seedling bench, stood up and brushed the cobwebs and dust from his sweatsuit. He pulled a wad of spider webbing from his beard and made his way over the broken glass to the door. The greenhouse, now without walls and a roof, left with only two doors, didn't hide her exit or conceal her path.

"*Come, come you wasp, i' faith you are too angry!*" he called.

"*If I be waspish, best beware my sting!*" she answered from inside the barn.

"*My remedy is then to pluck it out!*" he hollered, a finger waving flamboyantly in the air. He ran to the banging barn door and stepped inside.

"*Ay, if the fool could find it...*" she said, making sure he hadn't lost her.

He peered into the darkness of the barn and slowly took a step forward.

"*Who knows not where a wasp does wear the sting. In the tail?*" he asked, looking for a clue of her.

"*In his tongue,*" she whispered, seductively.

"*Whose tongue?*" he asks, picking up his line, while peering in the sunlit dust.

"*Yours if you talk of tales,*" she said, egging him one step further, "*and so farewell!*"

She had taken a hoe and hooked it to a loose board on the edge of the partial hay loft. As she said "farewell" she pulled hard on the hoe handle and swung most of her weight on it. The arthritic timbers gave way and thirty years of dusty hay enveloped him like a cloud.

He was coated in dust, hay hanging from his arms, his shoulders prickly with it, hay spokes exploding from his hair. He sputtered and shook the bigger pieces from his head.

He extended his arms to begin his next line, when she asked, "Where are we now?"

"Well, I'm standing in the orchestra pit, just in front of the front row of seats in the audience," he answered.

He extended his arms again.

"Be mad and merry, or go hang yourselves:
But for my bonny Kate, must with me:
Nay, look not big, nor stamp, nor stare, nor fret," he recited.

He took one step forward, brushed a clump of hay from his chest, clenched his fists and roared, *"I will be master of what is mine own!"*

He peered through the swirling dust.

"She is my goods, my chattels, she is my house,
My household stuff, my field, my barn, my everything!"

When he shouted "barn" he waved his arms wildly and leaned his head back.

"Did it really say 'barn'? Is that really in there?" she asked, hiding behind him in a cow stall.

"Rrrrrrgh! Yes, that's really in the play!" he roared, as he turned. Finding an old milk stool, he sat on it and continued: *"Come sit on me."*

"Asses are made to bear, and so are you," she said in sweet sarcasm. "What's here? Where am I now?"

"You're standing in the wings, so to speak," he prophesized. "Why don't you come out here into the stage area?"

With exaggerated stealth, she came out of the wooden stall and slowly walked to where he pointed. He waved her further away. She moved, as if looking for her mark on the stage floor. He held his palm up abruptly when she was correctly positioned.

"For she's not forward, but modest as the dove,
She is not hot, but temperate as the morn.
And to conclude, we have 'greed so well together,
That upon Sunday is the wedding day."

She crouched slightly, bared her teeth and held her hands up, claw-like. She watched him as he slowly stood up.

"I'll see thee hang'd on Sunday first!" she hissed.

"A bit more to the left," he directed. "There, perfect..." he whispered, looking up at the crusty beams and expanse of roof.

"Why there's a wench: come on, and kiss me Kate."

She couldn't have moved in time to sidestep his next move. The home run was Biasi's. He lunged into an instant sprint, hit her going about 30 m.p.h., and then slid them both into a leaning post, feet first. He rolled on top of her just as she heard a great cracking overhead. In slow motion half the roof collapsed. The leaning post flew horizontally and landed with a bouncing thud. Timbers, thin and rickety, gradually gave way and dropped like slow moving volunteers. The wall with the door in it was the first to fall over — it fell away from the inside of the barn. The other walls gently followed, one falling across Biasi's back side. Thin boards shattered all around them. When the dust settled, the only thing remaining in the pasture was the framework of the greenhouse and the maple tree.

Shingles and boards moved.

Biasi slowly pulled himself up as if completing a last push-up. His head wobbled slightly. Her eyes were wide with fear.

"My, God!" she said, "Are you all right?"

He seemed to be having a hard time focusing his eyes. Dreamily, he recited, *"Come my sweet Kate:*
    Better once than never, for never too late."

She held his face in her hands, her warm grey eyes pearlized by the setting Canadian sun. "Oh, Petruchio," she sighed as she kissed him just before he passed out.

Chapter 47

Those who shun the whimsy of things will experience rigor mortis before death.
— *Tom Robbins*

"**I** could have killed us both," says Biasi, rubbing the back of his head. "I still have a scar back here somewhere."

"What did the college do when they found out?" asks Lash.

"Well, nothing," says Biasi, "since they were going to have the barn torn down anyway. I just wrote it into my bill for architectural services..."

"You *didn't*!" squeals Hershell.

Biasi smacks his lips and nods.

"And they laughed at my hat story!" says Hershell sarcastically.

"Well, did you know that the building was going to fall that way?" asks Chadwick.

"Yeah...I could pretty much tell how the old girl was going to go ...it was a simple structure and I knew exactly which support would most likely do the trick. But it was a dumb stunt. I just got caught up in the moment. I wanted an *1812 Overture* ending to our spectacular rendition of *Taming of the Shrew*. What I got was six stitches in my head and we had more bruises between us than a train wreck. It was a glorious afternoon!"

"Sounds like a fine piece of madness to me," says The Wizard, with envy in his voice.

"You know what I liked most about Travis?" begins Biasi, not wanting or waiting for a response. "She could hold up her end of the madness. If I had played Dagwood Bumstead that afternoon, instead of Petruchio, she would have played Blondie."

"Chips, anyone?" offers Hershell. He passes the bag and there is great crunching. "What about the project? How did the new building turn out?"

"Just like Travis said it would...I only had to do the drawings once," marvels Biasi.

"So what happened between you...and...Travis?" asks Lash.

"More rum," Biasi requests, waving to his bottle at the other end of the table.

"No...that's enough. Finish your story first," parents Hershell.

"OK..." moans Biasi, "although answering that question without libation is cruel and unusual punishment...

"It's like this...in my own mind...Travis Duncan was an investigative reporter's wet dream. She made *60 Minutes* look like a sitcom. She used to tell me about how she tore her toys apart when she was a kid, just to see what made them work. We would analyze the universe together and then analyze me, since my favorite subject was me. I think that we tore me apart so many times, that we kind of forgot how to put me back together again!"

Biasi waved a bit in his chair; he was far from sober.

"God! I admired that mind of hers. There was no lid on her creativity. Sometimes I thought she was more of an artist than I was.

"Mind like a steel trap. She got more beautiful...that fascinated me. I'd see her two or three times a year. Usually at some social event. Lots of people around. We would flirt wildly in front of everyone. And I would lust after the sight and the smell of her. And then the next day I just didn't pick up the phone. Days went. Months went. And then I'd see her in a restaurant or somewhere. And she'd look even more wonderful than ever.

"I suppose that subconsciously I was getting the message that she was doing better and better without me.

"She's the only woman I've ever known, who, even though you didn't call her, loved you *anyway*."

The early morning hour at the Pittock Mansion was very quiet. Biasi sighed. They could hear the clock in the foyer, their own hearts... and the crinkle of Hershell's potato chip bag.

"Biasi, did you say earlier that you are also a pilot?" asks Hershell.

"I don't recall saying it, but...I used to have a pilot's license, yes."

"That's a rather unusual combination, isn't it? Architect and pilot?" asks Lash.

"Not really," interrupts The Wizard. "Both are always trying to put something between earth and sky."

Biasi flashes his great Franklin Roosevelt smile and his chest jiggles with laughter.

"You still fly?" asks The Wizard.

"Nooooo," answers Biasi, watching the rum gurgle out of the bottle and into his glass.

"Flying was a great escape," he says, eyeing his glass. "You might say I gave up one escape for another."

The four in the fraternity look at each other. They each have the same message, but none of them seems to have words.

"You're such a talent, Biasi. . . ." Hershell begins, sadly.

Chadwick interrupts, "Biasi, is drinking working for you. . or are you just going down Tunnel Number 4?"

Biasi pushes himself to his feet and angrily eyes Chadwick. "You're such a saint, goddamn you, you'll have to ride on the dashboard next time we go out!"

Biasi slumps back in his chair. He gives a half-hearted wave to Chadwick, the closest he will come to an apology.

"There's not enough time or money right now," Biasi says, "I know the routine. I've checked it out. I know that may sound like a cop-out, but I just can't do it right now. The firm's at a critical point. I can't. . . I won't take the two or three weeks right now. But, you know, Travis' money would get me off of several hooks right now. I could take a whole new direction with just a little time off. Money would get me that. And I'd take it."

"I believe you would," nods Hershell.

Chapter 48

*It is a funny thing about life; if you refuse
to accept anything but the best, you very
often get it.*
— W. Somerset Maugham

Like fawn-colored feathered fans waving over warm chocolate
pudding, Lash's lashes become the focus now.

"Guess it's my turn, huh?" he flutters, adjusting the Kenworth belt
buckle on his Levi's.

" 'Reckon so, partner," drawls Biasi, more than half drunk and
imitating Lash's country speech.

Lash has the longest fringe ever grown on human eyelids. His
eyelashes wave like huge fluffy awnings past his soft brown eyes. This
remarkable physical trait will stop a power-shopping female from across
a shopping mall. To make matters worse, he dips and waves the things
like Sally Rand fans. The rest of him is Chippendale Calendar quality,
but it is his eyes that cause other eyes to stare.

Lash sits up and rubs the tops of his thighs with the palms of his
hands, his only nervous gesture. He shrugs. His dialogue will require a
jump start.

"Well, tell us about what you do. . . ." helps Hershell.

"I drive," answers Lash. "I've driven over a million and a half
miles without an accident."

Chadwick whistles; he is impressed. Hershell applauds. The Wizard
does too. Biasi shakes his head, unbelieving. "Wow!" they all say.

"So you're a *professional* driver," says The Wizard.

"Well, 'professional' don't mean you're good at it, 'professional'
just means you get paid for it."

The fraternity gets a great laugh out of this.

"So you could say, I'm a professional *and* I'm good at it. Always
was. Just a knack for it, I guess."

"Chip?" offers Hershell, tipping his potato chip bag towards Lash.

Lash shakes his head and rubs his tummy.

"Well, I'm an owner-operator and Red Bessie out there is my whole business. I haul beer from L.A. to Vancouver, Canada. Then boxes of fiber optic stuff from Saskatchewan to Texas. Cosmetics from Dallas to the East Coast. Hardware from Florida to New York. Books from South Carolina to Boston. It could be candles or condoms next week, you know? Every haul's a different customer. The only difference between my job and being a proctologist is — a proctologist gets to deal with only *one* asshole at a time! I got two brokers on opposite ends of the United States and I spend a lot of time in pay phone booths."

Hershell har-har's; Biasi laughs and snorts until rum and coke comes up into his nose. Chadwick cackles and The Wizard leans back and whinnies in a high-pitched laugh.

"I been truckin' since before computers got into it," continues Lash more at ease with his monologue now. "I can remember when people filled out shipping tickets in five minutes. Now I get to stand around, roundin' the heels of my boots while somebody inputs into a computer. You notice how much longer it takes you to buy something in a store nowadays? They got to punch 38 numbers into a computer and that don't include the price!"

"Do you ever take your hat off?" asks Chadwick.

"Why?" asks Lash. "Somebody die?" The grey felt Stetson stays on his head.

"Don't mind him," says Hershell, throwing a Corn Nut at Chadwick. "Say, you got any of those Wheat Thins left?"

"One box," says Chadwick, "and I'm saving that for breakfast."

"Doesn't sound like you have much routine in your life," offers The Wizard, hoping to direct Lash to his path again.

"No, every day's different, that's for sure. I wouldn't like getting into a rut. You know what a rut is, don't you? That's a grave with both ends kicked out. Well, I like things best when I'm out on the road in that KW with the stereo turned up to about eight on the Richter scale, I've got a full tank, a full load, and good road. That would eliminate my bein' in Nebraska."

"So where's your home?" asks Biasi.

"You just rode in it," answers Lash.

"Don't you have some kind of a home base?" asks The Wizard.

"Got two post office boxes...one in Texas and one in South Bend, Washington. That's where I'm from originally — the Willapa Bay area."

"So you spend most of your time alone?" asks Chadwick, making notes on the pad in front of him.

"The way I figure it," drawls Lash, warmly, "is that God was able to make the world in six days 'cause He had the advantage of workin' alone."

Hershell snorts. "I can't believe that you spend all your time alone..."

"I guess people think that just because we're on the road all the time, that we truckers have a pretty active and well-rounded sex life." He makes a classic gesture with his hands as he says "well-rounded."

"Well," he adds, "that would be right."

Chadwick puffs little clouds as he laughs at Lash and writes on his pad. He touches his cigarette to the crystal ash tray.

"Have you noticed," says surly Hershell, "that everybody has moved down to this end of the room, Chadwick?" Hershell waves his hand as if to move a smoke screen.

"So what's your 'handle'?" asks Biasi, ignoring the old man.

The maribou lashes blink slowly and end wide. "Lash," he answers, surprised.

"What's your real name?" asks Biasi.

"Roger, but I couldn't use that. Besides, nobody's ever called me Roger. Not even my mama."

"Why couldn't you use Roger?" asks The Wizard.

"Don't know much about CB's, do you?" Biasi teases The Wizard.

"Oh."

"Yeah," says Lash, "and I got a CB that'll reach from here to Manilla."

Lash pops the top on another beer, then says, "There any more coffee? I think I'd probably better switch to coffee."

"You gonna drink that beer?" nudges Hershell.

Lash hands him the can and shakes his head at Hershell's capacity. The Wizard says, "Pass me your cup" and he fills it from the perking pot on the serving table.

"So where you from and what's your story. . ." says Biasi.

"Like I said, I'm from South Bend, Washington. That's Washington, the state. I'll tell you a true story about South Bend. . .Pacific County, that's our county, well, the county seat was located in Oysterville for twenty years and the folks in South Bend, well, that was a bit too inconvenient for the people in South Bend, so about a hundred years ago, they just got into a couple of steamers and headed out acrost Willapa Bay and stole the county records. So since 1889, South Bend has been the county seat. Around 1905, Raymond, the town next door, started getting real big because that's where Weyerhaeuser built a paper mill and, well, there was some talk of Raymond becoming the county seat. So the people of South Bend built a County Courthouse building to end all county courthouse buildings. It was called the Gilded Palace of Reckless Extravagance. . .'cause that's just what it was, but it *worked* because nobody's ever wanted to move the county seat again. So that kinda tells you about where I'm from. . .and South Bend is the Oyster Capital of the World. . .leastwise, that's what the sign says as you're comin' into town."

Hershell leans forward and ceases his munching. "Is it true," he whispers, "what they say about oysters?"

Lash repositions his hat. "I've never had any complaints from the ladies," he answers, modestly.

"So what else is in South Bend, Washington?" asks The Wizard. "Besides the county seat?"

"Well, the lady who wrote the state song lives there. There's a museum down on Main Street...it has the famous Forks River moonshine still in it and an old Studebaker wagon. There's about a two story stack of oyster shells by the bay at the Coast Oyster Company. You know, we got a Dairy Queen and everything, it's a real town. Also have about 98% unemployment rate, too. It's Washington State at it's loggin' best, I'll tell ya. See, our wise and wonderful federal government quit dredgin' the harbor so the big ships can't make it into port anymore. That and together with nobody building houses...well, if there's no building, the logs don't roll. Japanese driving up the prices, that didn't help matters much. And it's kind of a one-mill town. Anybody in the construction lobby sneezes in Washington and part of Pacific County goes into the bay."

"How come you ended up driving a truck instead of shuckin' oysters?" asks Biasi, familiar with the bivalve mollusks.

"My dad run a steam donkey in the woods for Weyerhaeuser and then he unloaded logs at the bayside mill. I'd hang out with my dad on weekends on the landing or run tools for my brother Blackie. I had three brothers and three sisters, all of 'em much older than me. Blackie, he was my favorite. He didn't talk much and he was really into old cars. Used to work on jalopies and I'd help him. I started driving a small tractor when I was 12, just around the acreage my folks had for like a little truck garden, earn some extra money with the place. Anyhow, when I got my drivers' license, I chased parts part-time after school and on Saturdays.

"I was the first one in my family to get a high school diploma. My grandfather, when he came west from Virginia, he couldn't even read. I really couldn't see much point in staying in school myself, though, when I could have been out on the road earning sixteen dollars an hour."

Lash's voice begins to dry up and he takes a sip of coffee. The clock in the foyer chimes four. "Boy, I'm glad they left us this coffee ...life wouldn't be worth livin' without this black stuff." He tips his moustache with his forefinger and smoothes his beard.

"Me and Blackie always had a way with wheels. There's a real art to driving something with a load on...like any fool who steps into an RV or tries to pull a simple trailer will show you. You turn the opposite way than you think you ought to...only my 'ought to' is right for movin' a truck. I won the Loggers Playday truck competition up in Hoquiam when I was about nineteen."

"Loggers Playday? What's that? Kentucky Fried Chicken putting spotted owls on the menu?'' chides Chadwick.

The little trucker scowls at Chadwick.

"You should be nice to Lash," advises The Wizard to Chadwick. "If it weren't for him, you'd look short."

It is true; Chadwick at barely five feet seven inches would still top Lash. Both men are muscular but Lash clearly has the chest of a well exercised bull dog.

"I don't need *you* fightin' my battles for me," Lash snips at The Wizard.

"Boys, boys!" interjects Hershell. "Just when we thought it was safe to start liking each other..."

"Go on," encourages Biasi.

"Well..." continues Lash, "you know, whatever you're willing to put up with is exactly what you'll have."

"Don't mind either one of them," advises Biasi, "they're both about a half bubble off plumb."

The "sophisticated" architect lapses into a forty-five year old speech pattern that is distinctively back woods, Columbia River.

"When it's time for you to pee," goads Lash to The Wizard, "do you go into the men's room or the ladies' room?"

"Good one," giggles The Wizard. "That's quite good."

"Mellow *out!*" bellows Hershell, jumping up and scattering the tiny broken pieces of potato chips that hide in the bottom of chip bags.

"So you're chasing parts," says Biasi, picking up the story. "Then what?"

"I got my combination license at 18, won the contest at 19 and next thing you know I'm haulin' gravel in a dump truck for an asphalt plant. I was makin' such good money about then and I'd had a bunch saved, I bought the truck, changed it to a log truck so that I could go either way with it. I could keep it busy hauling or logging. It was a good set up. Then what happened was...I was outside Skamokawa in the hills, loggin', when this powder monkey blows up my truck. To bits. There wasn't enough straight metal left of it to make one of these candlesticks here..."

Lash has turned a little pale just remembering the explosion that flattened the logging site, leveled the hillside and disappeared his Mack.

"Much as I hate to admit it, Chadwick is right...sometimes things work out for the best that at first seem to be the worst. I took the insurance and bought the Kenworth conventional cab with the sleeper, took it right off to the pin-striper to have the lettering put on it and I hit the road. Just when everything in Grays Harbor and Pacific County bottomed out, I got thrown a lifeline. Things were always touch and go financially with the Mack. I was just on the edge of havin' it repo'd once and I swore I'd hide it up in the mountains somewhere if somebody tried to take it. I would have too. Guy did me a favor, blowin' it up. But at the time, they just about had to sedate me to keep from killing him.

Dangerous Dan, they called him. And I found out why...anyway, he left for Alaska. Lots of guys who made mistakes in Washington ended up in Alaska. They used to have a liberal approach to safety up there.''

Lash looks at Biasi, and wonders what he wonders. Then he eyes The Wizard who sits listening intently. Lash goes to Chadwick with his eyes and watches the developer take more notes. He gets a question mark on his face and nudges Hershell. Hershell watches Chadwick writing for a moment.

"Probably just his grocery list," says Hershell. "Think nothing of it.''

Lash stretches his hands high above his cowboy hat and he yawns. "Know when I stopped worrying about money?'' he asks.

"When I had some," he answers himself. "Money calms my nerves.''

"Then Travis' millions should put you in a coma!'' cracks Biasi.

"I have every intention of making that happen, yes,'' grins the trucker.

"What would you do with that kind of money...?'' ponders Biasi, dreamily.

"I'd probably hire Dolly Parton to just sit in my truck and sing to me while I drive...just have her there live instead of on tape! Or maybe I'd buy Nashville. Tell you what I wouldn't do: I wouldn't fill out another form and I wouldn't ever drive at night again. No more weigh stations and no more scandal sheets. Life would be different, there's no doubt about that!''

"Yeah," dreams The Wizard.

"Yes..." sighs Hershell.

"Even after taxes, it's an impressive piece of money,'' says Chadwick.

Hershell stops munching as they all drift their separate ways, imagining the money. They have avoided talking about the money, as if it, instead of Travis, is the one dead.

"People do funny things with money,'' Lash observes. "A lot of folks would rather be envied than be happy. That makes 'em spend money in a funny sort of way. Travis and I talked about this; she had a handle on it...she'd spend money on things that brought her and other people some happy times...didn't matter about the status of the thing. I'd like to think that I'd do the same...but maybe I wouldn't.

"All I want is a chance to prove that havin' a lot of money won't make me miserable.''

It takes a moment for the fraternity to grasp what Lash has said and when they do, they laugh in chorus.

"You're a little philosopher, aren't you?'' admires The Wizard.

"I don't pretend to be anything that I don't know how to spell,'' answers Lash, modestly.

Hershell tugs at Lash's sleeve, using his beer can waving in the air for emphasis. "Don't worry if you're rich or not," Hershell advises, "just as long as you can have everything you want."

"That's marvelous advice," grinds Biasi, sarcastically, "but my tastes seem to exceed my earning capacity."

"There needs to be an adjustment somewhere, Biasi," says The Wizard, noting the empty glass in the architect's hand.

Chadwick flips through the pages of notes on his pad. He underlines on some pages. The others watch him.

"So..." he directs, "what was it like growing up in South Bend, Washington?"

Chapter 49

Nothing is impossible to the person who
won't listen to reason.
— Anonymous

Balloon-hustling clowns ambled down Main Street, their big yellow feet flapping on the blocked off, blacktopped street. One of them stopped to take a dime from a little brown-haired woman who was setting up two lawn chairs with her son. She handed the blue *Whitney's Chevrolet-Montesano* balloon to her tiny son and they took their places curbside, a thermos of Kool Aid between them. Labor Day Parade, South Bend, Washington, 1957.

The sidewalk, so infrequently used by Main Street patrons on any other day, became prime real estate once a year for the parade. It was best to get there early, sip your cool drinks, buy the good carnival popcorn and wait for the Big Moment. The clowns relieved both the wait and the coin purses of the spectators.

The tiny brown-haired boy held his balloon string tightly as his mother tied the end of it around his wrist. "Careful, Mrs. Lindsay," the clown, who was really Leon the barber, said, "the little fellow might blow away!"

Mrs. Lindsay managed a polite smile. Just barely five feet tall herself, she had heard enough small people jokes to last her a lifetime. She checked her watch; the parade was always on time. Today it was 1:15 and still no color guard appeared from around the Standard Oil station. A baby squalled and two dogs on leashes got into a fight. All the park benches along Main Street were full and a hundred aluminum lawn chairs dotted the parade route. Cushions and blankets were low rent seats for the annual spectacle.

Suddenly a squat man in a green military cap popped through the crowd and tapped Mrs. Lindsay on the shoulder. It was Joe Jenson, the owner of the Coast to Coast store; Mrs. Lindsay had bought all of her seeds and garden tools from him. He was nearly out of breath and his face was red and sweaty. "Mrs. Lindsay, can I see you for a moment?" he asked.

Alice Lindsay straightened the collar on her cotton print dress, pointed a "stay" command to her young son and then disappeared into the crowd following Joe Jenson. In a moment they both returned, Joe wringing his sausage-like fingers and Alice Lindsay as pale as the hardware store owner was flushed.

Alice Lindsay wore a hat and gloves 53 times a year, every Sunday and to the Labor Day parade. She never missed the parade, not since she had been crowned Miss Oyster in 1928 and presided over the event, the closest one could come to royalty in South Bend...

"Come with me, dear," she said to her son, an unusual tenseness in her voice.

"But, Mama, I want to watch the parade," he answered, softly.

"Just come with me, *now*," she whispered, sternly, trying not to attract attention. There had already begun a low grumbling in the crowd, something like first gear on a log truck.

Even though he was six years old, Mrs. Lindsay could still pick her son up and carry him. She whisked him through the crowd of people, following behind Joe Jenson. The balloon knocked several taller spectators in the head. The little boy made no effort to curtail the balloon, he just smiled a pretty smile and batted his eyelashes.

When they rounded the corner of Fanny's Floral Shop, they could see the anxious color guard and the Coast Guard band. "It'll be just a minute, folks, just a minute!" Joe Jenson reassured the participants. He trotted and Alice Lindsay began to jog behind him, carrying her son. They went nearly the full length of the parade, past the mayor in the town convertible, past Gladys Ray's School of Dance performing dancers, past the sheriff's mounted posse, past the antique cars and the dog carts.

"Are we going to go see Daddy?" asked Alice Lindsay's little boy.

Bodie Lindsay was driving the volunteer fire department's red utility truck in the parade. He and his son Blackie threw candy out the windows for the kids and they would sound the siren as they drove the length of Main Street. The fire truck was the last parade entry and when everyone saw Bodie and the fire truck they knew the parade was over.

"No, Daddy's further down that way," puffed his mother.

Joe Jenson stopped beside a huge flat trailer hooked up to a powerful Freightliner truck. Alice Lindsay looked at the strange contraption on the flatbed. Tubes of chickenwire surrounded what may have been a small backhoe. Thousands of tissues had been stuffed in the chicken wire and then spray painted brown. Construction paper leaves were stapled and taped to papier mache "limbs" and attached to the chicken wire "trees." Someone in a beaver costume toting a chain saw sat impatiently on one of the branches. A large laundry basket was suspended by two metal cables from a major limb. The cradle, except for pink and white baby bunting, was empty.

Jeannie Petrie was nearly hysterical when Joe Jenson and Alice

Lindsay arrived. She was atop the flatbed, microphone in hand, dressed as a pioneer woman. She was supposed to play her guitar and sing "Rock-A-Bye Baby" while the beaver sawed the "limb" from the big tree. Now their whole moment of glory was ruined. Baby Petrie, Jennie's four year old sister, had come down with chicken pox just that morning. With no baby, the VFW float, complete with tree limb that "collapsed" and then righted itself, would be woefully incomplete.

They had tried using Bosco, the Petrie's mutt dressed in a baby's bonnet, but the dog wouldn't stay in the cradle. Neither would the cat, Calico Kitty. No one else was small enough to play the part of the Rock-A-Bye Baby, a load limit of 50 pounds required. No one until Joe Jenson, float chairman, remembered the tiny six-year old Lindsay boy who was sure to be waiting on Main Street to watch his father and brother drive by in the red fire truck.

When Alice Lindsay saw the "forested" backhoe, she was skeptical. "How does it work? Is it safe?" she asked. The beaver gave a hi-sign to a hidden operator as he pretended to saw the big limb. Sure enough, the basket dropped three feet as the limb appeared to collapse. Slowly the hydraulics brought the limb back into position again, the cradle and contents perfectly safe.

Alice handed her son to Joe who boosted him up to Jeannie. "Oh, thank God, thank God," praised Jeannie, out loud. The cradle was lowered and the boy hopped in, Keds and all. Everything was going fine until Jeannie tried to put the baby bonnet on his head. "Nothin' doin'!" he squealed, escaping from the basket. He stood defiantly at the edge of the flatbed trailer.

"Come on, dear, do it for Mama, OK?" Alice Lindsay pleaded with her son.

"Not with that baby thing on!" he protested.

"He's *got* to wear it!" screamed Jeannie, breaking out in tears. "Or nobody will know he's a baby!"

"Please, please," begged Joe Jenson, sweating through his uniform. "I'll do anything. We have to start the parade or people are going to start going home!"

The tiny boy stood, little fists on his hips, still tied to his Whitney's balloon.

"What'll it take?" Alice Lindsay asked, addressing her stubborn son.

The little boy looked at the bonnet and looked at his mother. He looked up at the waiting beaver and he looked at the crying pioneer girl. He looked at the mayor turned around on top the blue '55 Chevy convertible. He looked down at the fluorescent pink skirts of Gladys Ray's dance team. He looked at the dozen uniformed members of the Veterans of Foreign Wars.

"I want to throw candy like Dad does," he said.

"Candy! Candy!" Joe Jenson started to yell as he turned in circles.

"Where can we get candy? The stores are closed! The stores are closed!" The panic for candy was on.

Alice Lindsay patted Joe Jenson on the arm with a gloved hand.

"Tell everyone to get back in line and get ready," she commanded. "This parade will start in two minutes."

Alice Lindsay trotted towards the back of the parade, past the Hoquiam High School band, the Afifi bicycle clowns from Astoria and the 4-H Shetland pony troop. Her hat was askew when she reached the fire truck.

The color guard rounded the corner at the Standard Oil station, their brass buttons sparkling in the Indian summer sun, their white spats brilliant on their polished black boots. The Coast Guard band launched into "Stars and Stripes Forever" and the crowd on Main Street stood up for the passing of the colors.

"Elect Vern Putka — Auditor" the hand painted sign read on the side of the brand new parading 1957 pink Cadillac sedan. Vern and Mrs. Putka waved from the back seat while their son Vernon drove the car.

The children's bicycle parade wobbled by next, crepe paper woven in the spokes of Schwinns, plastic streamers fluttering from handlebars. Children with painted faces rode past the parade crowd. Occasionally one bike would hit another or run into the auditor's Cadillac. Vern would lose his parade smile temporarily.

A 1919 Kissel car, black and dented, proudly putt-putted down the street followed by a '29 Ford roadster carrying Judge Brown and Mrs. Brown. Their cocker spaniel sat between them, periscoping from side to side, wondering about the applause. Parade-watching dogs barked at the cocker.

A rickety 1930 Ford touring car rolled and coughed down the street driven by Miss Dixie, the 250-pound owner of Miss Dixie's Spit Curl, the local beauty shop. The other Spit Curls waved from the open car: they were all dressed as 1920's flappers, with headbands made of sequins, wrapped in purple and red feathered boas and waving strands of plastic "pop beads." Miss Dixie honked the ah-oo-gah horn every twenty feet or so and several men shouted propositions to the flappers.

The Lions Club flatbed pick up truck came next with the old school bell anchored and clanging. Several of the Lions kept it going. Anything that could make noise, any siren, any horn, any noisemaker of any kind was lifted, hauled and set off at the Labor Day parade — much to the annoyance of the Sheriff's Mounted Posse, whose palominos pranced nervously on the pavement, twisting the officers from side to side. Reins pulled back, the five horses held their heads high, watched the people wild-eyed and frequently left fat clumps of grassy horseshit in the street.

The person in charge of organizing the parade every year, Henry

Failing, owner of the Failing Butcher Shop, had never marched in a parade or he would have done something about the horses...or planned for the horses to go last. It was Gladys Ray's unfortunate duty to lead her dance troop down Main Street, performing their precision marching routine right behind the sheriff's posse. The soft black leather ballerina-type slippers kicked and stomped in the horse dung while the dancers kept their pasted smiles square on their faces. Their brave rows filed and twirled, kept their white-gloved fingers stiff as well as their lips, swirled in their short bright pink skirts and made the best of it. Gladys vowed, as she did every year, to murder Henry and display him in his own meat cooler.

The first of the log trucks turned the corner narrowly missing the Standard Oil sign. Four enormous logs were strapped to the long trailer. The tires were spotless and painted with a shiney black paint. Chrome lugnuts sent sparks of light into the applauding crowd. The yellow cab of the Weyerhaeuser Company truck was polished like a Corvette. The loggers in the cabs wore their new Oshkosh overalls and the creases still shown in their J.C. Penney plaid flannel shirts. They waved and called to their friends on the street. The truck growled in low gear and the air brakes hissed.

Another log truck followed. And another log truck. Peterson's Trucking from Raymond. Daline Transportation from Aberdeen. The two brown Kenworths of Salick Brothers Trucking from Central Park. Log trucks, common as cranberries, plied the streets and highways of Pacific and Grays Harbor counties every day, 365 days a year with no particular notice. Today they drew applause and waves from the crowd, their neighbors. Radiator grills, wheels, trailer hitches and even the logs themselves were power-washed, steam cleaned, dried, wiped and buffed. A final wipe down with Pledge sprayed on a kitchen towel was essential before entering the parade route.

Then, unexpectedly, a truck not on the program appeared, nuzzling its way in front of the mayor's convertible. Blowing its impossibly loud air horn, the uninvited truck started down Main Street. Five loggers dangled from the running boards whooping between horn blasts. Their jeans were patched and oil-stained. A thick layer of mud coated the cab of the phantom truck like icing on a store-bought cake. Clumps of dirt fell from the logs as the truck rumbled past. Black and red clay was caked to the wheels and there was so much road grime on the cab door that the identifying name was unreadable. The loggers waved their fists and cheered, thumping their filthy plaid shirts and showing off their suspenders, formerly red, now a dead blood color. The crowd stared. A paper banner stretched between the exhaust pipes above the cab read: THIS IS WHAT A REAL LOG TRUCK LOOKS LIKE!

The truck received a standing ovation all the way down Main Street. It was followed by the horrified mayor who was also South

Bend's dentist. Behind the mayor came the red Chevy longbed with Miss Oyster 1957 seated on a throne made out of a rose trellis from Jenson's Coast to Coast. Paper roses surrounded the Labor Day princess who demurely repositioned the spaghetti straps on the formal her mother had bought in Olympia. Her pink nylon net gown got the admiration of the womenfolk lining the parade route and her 36D's straining the seams got the nod from the menfolk. She waved her wrist-length lace gloves as if she were washing a large window. She smiled bravely and brushed the blond curls from her face. She was the 35th Miss Oyster, a county position of immense responsibility. She would go on to appear in the Loggers Playday parade the next week in Aberdeen and have to cut the ribbon at a car care center. She would learn to fend off the advances of councilmen and business owners. She would no longer be Debbie Grisholm; for as long as she remained in Pacific County, she would hold her title and the shopkeepers and gas station attendants and teachers and neighbors would refer to her as the Oyster Princess of 1957.

Behind the reigning 16 year old came *the* float. Pulled by the biggest Freightliner in the county, the flat trailer was draped with green indoor-outdoor carpeting and held a strange looking tree forest. Jeannie Petrie sat on a bar stool with her guitar and hooked her foot around the microphone stand to steady it. She strummed her best and leaned down into the microphone to sing. The driver tried to keep an even pace but when he didn't, Jeannie toppled on her stool and had to stand up to keep from falling over. She never lost a beat to the music though, a real trooper.

"Our Abundant Forests" read the large letters covered with aluminum foil and glued to the carpet. "VFW" read the emblem in the forest. The beaver, Joe Jenson's oldest boy, fired up the chain saw and pretended to lay waste to the largest tree limb.

The crowd gasped as the limb did actually fall. And then they noticed the cradle hanging from the two "ropes" and swaying, the baby blankets fluttering in the breeze. As the cradle "fell" the baby's head in a bonnet popped up.

"Look at *that*!" a child yelled from the crowd, pointing to the large laundry basket on the float.

"There's somebody in there!" a man said.

Two brown eyes peered over the fluffy baby blanket and blinked at the parade crowd. The hydraulics kicked in and the limb slowly righted itself, ready for another "cutting" by the willing beaver. As the cradle went up, a little fist, wrapped around a Tootsie Roll, appeared and let fly. The first piece hit Stu Jenson, Joe's brother, in the head with a "pluck!" and other pieces soon littered the sidewalk and the street. Children started to scream and broke loose from parents' grips. Scrambling boys pushed grade school girls as they raced and fought for the candy pieces. Licorice, Bit-O-Honey, hard candies, red hots and penny bubble gum sailed through the air and landed like hailstones.

"Hurrah for the VFW!" a man cheered. The children squealed and the adults applauded and waved to Jeannie and the beaver.

Alice Lindsay stood and applauded with her gloved hands, her eyes filling with proud tears.

After Stu Jenson had been hit for the third time, he said, "I don't know who that baby is, but they could sign her up for the Yankees. Jees, that kid's got an arm!"

The proud marching troop of VFW members, led by a smiling Joe Jenson, followed the float and waved happily. The Hoquiam High School band played "When The Saints Go Marchin' In" and the "Battle Hymn Of The Republic." Only three members were out of step, a record. The bicycle clowns were a hit, circling and gyrating in their uneven wheeled bicycles. The 4-H ponies were admired for their perfectly coiffed manes. And the South Bend volunteer fire truck brought up the rear.

As the parade approached the sixth and last block of Main Street the crowd was on its feet cheering wildly, the children protesting its end. The VFW color guard in the lead was now one block over and nearly parallel with the Freightliner pulling the float. One of Miss Dixie's girls had hopped out of the touring car and, feathers flying, ran up to Joe.

"It's been so much fun, Mr. Jenson, let's just go around the block and do it again! Huh, can we?" she puffed, nearly out of breath.

Joe looked at the street of scrambling children, watched little Lash Lindsay as he erupted with another fistful of penny candy, heard the air horn of the uninvited log truck and looked at the painted cheeks of the flapper in front of him.

"Sure!" he said.

So the parade went around the block and did it all again.

Chapter 50

Why should we be in such desperate haste
to succeed and in such desperate enter-
prises? If a man does not keep pace with
his companions, perhaps it is because he
hears a different drummer. Let him step to
the music which he hears, however meas-
ured or far away.
— *Henry David Thoreau*

"Travis used to say that South Bend wasn't the end of the earth, but you could *see* the end of the earth from there..." smiles Lash.

Biasi has warmed his glass by fondling it, rolling the last drop around in the bowl of the goblet. "Nothing quite like a small American town," he sighs.

"You know," says Lash, touching his cheek with his finger, "there are millions of people living in New York City; there's millions living in between the palm trees in L.A....but there's also millions living in tiny towns like South Bend. And we have heart attacks and kids on drugs and love affairs and overdue bills just like everybody else."

"So what's your point?" asks Hershell.

"Well, I suppose...that Life's gonna get ya, no matter where you go. Like somebody said, 'No matter where you go, there you are.' I go all over the place...my there is pretty soon my here. And I'm still me, carrying around the stuff I've always carried around. You know, I sometimes have the perspective that we're all on a trail. We each have a horse and saddle bags and packs on our backs and we're wandering down this trail. And then you meet up with somebody and the two of you ride along together for awhile...maybe even for a long while. But night comes and you build a camp fire and you each open your packs. Now some of us are carryin' around some rocks in our packs. I call 'em the Rocks of Negativity...stinkin' thinkin' that doesn't do us much good. Anyway, you can take a rock out and show it to your trail buddy and then maybe you leave it behind. Sometimes you take a rock out and look it over and talk about it and decide to keep it awhile longer.

"Anyhow, you load up and continue on down the trail. There are some people who like to stick to the main trail; there are others who go wander off into the thicket every chance they get. Sometimes you blaze your own trail. Side trips are always possible. You can always come back to the main trail later.

"And then a time comes when maybe your trail partner wants to go one way and you want to go another. Or maybe you just started gettin' on each other's nerves. It's possible to meet up with a partner early on and go the entire distance together, but it ain't bloody likely. Anyway, I think the thing to do is to wish 'em well, wave a good wave and keep goin' down the trail.

"And once in a blue moon, you'll meet somebody and you'll travel awhile with them and you never want it to end. But something happens. Who knows what? And it's just not possible to continue. There's a lot of pain in that. . . for me, anyhow. I finally developed the perspective that I'm going to see them again on the trail. And I don't know how or when or where. . . but we'll ride together again some day.

"I can let go after that. I can wave the good wave. I can get on down the trail.

"All this makes me less afraid to say, 'Howdy,' to a new person, a new trail or a new adventure. And meetin' you guys, we've come together. . . the five of us anyway. . . and we've come down this trail together, just this one night. The colonel opted not to go. That's his choice.

"I, for one, am glad I came. . . this has been an interesting side trip. I never thought that, under the circumstances, I could think any of you was even OK. But now that I've heard your stories. . . well, even The Wizard makes a little sense some of the time. And Chadwick, as much as I hate New York and big business, you really hit home with that Tunnel Number 4 story. Biasi, you're one wild comanche, that's for sure. And Hershell, I hope I grow up to be just like you. . . "

Lash smiles at the old man.

"Actually, I just been waitin' to grow up!" he adds, pulling himself up tall in his chair.

Biasi wears a dazzling smile. "It is interesting that we should 'meet up on the trail' like this," he says. "Quite a perspective, Lash Lindsay."

"It also means," adds Lash, "that you can choose to go down a different trail whenever you want to. . . there's lots of 'em out there."

"Lash. . . " says Chadwick, quietly, "what was it like for you to meet Travis 'on the trail'?"

Chapter 51

There's no traffic jam on the extra mile.
    — *Anonymous*

It had been dark in October for hours when he pulled Red Bessie in off Interstate 5 at the Stafford exit and into the lit Sinclair station. He eased the rig towards the diesel pump, sitting high in his chair to see over the Kenworth's nose. There wouldn't be a wait; no trucks were in sight.

He walked around the station towards where he remembered the restrooms to be. As he came around the corner he was surprised and delighted to see a grey 1940 Ford parked at the gas pumps. White-white outdoor fluorescent lights bathed the car, the pumps and the station. The car's hood was up. A figure, draped in black, leaned inside the engine compartment.

His eyes caressed the fat fenders with appreciation. The chrome glistened in the moonlight effect of the gas station floodlights. Wide whites set the coupe up, as if it were going to drive through high water soon. Baby moon wheel covers, chrome beauty rings, "Ford Deluxe" emblems on the raised hood, good rubber on the running boards. He got closer. The black figure, hidden under the shadow of the hood, wiggled cables on the engine.

"Nothin' serious, I hope. . ." he volunteered.

The cable-wiggler stopped and leaned out into the light. The white around the face, the large white collar and the black headpiece startled him: it was a nun.

Lash took a step back and removed his Stetson. "Beg your pardon, ma'm," he said.

Her glance hit him about mid-thigh and travelled northward ending with his eyelashes.

"Bless you," she said and went back under the hood.

"Nice car, sister," he offered.

"Yeah," she answered, absently. Then she sighed, the disturbed and frustrated universal sigh of car owners everywhere.

"Excuse me," she began, "the gas station guy has been no help.

Do you know anything about engines?"

Lash was still standing, hat in hand, taking in the coupe's condition. The chrome looked fairly good...the grille needed replating. The door handle hung limp as a spaniel's ear, like they always did on old Fords.

"Is the Pope a Catholic?" he answered her question. "Here, let me take a look at 'er."

The nun waved her greasy fingers in the air and he handed her a paper towel from the dispenser above the gas pump. His hand went long into his pants and pulled out a tiny flashlight. He set his Stetson on the top of the Ford and walked to the front bumper. She stood back, an apologetic look on her face.

"It started to sputter. I pulled it in here. Now it won't start. It's got fuel."

He leaned in under the hood flooding her view with his tight jeans. Like two cantaloupes pressed together with denim, his firm posterior presented itself. The muscles that stretched from his chest around his sides pulled tightly against his shirt. She closed her eyes for just an instant, mumbled "Oh, my God" and clamped her hand over her mouth. She made the sign of the cross.

"You say something?" he asked.

She had inhaled and seemed to have trouble exhaling. "No, no," she said, "nothing important."

Her eyes followed the seam in his jeans as it disappeared between his legs.

"Uh, see anything?" she asked.

The darting little light danced over the black engine. Finally he pulled his head out from under the hood. He looked her over. She stood self-consciously wadding the blue paper towel in her hands.

"You're not a real nun," he said, suspiciously. "Nuns don't drive 283 small blocks with four barrel carburetors on 'em."

"Ah, well," she began, nervously, "it's a new image for the church. We've updated things. Keep up with the times, you know?"

He leaned on the fender of the grey Ford.

"And now that I think of it...grey wasn't a stock color in 1940, either..."

Her burning cheeks scrunched around her eyes. She shrugged.

"So it's not stock."

"I'll tell you what's not stock," he teased. "You aren't."

"Yeah, well..."

She twisted the blue paper towel into a roll, trying to look anywhere but into his eyes. Finally she wadded the paper up and heaved a perfect 3-pointer into the white metal garbage drum.

"You got a good arm, Sister Fly-the-Coupe. I think you may need a fuel filter. Let's try that."

He marched off into the office of the gas station and woke the attendant, motioned to a part on a shelf, pulled bills from his wallet and returned to the Ford.

"Hold the light," he said, handing her the flashlight.

He unclipped his key ring from a loop on his jeans, opened his pocket knife to the screwdriver end and leaned inside the engine compartment. She leaned in with him to put the little light where he was working. He loosened two hose clamps. The powerful little light in her hand lit a good deal of the engine and reflected up into his face. The shadows of his eyelashes made giant black fans on his face. She stared.

"Excuse me," he said, "the light...."

"Oh! Sorry..."

He fiddled with the clamps on the gas filter.

"You going to tell me what you're up to tonight?" he asked, never taking his eyes of his work.

"What, are you from Mars or something? Don't you know what day it is? Tonight's Halloween. I'm on my way to a party."

"I'm a trucker. We don't know about holidays. So is this your husband's car?"

"It's *my* car! I bought it myself a couple of years ago!"

"You restore it yourself?"

"No, it was like this when I got it."

"What possessed you to buy a '40 Ford?"

"A car is a necessary evil. Well, just like now, you gotta have a car but sometimes they're a pain in the ass...tires, insurance and all. So I figured if you're going to have to have a car, it might as well be a fun one, something a little different...with some style. Anyway, this is the first break down I've had with it. Ran like a Swiss watch until tonight."

"There," he said. "Get in and fire it up."

She handed him the flashlight, opened the driver's door, slid in under the steering wheel and started the car. The tenor rumble was instant. He slammed the engine hood and clamped the chrome clamp on the nose. He stepped around the car and shut the car door for her.

"Well, I guess that's it!" he said, cheerfully.

She put one hand on the car door. She watched as he put his Stetson on. "I don't want that to be it..." she said. Then she looked at her lap, embarrassed.

"That's my rig over there," he said, pointing to the nose of Red Bessie.

"Come to the party!" she said.

"I don't have a costume."

"Sure, you do. Bring your truck and come as a trucker."

He tilted his hat back on his head and bent his knees to look in through her window. Only a five inch square of her face was visible to him.

"What color is your hair?" he asked, slowly.

"Suppose," she teased, "that you just 'get in the habit' of finding out for yourself.''

The empty trailer on the back of the Kenworth had a ramp. He set the ramp out, drove the Ford into the trailer, fueled the tanks, helped her up into the cab, paid the astonished gas station attendant and pulled Red Bessie into gear.

"Where to?''

"Right down this road,'' she pointed.

He went through the gears and Red Bessie started to hum.

"You really had me going there for awhile...in that outfit,'' he finally said, a big smile on his face.

"I tried celibacy once, you know,'' he offered. "Worst 25 minutes of my life.''

"Celibacy,'' she answered, "is a matter of time.''

"What are you talking about? You mean it's only a matter of time before you're celibate?''

"No, no, no,'' she flapped, "I mean that the definition of celibacy is really hinged on the aspect of time.''

"Why do I get the feeling that we're both talkin' about something that neither one of us knows anything about...?''

Undeterred, she continued, "Look, if I say I've been celibate for a year, do you agree and say, 'yes, you're celibate'?''

She waved her fingers indicating that she wanted no verbal response from him.

"Or if I say that I've been celibate for 20 minutes...you'd laugh and think, 'That's not celibacy.' So when *is* it celibacy? Two weeks? One month? Six months? How long do you live without sex before someone says 'Yep, you're celibate, all right'?''

"You're making me nervous, Sister Fly-the-Coupe.''

"Yeah, well, so many things are determined not by their condition but by how long the condition exists. If you sneeze, it's a sneeze. But if you keep sneezing, it's an allergy. Celibacy is not so much a state as it is an amount of time. And the amount of time varies from person to person and the definition changes. For instance, you'd have to be celibate 20 years for my mom to say you're celibate.''

"There's a reason that you're here instead of your mother...''

"And promiscuity — that's *another* thing that's not really a condition as much as it is an *amount*. Ever think about that? I mean, what is promiscuous? Three sex partners in a lifetime? Three in a week? Three all at once?''

"Lady, you're embarrassing me, I thought you'd like to know that.''

"Well, some words are judgement calls, you know?''

"So what do you do for a living...write dictionaries?''

Passing headlights would momentarily fill the inside of the truck with light and he could see her eyes spark as she explained her thoughts.

"You like definin' things so much, I've got a word for you..."

She folded her hands in her lap, pretended to look composed and gently focused on him. If halos were possible, one would have fit on her head just then.

"How about 'love'?" he suggested.

"How *about* love!" she raged, instantly finding a soap box.

He winced, looking back to the road.

" 'I'll be true forever...I love you,' " she quoted. " 'I love you so much I would move mountains for you. Swim oceans for you. I love you so much, I would die for you!' "

Her hands made two little fists.

"Yeah, but would you take the garbage out every Tuesday morning? Would you hang the toilet paper on the roll the way I like? Forget oceans! Would you love me enough to let me be a vegetarian without making jokes about what I eat? Would you mind if I wore my jeans *inside* my cowboy boots like a city slicker? Would you let me play the sound tracks from 'Camelot' and 'West Side Story'? Would you get upset if I used your razor? FUCK LOVE! HOW ABOUT A LITTLE *TOLERANCE*?"

The ride was bumpy without much of a load on. They bounced in the truck seats, despite the seatbelts.

"Well," he said, "I don't own a razor...and I loved ya enough to fix your fuel filter."

Chapter 52

We can see the stars and still not see the light.

— Eagles

"**I** took second place at the Halloween party that night," reminisces Lash. "Got a bottle of brandy as a prize for just showin' up as myself. I think it was my extra prop that did it...Red Bessie. And you know, if I hadn't looked inside that Ford, I never in this world would have figured out that she wasn't a nun. It was a very convincing costume."

"Travis was a very convincing lady," says Chadwick.

Lash stands and begins to make his way to the men's room. "Travis said something else I haven't ever forgotten..." he drawls. "It went something like this... 'Do not mistake trust for control.' People say, 'I can't trust you' when what they really mean is, 'I can't control you.' Or, 'I can't live with someone I can't trust' when it is more accurately, 'I can't live with someone I can't control.' She was talking about parents when she told me all this, but I always thought it was a good observation about people, no matter what the relationship."

He turns, takes a few steps, stops and turns back to the Fraternity. "I made an effort to pick up on all the waybills for Portland, Oregon," he says, a little shyly. "Sweet God in heaven, I'd give my Mack truck just to hold her in my arms again."

"Easy enough for you to say," observes Hershell, "since your Mack is in pieces all over Skamokawa!"

Chapter 53

The person who is never wrong is the
person who never risks or decides.
— Anonymous

"Gentlemen," begins Biasi, "I don't know about the rest of you but I have breathed the same air long enough. I need to get outside, walk around, do some thinking on my own now."

The Wizard rubs his eyes and scratches his thinning hair. "I'm sure all the clues are here," he says. "Now all we have to do is make some sense of it."

Biasi stretches, his hands gripping his back. "I am dog-tired," he says, "and I feel about as dumb as a dog right now, too."

"Hey, dogs ain't dumb," says Lash. "Ever see one get up early to go to work? I'm gonna go walk around this place and see what's here. How 'bout you, Hershell?"

"I think I'll just go sit on the porch. I have a tendency to walk off cliffs in the dark."

"How 'bout you, Chadwick?"

"I think I can think better in here, thanks."

"You won't mind if we leave the front door open to air out the place, then?" needles Hershell.

Chadwick waves and goes back to his notes.

Biasi leaves the foyer, presses open the hefty oak door, rubs his hands appreciatively over the wood finish and steps across the portico. Hands in his pockets, shoulders braced against the cool October morning air, he walks to the fenceline and looks out across the city of Portland. The river is blue-black and waving trees cause the city lights to seem to twinkle. He leans on the fence and holds his head, studying the cranes far below working in the ship repair yard.

"Travis, damn you," he says aloud, "I really need that money, sweetheart. You would force me to *think* to get it, wouldn't you...?"

The Wizard crosses the portico and once his eyes adjust to the darkness, he takes the asphalt path that leads to a park bench and the scenic overlook. He strolls carefully along the path, feeling the coolness around him, the damp early morning breeze chilling him. More than 180 degrees of the Willamette River is visible from the overlook. The Wizard takes it all in, a stirring wind pulling his hair from his ponytail. He holds his hands out, stretches his long skinny arms and leans his head back as if to release something inside himself. He holds the pose, open and vulnerable.

Lash has walked to the parking lot and he stands by his Kenworth. He absent mindedly kicks the 44 inch tall tires and checks the hood latches. He bends to touch the fat chrome lugnuts; they're all secure. "I don't know why I came out here to see you," he says softly to Red Bessie.

"Yes, I do," he corrects himself. "You're my comfort zone. You make sense to me. And *you* knew Travis. What on earth do we have in common with these guys...other than the fact that we're all just a tad nuts. But just a tad. What did Travis have in mind when she put this together? What's her point?"

Hershell pulls a candy bar from the pocket of his swaying palm trees and sits on the stone porch to tear the paper wrapper. He whistles the melody to "You're An Old Smoothie" while he inhales the aroma of chocolate and pine trees. He nods his head in time to his music, his eyebrows orchestrating. Suddenly he stops whistling and snaps his fingers.

Chadwick places five sheets of paper in a row across his end of the Pittock's dining table. He arranges them, then rearranges them. He begins to take more notes on a fresh sheet of paper. He sketches lines and begins grouping and cataloguing his facts. He glances at his Rolex and writes quickly. Once he stops to rub his chin thoughtfully, feeling a very slight morning stubble. He winces. He strokes his face. "A hundred bucks for a shave and a hot shower right now," he says aloud.

Chapter 54

Cabbage, n. A familiar kitchen-garden vegetable about as large and wise as a man's head.

— Ambrose Bierce

The Scripto inky blue sky lightens to indigo. The outline of Mount Hood is visible to the east, a pink halo registering to her left. A tan Budget Rent-A-Car appears in the Pittock Mansion driveway, rounding a corner and parking near the truck. Col. Williams steps out of the car and locks it. He gives a tug to his uniform jacket and starts towards the mansion when he is startled by a greeting.

"Good morning, Colonel."

Lash, arms folded, leans on the truck's fender, his cowboy hat squarely on his head. Lash straightens and extends his hand.

"Lash Lindsay, if you recall from last night?"

Col. Bobby Williams grasps the handshake and nods, the shiney leather bill of his cap catching the impending pink sunrise of Mount Hood.

"Yes. Been here all night, have you?" asks the colonel, slightly uncomfortable.

"Yep, all night long. My eyes are anxious to see the inside of my eyelids, that's for sure."

Col. Williams has jammed his hands deep into his pockets.

"Yeah, me too. It's been a night," he comments. "This your truck?"

"Yessir. Mine and the bank's."

The colonel leans down towards Lash.

"Aren't you kind of small to be a trucker?"

"I drive it, I don't have to lift it," replies Lash, turning on his heel and walking towards the Pittock.

Biasi joins Lash under the portico and wraps his big bear arm around the little cowboy-trucker.

"Ya got it all figured out, Mr. Lindsay?" asks Biasi, great cheer in his voice.

"Boy, I don't know, Mr. Biasi," says Lash shaking his head.

"Hershell, how 'bout you?" Biasi greets the old man. Lash extends a hand to help him stand up. Hershell rearranges his palm trees and spies the colonel.

"Well, look what the cat dragged in..." he says.

Col. Williams gives a little salute to Hershell and nods to Biasi.

" 'Mornin', Colonel," says Biasi, dropping his hold on Lash's shoulders and extending his hand. The colonel politely shakes Biasi's hand and waits to see if Hershell also wants a handshake. Hershell folds his arms.

The Wizard appears on the path to the portico, his arms wrapped tightly around him. "Brrrrrr," he says, "even my goose bumps have goose bumps. Oh, it's the colonel...we'd about forgotten about you."

The Wizard floats past, his caftan dragging on the stairs. Lash looks towards Mount Hood and watches the pink turning to white-yellow.

"It'll be dawn soon," he says.

They follow The Wizard through the oak door and across the foyer into the dining room. Biasi returns to his place next to Chadwick. Hershell stands next to him. The Wizard and Lash go around the table to Chadwick's right. When the colonel enters the room, the Fraternity is gathered on one side of the table. They are all standing, except Chadwick who still sits with his pages.

An uncomfortable silence happens. The colonel removes his hat and tosses it gently in his hands. The Fraternity watches him; no one speaks. The colonel holds his hands out as if to explain something but no words come from his mouth. He strokes his short blond hair with one hand.

"I know," says Biasi, finally, "this night has hardly been 'regulation.' "

The colonel takes a step forward.

"Is there any coffee?" he asks.

"It should be about the consistency of maple syrup by now," comments Lash, "in other words, just the way I like it."

Lash, nearest the coffee pot, begins to pour cups. "Come on, guys, it won't hurt to be nice to the guy. What have we got to lose?"

Hershell growls a low growl.

"Mellow *out*!" Lash mimics. "I believe that was your own advice...?"

Hershell takes his coffee cup, spills most of it and sits in his position next to Biasi. He rifles through the bags on the dining room table. A Corn Nut rolls out and he picks it up and pops it into his mouth. He checks the other bags; all empty.

"Chadwick, where are those Wheat Thins?" he demands.

"Not on your tin-type!" says Chadwick. "You're the Imelda

Marcos of Junk Food.''

"Come on, man,'' encourages Biasi. "Where are they?''

"No.''

"Just a lousy handful of Wheat Thins, Chadwick, for Chrissake!'' says Lash.

"No!''

"Here they are!'' yells The Wizard, pulling the box of Wheat Thins from a grocery bag under the table. Chadwick reaches for the box. The Wizard throws the Wheat Thins to Biasi. Chadwick reaches to his left. Biasi pulls back with the box.

"Go out for a long one,'' he hollers to Lash.

Lash lopes across the dining room as the box of Wheat Thins clears the chandelier and lands cradled in his arms.

"Come on now!'' protests Chadwick.

Lash opens the box, hands 20 or so crackers to Hershell and then throws a dozen at Chadwick. The Wizard and Biasi jump at the table, scarfing up little square Wheat Thins. Chadwick gets two of them for himself.

"That'll teach you to *share*,'' admonishes Biasi to Chadwick, as they all munch.

The colonel, not included in the sport, stands an outsider. Lash, still clutching the captured box, holds it out to Bobby Williams.

"Wheat Thin, Colonel?''

The military man looks at the trucker for a moment. He doesn't know why the Wheat Thins are important.

"It's OK, they're not poisoned,'' encourages Lash. He shakes the box towards the colonel as if he is encouraging a wild animal to come to him.

"Thank you...and why don't we just make it Bobby, instead of Col. Williams.''

"OK, Bobby,'' Lash says. He turns to the group. "Hey, guys, this here is *Bobby*.''

"I'd...I'd like to talk to ya'll for a bit before the attorney gets here...'' starts Bobby Williams.

"Well, will wonders never cease,'' Biasi barely whispers to Hershell. Lash and The Wizard take their seats. Chadwick flips a page on his paper pad. Hershell settles back.

"This isn't easy for me,'' Bobby says, looking down at his hat.

"Well, why don't you sit down and just start somewhere,'' says Hershell, merrily. "Get the man a cup of coffee.''

The Wizard hands the colonel a cup. Bobby takes George Sam's place.

"Take your jacket off and get comfortable, Bobby,'' encourages Biasi. "It wasn't easy for any of us, man, but here it is...morning... and we're all still alive...''

"I'm sure you've spent a better night than I have,'' says Bobby.

"Don't count on it," comments The Wizard. "None of us came to any agreement about anything."

"Yeah, we did!" corrects Lash.

"What!?" asks Hershell.

Lash turns to the colonel as he is hanging his jacket on the back of a chair. "We all agreed," says Lash, "that whoever wins the money will go back down to the Kash 'n' Karry on Burnside and buy Rhonda her very own wrestler."

"Oh, yeah! Oh, yeah!" they all cheer.

"Looks like I missed quite a party," grins Bobby.

"This is nothin' compared to the party I'm gonna throw when I get my hands on all that money!" beams Lash.

"On *my* money, you mean," adds Chadwick.

"Nope," says Hershell, a Cheshire cat smile on his face.

"Quiet, quiet!" asks The Wizard. "Let's hear what the colonel... er, Bobby...has to say!"

"Give me my goddamed Wheat Thins!" demands Chadwick.

Lash tosses the box to him.

"OK, now start," says Chadwick.

The colonel, looking less militant in his plain shirt sans rank, takes a deep breath and lets it out in puffs.

"I realize that I don't owe any of you any sort of explanation," he begins, "but I'd like to explain...some...things."

He sees the melted wax on the table cloth, the empty beer cans, chip bag wrappers, apple cores, cigarette butts, fallen glasses and half of a head of cabbage.

"Looks like my old fraternity house in here!"

"Yeah, well, that's what it is. We're a fraternity," explains Biasi. "Jees, it does look like Dinner From Hell, doesn't it?"

Biasi looks back at the colonel. "Yes?"

Bobby sips the strong, hot coffee and winces.

"My story wouldn't have done you any good, even if I could have shared it with you. Please..." He holds up his hand.

"I haven't seen Travis Duncan in fifteen years. That's an awfully long time ago. Can you remember anything about your life and what it was like fifteen years ago? Names like Phu Cat, Qui Nhon and Phnom Penh were in the news. I was a 27-year old captain stationed at Fort Benning, Georgia when I met Travis. She was working part-time at the officers' club and working part-time for political interests like the McCarthy campaign."

"What?" asks Biasi.

"That's right. She was working both sides of the street, so to speak. I remember when she was stopped at the front gate for having a peace symbol stuck on her windshield."

"Travis wasn't political," comments The Wizard, scratching his head.

"Travis wanted to know things," continues the colonel. "She wasn't on output, she was on input. She listened. To everything. She thought that she owed it to herself or someone...who knows?...to have an open mind about *everything*, everybody and everybody's idea and opinion.

"Well, bullshit on that! That was my thoughts at the time... except when she was listening to my opinion, of course. That was her magic. She used to listen real hard. She paid so much attention to what I was saying that, of course, I...was...interested in her. Nobody no where and not since has ever listened to me like Travis did. I don't know what she found so damned interesting..."

His memory becomes so vivid that his speaking slows. His fingers play with the edges of the Wheat Thins.

"Eat some Wheat Thins," encourages Hershell. "Chadwick swears by 'em. Says they'll make you remember Travis..."

Bobby WIlliams drops the crackers.

"I don't want to remember Travis," he says.

Hershell looks over his shoulder at Biasi and Chadwick.

Bobby drinks more coffee.

"I took Travis to Viet Nam with me," he says.

"Say, what?" exclaims The Wizard.

"I mean, in my mind," says the colonel, anger rising in his voice. "For eleven months, three weeks and five days. And she was with me every minute. Helicopters, supply boats, flooded tents, ammo clips, her face is indelibly etched in all of it for me. I was terrified. Your mind will do anything when it's truly terrified. I kept my sanity by talking to Travis. It was the only thing that got me through. I swear, I could pass a lie detector test saying that she was actually there with me. To me, she really was.

"So you see, for me to remember Travis, I have to remember Viet Nam. Not just Viet Nam in general, the way most Americans remember it, but I get to remember it in detail, like I lived it. Well, I don't want to remember.

"Travis was special. What I had with Travis was special. There was nothing that happened with Travis that wasn't special. And unbeknownst to her, her face and her voice got imprinted on some stuff of mine that's going to remain buried. No amount of money can get me to dredge it up either."

Bobby Williams stares into his coffee cup, then drinks. He looks up at the Fraternity. They are completely still, riveted on his commentary.

"So I just wanted you guys to know..." says Bobby, a little lighter now, "that I didn't mean anything personal by the way I acted last night. It's not you. It's me. I knew I was going to have trouble with this the minute I got the letter from the attorney. Seeing her name typed on that letter...just seeing her name again...set me off."

He rolls the small cabbage head towards himself and begins pitching it in the air like a softball.

"Ordinarily, I'm just a regular guy doing my job and serving my country. Looks like ya'll had a pretty interesting time here last night. I wish I could have stayed...but I couldn't.''

The other five exchange sympathetic and uncomfortable glances. The colonel stands, still tossing the cabbage. "Volleyball, anyone?'' he asks.

"Sure!'' says Chadwick, dropping his pen.

Bobby Williams sets up the cabbage by tossing it flathanded into the air. As it begins to come down he swats it. The pale green vegetable sails within inches of the chandelier and Chadwick is under it in an instant.

"Set up, Biasi!'' he shouts, bouncing the cabbage toward the architect in an easy lob.

Biasi hits the cabbage underhanded. It narrowly misses Hershell's head and Lash pops it back across the table. He is on his feet, joining Bobby's team. Chadwick hits the thing hard and the cabbage blasts into The Wizard's space. He hits it with his open forearms and sends it flipping through the air, losing a leaf as it comes down in Hershell's lap.

"All right, you guys!'' yells Hershell, on his feet. "You're playing my game!'' He sets up the cabbage and spikes it to Chadwick. Chadwick takes two fists and pummells the vegetable again in The Wizard's direction.

"Set it up!'' cheers Lash and The Wizard does an easy lob in Bobby's direction.

"Good one!'' says Bobby. "Here it comes, Lash!''

Lash has the third hit. He jumps and hammers the cabbage in Biasi's space. It hits the floor with a splat.

"Our point!'' says Bobby.

"We need some rules here,'' says Chadwick, picking up the cabbage.

"Oh, jeez, you and your rules,'' whines Hershell.

"The chandelier is out of bounds,'' announces Chadwick. "You lose a point if you hit the chandelier.''

He tosses the vegetable upward and openfists it across the table.

"Set it up! Set it up!''

The Wizard is under the falling cabbage and lifts it in the air in Lash's direction.

"OK, Bobby, it's all yours!'' says Lash, making an easy set.

Col. Williams blasts the cabbage with two fists, it rockets through the air past Biasi's outstretched arms just as George Sam and Timothy walk through the door.

Chapter 55

*A man is about as happy as he makes up
his mind to be.*
                        — *Abraham Lincoln*

"**Y**ou guys are friends of Travis Duncan," says Timothy,
eyeing the flattened cabbage on the floor. "Now how
did I know that?"

He walks briskly to the head of the table and pulls his chair out. He
reviews the table, once pristine with formal china.

"Looks like the place has been decorated by her too, I see," he
comments.

George Sam turns his head to keep from snickering.

Like guilty choir boys caught sipping the sacristy wine, the six are
quiet and obediently find their chairs and sit down. George Sam clears a
place on the table for his brief case.

"Good morning," says George Sam to the Fraternity.

"Now that depends entirely on you, doesn't it?" suggests Hershell.

George Sam pulls a file folder and closes his case.

"Now I see where she got it . . ." he smiles at the group.

Timothy is dressed in a severe black suit, white shirt and dark tie.
He appears to be dressed for a funeral, and it *is* a funeral of sorts for
him. He will be witnessing the departure of Travis Duncan's money into
another world. He is in a state of profound grief and he has no humor.
He is prepared to mourn.

"Gentlemen, we won't take much more time. I'm sure you're anxious," says George Sam. "All you have to do is to write your supposition on a piece of paper. One guess per participant, that's all that is allowed. If you make more than one guess, you will be disqualified.
Please write clearly. Again, the question before you is: what do you all
have in common?"

Timothy scowls. He mouths the words "all pigs" but he doesn't
really speak. George Sam hands out pads of paper. They pass them,
bucket brigade-style, around the table.

Chadwick gets fresh paper and immediately begins to write. Biasi takes his page and taps it with his pen. He looks at Hershell. The old man is slowly scripting a guess. Lash looks at Biasi and shrugs. Bobby Williams sighs as he picks up his pen. The Wizard bites his lip, staring at the blank sheet.

"Names on paper," adds George Sam.

Everyone writes. There is quiet. The foyer clock very softly chimes seven.

Lash gets an inspirational glint in his eye and he scribbles on his page, "We're all great lovers." He looks up and through the chandelier he sees The Wizard. Then he makes pen strokes over "great lovers" and he sighs a worried sigh. Everyone else is writing. Lash writes and folds his page.

"Hand 'em in, gentlemen, it's that simple."

"Yeah, well, when do we get to know?" asks Biasi.

"Patience, Mr. Biasi," says Timothy.

"Easy for you to say," protests the architect, "you're not the one waiting at the dock for your ship to come in!"

George Sam lifts his right index finger and speaks softly, "Hell hath no fury like a woman mourned."

Six sheets of paper, each folded, sit before the attorney.

"I will read each answer," says George Sam, "and then I will read the final pages of instruction from Travis Duncan's last will."

The Wizard closes his eyes and bites his lip harder. Chadwick's jaw muscles work back and forth like pistons. Biasi rubs his forehead until his skin turns red.

" 'Lash Lindsay,' " reads George Sam. " 'We're all *honest*.' " Five surprised pairs of eyes look to Lash.

"Calls 'em like I sees 'em," shrugs Lash.

George Sam puts the sheet down and picks up another.

" 'Colonel Bobby Williams: we were all *lessons*; she was on the 'road to find out' and we were sign posts.' "

Hershell's eyebrows go up. "That's a good one," he says.

" 'The Wizard: we're all *philosophers*,' " reads George Sam.

Lash looks warmly at The Wizard. "Yeah?" he asks. "Yeah," The Wizard responds.

" 'Holbrook Biasi: we're all *good at what we do*.' "

Timothy's eyes widen with new respect. This is not what he expected.

George Sam picks up the fifth sheet. " 'Chadwick Ollander: we are all *lone stars*.' "

Heads turn to Chadwick. "You mean after all that analysis, that's what you came up with?" gasps Biasi.

George Sam picks up the last sheet.

"What if nobody guesses correctly?" asks Bobby Williams.

"Then," says Timothy, nastily, "none of you gets the money. It goes to the scholarship fund."

There's not a breath, not a heartbeat, not a quiver in the dining room. George Sam holds the last sheet.

" 'Hershell Kaye,' " he reads. He looks up from the paper. They are all leaning slightly towards the attorney.

" 'We've all had the *courage to run our own race*.' "

Chapter 56

We live our lives in chains and never
realize we have the key.

— *Eagles*

Gale force winds blew in off the Oregon coast and rattled the shutters on the cabin at Neskowin. A pot full of geraniums flipped off the deck railing and landed in the sand. Travis Duncan watched the flowers leap to their death and said, "Damn."

Some Oregonians make a special effort to get to the beach just for the coastal storms. Travis wasn't one of them! The grey sea pitched and churned outside her picture window; it roared incessantly and threw logs, styrofoam floats, plastic bottles and kelp onto the sand. The sky was grey and white from north to south, not the slightest indication that it would ever be blue again.

Travis stood safely behind the bending glass watching the ocean's terrible fit. There was an eight quart plastic bowl in her arms, full of fresh, hot popcorn. Travis sighed and stared and aimlessly threw popcorn towards her mouth. Salt crumbs dotted her flannel shirt. A typewriter was nearby on a table, its inserted and blank sheet waving at Travis like a mocking, teasing tongue. She looked at the typewriter, its little black keys anxiously waiting to be tickled and she wished she could be the pot of geraniums.

"OK, here goes," she said aloud.

She padded over the the chair next to the typewriter, her grey wool socks catching minute splinters off the wood floor. She sat down, arched her back, sighed and picked up the hand cuffs. One cuff was already firmly attached to the typewriter. She snapped the other onto her left wrist. Engraving on the stainless steel cuff read: Property Oregon State Penitentiary.

"In order to write this, I have to presume that I am mortal. I am, of course, immortal as we all believe that we are," she typed.

"Just in case I'm wrong, which will be the first time this year, I will finish the instructions for the distribution of my estate.

"Why did I do it this way? You may be asking yourselves this question. Because, I'm rich, that's why...if I'd been poor or even moderately wealthy, you wouldn't have come.

"I can't be precisely sure who is there, listening to George Sam read this to you. But I can hazard a guess.

"And hazarding guesses is what you've all been doing. And to what purpose? I'll tell you: I wanted to set up the *possibility* that you might, by meeting each other, learn something.

"Now, learning is an interesting activity since it depends primarily on the learner and rarely on the teacher. I can't teach you anything... not because you're stubborn, although you are, but because learning does not occur that way.

"Having spent most of my life as a Student of the Universe, an activity I may retire from at any time...it is not a particularly comfortable past-time...I have learned lessons from you all. You were my teachers. Since you were ignorant of this at the time, it made teaching easy for you and learning delightful for me.

"Knowing, as I do know, that you can't teach anybody anything, I just wanted to set up the *possibility* that it may occur among you. The lessons I learned from you (plural) were not just important, they were critical. A miracle could happen and you might actually share these lessons with each other. What better legacy could I leave you? More valuable than the money, I leave you each other."

Travis' right hand dipped into the popcorn. She looked out at the pewter sea and watched a Clorox bottle roll down the beach. The picture window bent under the strain of the wind. She shivered and rolled the sleeves down on her flannel shirt.

"Did anyone make the guess that you are all obnoxious assholes?" she typed. "Because it takes that quality to find your own way and have a good life.

"I asked you to look for what you have in common. I suspect that when people look at their common points instead of their differences, magic can happen. What do *you* all have in common? Damned if I know...

"The directions state that the person who answers the question correctly, would win. So if you guessed something, you must be right. If you think you have something in common, you do.

"So here's the deal:

If you showed up for dinner,

and if you met the others,

and if you did hazard a guess *in writing,*

then the monetary portion of my estate shall be divided equally among those in attendance. Follow your bliss, boys. And remember, money is like manure, it doesn't do any good unless it's spread around.

"In the meantime, I will make every effort to spend every last dime myself."

Chapter 57

*The bond that links your true family is not
one of blood, but of respect and joy in
each other's life. Rarely do members of
one family grow up under the same roof.*
— *Richard Bach*

Biasi picked Chadwick up and threw both him and his box of
Wheat Thins in the air.

"So how much is it?" Lash shouts over the celebrating fraternity.

Timothy and Chadwick chime together: "Three million, eight hundred thirty three thousand, three hundred thirty three dollars and thirty three cents!"

The Wizard's fists are in the air and he dances like a Super Bowl quarterback in the end zone. Tears run down Hershell's face as he laughs and laughs. Lash and Bobby Williams hug each other and dance.

"You were right about the lessons, Bobby!"

Biasi lobs the cabbage across the room. Timothy ducks to avoid it. Biasi screams and stamps his feet on the floor. Chadwick falls back into his chair, his tie pulled from its knot.

"Well, it's not twenty three million, but it will do. It will do nicely. Do you realize that if the other three guys had been here, it would have cost each of us a million bucks?"

"Chadwick," says Hershell, wearily, "you are a blood-sucking, materialistic bastard."

"Thank you," says Chadwick.

Amidst the shouting and laughing and stomping and pounding, George Sam quietly hands Timothy an envelope.

"I don't know what this is, Timothy, but Travis wanted me to give it to you."

Timothy's eyebrows come together and he scowls slightly. He takes the white business envelope from the attorney's hand. He can feel a stiff weight through the paper.

"Excuse me, gentlemen!" he announces loudly. "The bank is prepared to cut checks today after one o'clock. Here is my card with the address of the downtown branch headquarters office. You are expected. Identification will be required. Eighth floor, estate department.''

Timothy sets several business cards on the dining room table as he stands to leave. He walks to a corner of the room and rips the flap of the envelope. A key falls and tinkles on the wood floor. Timothy reads to himself:

"Dear Timothy, my financial Archangel, the Bulldog of My Bucks, Mr. Stress, my dear friend, Timothy. Here is a key. It fits a locker at Portland International Airport. Inside you will find $1,000,000 in currency — cold, hard American cash, Timothy, and it's all yours tax free. You may wonder where this money came from since you kept such close tabs on things from the very start of the Cuban inheritance. What you didn't know was that I had my own money, stowed away before I believed in banks and banking. This million is my own and not recorded anywhere. I knew you'd miss taking care of the money so I've decided to give you this for your own. Love, Travis.''

Timothy's arms quiver and he looks up from the page, an iridescent glow coming from his cheeks. His eyes are glassy and he doesn't breathe.

George Sam has shut and locked his briefcase and he prepares to leave. He passes by Timothy and says, "See you down at the bank later, eh?'' In the background, the Fraternity still screams and dances.

Timothy stares into space. Then a very slight smile comes to his face.

"I won't be going into the office today,'' he says.

Chapter 58

The secret is: There is no secret.
                                    — Zen quote

Chadwick executes a perfect cartwheel over the little hedge hugging the Pittock's lawn. He lands on his wing tips and then does a Spud Web, leaping three feet in the air, slamdunking his fist.

The Wizard waves his fingers and dances folk-style while singing "Happy Days Are Here Again." He pirouettes off the porch, the yards of fabric making a loose and victorious flag.

Three million dollars has just taken 20 years off of Hershell Kaye, who does a good George Burns tap dance on the asphalt.

Col. Bobby Williams loosens his tie, stretches an alleluia to the Oregon sunrise and sighs, shaking his head.

Biasi and Lash are already in the parking lot near Red Bessie. Lash tosses his keys to the architect. Biasi looks in his hand, the Caterpillar key fob staring back at him.

"Go on, Biasi. Hop in the driver's seat and I'll show you what driving real power is. Once you drive this KW, you'll never be able to drive that Jaguar quite the same again."

Biasi hesitates, awed by the offer.

"Now where's your guts?"

Biasi looks at the white Jaguar sitting directly behind the Kenworth which looms above them as big as a building.

"I could stand to say 'good-bye' to part of my ego. . ." says Biasi.

The two crawl up into the truck while the others stop to watch. The body of the truck shakes when the engine springs to life with a great growl. The morning sun ignites the gold leaf in the pinstriping.

Lash makes sure Biasi understands the air brakes and the gears.

"This steering wheel is bigger than the tires on my car," says Biasi. "This is reverse, right here, you're sure?"

"Is a frog's asshole watertight? Of course, I'm sure. I live in this truck!"

"OK," says Biasi, checking the outside mirror.

"Now there's about 120 pounds built up in the brakes, you can put it in gear now," instructs Lash. He waves to the others from his perch in the passenger's seat.

Biasi taps the accelerator twice and Red Bessie snores like a dragon. "This is reverse?" he asks again.

"Goddamnit, yes," says Lash.

The big tires move slightly. Then Biasi puts his size 13 foot in it and pops the clutch. Lash flops forward into the windshield and then flips back into the seat. The Kenworth hits the Jaguar as Biasi watches in the wide side mirror. He holds his foot to the accelerator and his right hand turns white gripping the stick shift. The huge back tires of the Kenworth climb the frame of the dwarfed white car. It sounds like a hardware store being thrown into a garbage disposal. Hubcaps pop and fly off the tires of the Jaguar as it flattens under the rolling pin power of the truck.

Biasi pulls the truck into first gear and rolls it off the squashed car. He grins as he checks his view in the mirror. The Fraternity stands in white horror at the edge of the parking lot.

"And you all thought *I* was nuts," says The Wizard.

Lash has all the air taken from his chest. He has been pressed into his seat and his grey Stetson rolls around on the floor of the cab. His beautiful brown eyes are ringed with terror.

"You're right, Lash," says Biasi, shrugging. "You said that once I drove this Kenworth, I'd never be able to drive that Jaguar again...!"

Lash's voice comes out like a cartoon mouse. "What the hell did you do that for? Have you lost your mind?"

"I've never been more sane. I've never trusted anybody enough to even let another soul drive that stupid Jaguar. And you hand me the keys to...not just your rig...but to your livelihood. That Jag meant a lot to me...meant a lot of stuff that I don't want right now. If there's any damage to your truck, I'll pay..."

"There ain't no damage to the *truck*!" says Lash, looking into his side mirror at the Jaguar, its doors flung open like a dead bird.

"Lash!" calls Chadwick. "You may be a good driver, but you probably shouldn't try to find work as a driving instructor!"

Lash glares at Biasi and picks his hat up.

"Biasi, get out of that seat before I start wantin' to use you for a mudflap."

"I suppose this means," says Biasi, sweetly, "that I'm buying breakfast?"

EPILOGUE

Chadwick Ollander started a new business, the New York Super Sausage Company, "when ordinary sausage won't do," gained fifty pounds and married the star of a Times Square nightclub review. They had seven children all after he was 50 years old.

Holbrook Biasi went immediately into an alcohol treatment center and remained sober the rest of his life, which he spent hand building ("without the use of power tools") a house of his own in the mountainous area of the Columbia River Gorge ("where the people are spoiled, not the environment").

Hershell Kaye bought a pink Cadillac convertible (with emblems) and added an Olympic-sized swimming pool, a bath house with sauna, a new snack bar, a 6-room motel, a Kash 'n' Karry, a 9-hole golf course, and horseshoe pits to his Phoenix, Arizona nudist resort.

Lash Lindsay became the mayor of South Bend, Washington where he put together a joint venture with Weyerhaeuser, the Port of Willapa and Japanese timber interests for the dredging of Willapa Bay. He married the daughter of Miss Dixie and had one child, a daughter named Travis, who became the first granddaughter of a Miss Oyster to also hold the title. Red Bessie, dressed in crepe paper and balloons, was driven once a year on Labor Day.

Colonel Bobby Williams left the military, received his Ph.D. in psychology, specializing in the treatment of post traumatic stress syndrome. He and The Wizard co-founded a retreat center in Dufur, Oregon where The Wizard was particularly effective in developing a program for burned out female executives. He finished his work on creating a mind-altering language which was published and won him a nomination for the Nobel Peace Prize.

George Sam became the proud and lifelong owner of the red deuce roadster, the 1940 Ford coupe and the 1937 Packard sedan.

Timothy Anzil was never heard from again.

"If you don't like my book, write your own. Find a book you do like. If you like my novel, I commend your good taste."
--Rita Mae Brown

"Ditto."
--Alyce

ABOUT THE AUTHOR

Procrastinator's Success Kit
Teamwork & Team Sabotage
Take Your Hands Off My Attitude!
Alyce's FAT CHANCE
Why Winners Win
I Don't Have To & You Can't Make Me!

Alyce Cornyn-Selby

Dr. Alyce Cornyn-Selby has devoted her research career to the study of human motivation and communication. It royally *shows* in her first novel--a philosophical comedy that teaches and touches. A successful non-fiction author, Alyce was surprised when three different CEO's quoted from *this novel* to their management and sales staff.

A pioneer researcher of American attitudes and behaviors, Alyce has presented her research for colleges and corporations from Honolulu to London. Consistently rated one of the top keynote speakers in the United States and Great Britain, Alyce has 12 years of corporate management experience and headed a successful marketing firm with clients AT&T, Boeing and Kaiser-Permanente.

An award-winning scriptwriter and multi-image film producer, Alyce brings drama and comedy to her presentations. **Now one of the best keynote speakers in the country, you probably need to hear her speak, if you haven't already.**

To schedule: 503-232-0433 (Oregon)

BOOKS AND TAPES
by Alyce Cornyn-Selby

_____**BOOK:** *Procrastinator's Success Kit*
How To Get Yourself to
Do Almost Anything....................**$10.95**

_____**BOOK:** *Alyce's FAT CHANCE*
Taking off 100 pounds and
keeping it of (she's *done it!*).............**$7.95**

_____**BOOK:** *Take Your Hands OFF My Attitude!*
Getting better *behaviors* from others &
your right to a bad attitude................**$7.95**

_____**BOOK:** *Teamwork & Team Sabotage*
New and unusual look at teams
& people who sabotage them.............**$7.95**

_____**BOOK:** *Why Winners Win*
6 things winners have;
3 things they don't have...................**$7.95**

_____**TAPE:** *I Used To Be Fat*
The Weight Sabotage &
How to End it..............................**$9.95**

_____**TAPE:** *Teamwork*
New look at what it is
and how to get it...........................**$9.95**

_____**TAPE:** *Self-Sabotage*
What it is, how to
end it for self and others...................**$9.95**

_____**TAPE:** *Why Winners Win*
6 Things winners have;
3 things they don't have...................**$9.95**

Orders under $35, **SHIPPING $2 PER ITEM.**
Orders over $35, SHIPPING IS FREE.   TOTAL:_____

Check payable: **BEYNCH PRESS PUBLISHING**
                1928 S. E. LADD AVENUE
                PORTLAND, OREGON 97214

*Name*_____

*Address*_____

_____*Zip*_____